NINE

DAYS

NINE DAYS

MINERVA KOENIG

MINOTAUR BOOKS

A THOMAS DUNNE BOOK
NEW YORK

A THOMAS DUNNE BOOK FOR MINOTAUR BOOKS.
An imprint of St. Martin's Publishing Group.

NINE DAYS. Copyright © 2014 by Minerva Koenig. All rights reserved. Printed in the United States of America. For information, address St. Martin's Press, 175 Fifth Avenue, New York, N.Y. 10010.

www.thomasdunnebooks.com
www.minotaurbooks.com

Designed by Steven Seighman

Library of Congress Cataloging-in-Publication Data is available upon request.

ISBN 978-1-250-05194-3 (hardcover)
ISBN 978-1-4668-5266-2 (e-book)

Minotaur books may be purchased for educational, business, or promotional use. For information on bulk purchases, please contact Macmillan Corporate and Premium Sales Department at 1-800-221-7945, extension 5442, or write specialmarkets@macmillan.com.

First Edition: September 2014

10 9 8 7 6 5 4 3 2 1

NINE

DAYS

THURSDAY, NOVEMBER 1

———— ◆ ————

I

"Recognize this?" says the redhead, raising a nine-millimeter pistol to my husband's face.

It's late. We're walking the scenic route home after closing the bar. Joe stops, watching the redhead's partner come around on my left side. They're both under twenty years old, with stubbly heads and slow, mean eyes.

"Sorry, guys," Joe says, showing them his handsome *fuck you* grin. "We're dry."

"We don't want your money, *guido*," the redhead sneers. "It's too late for that."

A cop car ambles through the intersection at Twentieth and B, half a block behind the man with the gun, and a familiar dread tickles the bottom of my stomach. I'm not really here, but I've been here before. I know what's coming.

My hands jump to my ears seconds ahead of the shattering blast that takes half Joe's head off, and I brace for the two slugs that are coming my way. I remember that they won't kill me.

The cops will make the far corner in four and a half seconds and save my life. Not Joe's. He's already gone.

God damn it. Living through it once wasn't enough?

II

"That's gotta be her," somebody said.

I surfaced from the dream and found myself beached on the rear seat of a black Chevy SUV, blinking at the back of some guy's head. We were parked in a dark loading bay next to a bus station. Through the plate glass window, I could see a big woman dressed in a gray button-down shirt and pressed navy twills coming in from the back.

The head—Kang, his name was—folded up yesterday's *Washington Post* and sat tense while his partner, Buford, traded identification with the woman inside the station. I don't know what the hell they were worried about. Black tactical boots, paramilitary swagger, dark hair pulled back tight—she might as well have been wearing a sign that said COP, for Christ's sake.

After a couple of minutes, Buford turned and jerked his thumb at us. Kang and I got out of the car.

Nobody had told me where I was going—security, they said—but we had to be south of the Carolinas. The air was warm and thick, with a moist, grassy smell. Florida, maybe?

It had been forty degrees and raining when we'd left Virginia on Tuesday morning, and I'd dressed for the weather. I took off my coat as we went into the bus station, shifting my travel bag from one shoulder to the other.

The woman was bigger than I'd thought at first—close to

six feet and heavily broad, the smooth column of her neck rising from her shoulders like a mast from the deck of a ship. Her eyes were a nice golden brown, but they weren't friendly.

"I'm Teresa Hallstedt," she said, giving me a frank once-over. She seemed slightly puzzled.

"Want your money back?"

"No, but you might," she murmured. No pause, like she'd had ready.

Kang guffawed and swatted the *Post* into my midsection. As a parting gift, I took it away from him without breaking any of his fingers. He and Buford muttered some farewell platitudes, shook hands all around, and beat it. My ears did a little victory dance. The two of them had been yammering nonstop since Knoxville.

The Amazon headed for the door she'd come through, without any more talk. I followed, liking the way she maneuvered herself—plenty of swagger and taking up space like she deserved it; none of the shrinking, minimizing mannerisms that big women so often resort to. For about the millionth time since puberty, I wondered what it felt like to be tall.

Outside, I had to stop momentarily to steady myself. The night sky, no longer hidden by the loading bay roof, blasted into infinity overhead, impossibly vast and ending at a horizon that seemed very far away and too low. A weird lifting sensation, as if I were falling upward. It felt like a stiff wind could come along and blow me straight to Canada.

"You coming or what?" the Amazon called across the empty parking lot.

Two and a half years cooped up in various secure locations with cops and lawyers had made me a stranger to the outdoors.

I shook off my vertigo and made tracks for the burgundy four-door Pontiac. We buckled up and pulled out onto a narrow two-lane road. She eyed my sweater. "You want the air?"

Before I could answer, a burbling chirp sounded, and she brought out a slim black rectangle with a glowing blue face. I glared at it, irritation crawling up the back of my neck. I'm not a fan of the telephone, in any configuration. For my money, Bell attached his invention to the wall so you could get the hell away from it.

The Amazon listened, her lips compressing. "Fire there yet?" More listening, then, "Did she get a look at the guy?"

A green and white sign flashed by: AZULA, TEXAS. POP. 5,141.

"I'm about five minutes out," the cop continued into her phone. "Yeah. OK, Benny. Thanks."

She beeped the thing off and put it away, seeming to forget that I was there. I didn't remind her.

We hummed along in silence for maybe half an hour, the sparse ghosts of small houses sliding by out in the landscape; then the Pontiac slowed and rattled over a low bridge into a town square. A stone courthouse held down the patch of dry grass at its center, a couple dozen weathered storefronts huddled around it like campers around a fire. The place could have done time for cuteness if half the buildings hadn't been boarded up or vacant. I felt the thing between my ears boot up the automatic cost-benefit analysis it always runs through when I lay eyes on derelict real estate. My mood started to lift. Maybe this exile to the sticks didn't have to be the end of life as I knew it.

A thick plume of gray smoke twisted up into the sky from a building on the far corner, to our left. Two fire trucks were parked at the curb in front, and a couple of guys in full hero regalia stood on the courthouse lawn, one with a radio pressed to the side of his face. A short way off, closer to us, a uniformed cop was talking to a tiny old woman at the open driver's-side door of a police cruiser. They shaded their eyes against the headlights and stepped back as the Amazon pulled up alongside.

"Hey, Chief," the uniform said, walking over and laying his arm on the Pontiac's roof. He was maybe thirty-five—small, dark, and wiry—with a bristle of black hair growing low on his forehead. Second generation, I bet myself.

"Anything?" the Amazon asked him.

He shook his head. "911 caller gave the same description as Silvia did—Caucasian, blond, red gimme cap—but he was long gone by the time we got here." He jerked his chin at the firefighters. "First-in found point-of-origin indicators that look fishy."

"Damn it," the Amazon growled. She put the car in Park and got out.

As the cops strode toward the firefighters, the old woman—Silvia, I presumed—inched over and peered in at me. Her face was lined and folded like one of those dried apple dolls, with shiny black raisin eyes. Thin braids the color of sheet metal lay down the front of her patterned housedress.

I gave her the eyebrows, and she said, in a surprisingly deep voice, "What did you do?"

I considered telling her I'd just killed somebody's grandmother, but decided it was a little early to go off script. I hadn't even been in town for fifteen minutes.

"Nothing," I said. "I'm a friend of Teresa's."

The raisin eyes moved off my face to the suitcase in the backseat. "From where?"

"Boston," I said.

She smiled as if at a joke, and my radar went off.

"What's funny?"

The cops were back before she could get an answer out, the Amazon asking her, "Silvia, you sure you didn't recognize this runner?"

"All them white boys look the same to me." She shrugged.

The Amazon got back into the car, saying to the uniform, "Keep everybody here, will you, Benny? I'll be right back."

We bumped over the fire hoses crisscrossing the street and passed along the front of the courthouse. The Amazon nodded toward the row of buildings facing it and said, "You've got a job interview there tomorrow afternoon."

The buildings she'd indicated were all dark except for a two-story place with a row of Harley-Davidsons parked at the curb in front and a neon sign in the window reading GUERRA'S. Open at this hour, it could be only one thing.

"Get bored halfway through?" I asked the cop.

She cut her eyes at me. "What?"

"If you'd read my whole file, you'd know that I was just stop-gap help in the bar, as a favor to my father-in-law. Construction is my field, not slinging booze."

She made a face and started shaking her head before I'd stopped talking. "You're not in California anymore. Girls don't do that kind of work around here."

I gave her back the face. "But they're allowed to run the police department?"

"I'm not in hiding from a bunch of neo-Nazis who want to kill me," she pointed out. "I can afford to be weird. You can't."

Fucking cops. Everywhere you go, they're the same.

Away from the square, there didn't seem to be much of a town. We drove maybe half a mile on a curbless, pitted strip of asphalt apparently unrelated to the sporadic buildings in its vicinity, some of which might have been houses. After we turned right at a small church with a big graveyard, signs of habitation disappeared entirely except for a big white house up ahead on the right.

The Amazon stopped to let a car coming toward us exit the narrow gravel driveway before turning in. There was a young woman at the wheel, too busy keeping her beige four-door out of the ditch to acknowledge us. I felt a little zap of something come off the Amazon as we passed, but it didn't last long enough for me to classify.

We parked on a bare patch of dirt under a low-hanging tree, and I followed the Amazon up onto a long screened porch facing the driveway. She unlocked a door and flipped on the lights, illuminating an antique kitchen with a Formica dinette against the wall, between two tall windows.

"I've gotta go deal with this fire situation," she said, twisting a brass skeleton key off her ring and handing it to me. "I'll come by in the morning so we can get each other up to speed. Call me on my cell if anything needs attention before then." She scribbled on the back of a card with a green ballpoint. I took it, and she disappeared down the porch steps.

In addition to the kitchen, there was a bathroom with an Olympic-sized claw-foot tub, and a room barely big enough to contain the queen-sized bed shoved sideways against the wall under a high window. Another door faced me across the narrow space alongside the bed, but it was locked and didn't open with the key. I decided I could survive the night without seeing my living room, and tossed my stuff into the closet. Then I went out to sit on the porch steps and take another look at that sky.

III

The heat woke me late the next morning. I lay there listening to the unfamiliar silence, wondering if I'd gone deaf in my sleep. Then I remembered where I was.

Wrapping myself in the bedsheet, I got up and went into the kitchen to forage. A rattle at the apartment door sounded before I could get the refrigerator open. Figuring it was the Amazon, I opened up and found a man standing there instead.

"Sorry," he said, taking a step back. "I didn't know Teresa had rented the place already."

He was whip-thin but expansively framed, big bony shoulders pushing at the seams of his snug-fitting T-shirt, with frankly dyed black hair and light eyes that didn't quite connect with mine. He gave off sex like church incense, and I felt myself remember that a few of my favorite condoms were still floating around in my bag somewhere. I'd just started thinking about asking him in when the Amazon appeared from a door at the far end of the porch.

Her hair was wet and she wore an exasperated expression. "Don't you answer your phone?"

"I didn't hear it," I said, privately amused by the technical truth of the statement. I'd unplugged the loathsome instrument before falling into bed. An old habit and a good one.

"Hey, Teresa, is Richard around?" the guy asked her. "I need to get into the basement."

"I don't keep track of him anymore, Jesse," she said, a stain of irritation on her voice. "Let's go inside," she said to me.

He put a hand out, saying, "I'm Jesse Reed, I live upstairs."

"Julia Kalas," I replied, shaking.

"Like the opera singer?"

I spelled it and his expression went curious, his eyes hovering somewhere around my chin. "What is that, Greek?"

"It's Finnish."

The feds had fought me on it at first, but there was no way I was spending the rest of my life named Smith. It wasn't as if the name Kalas were traceable to me—at least, not by anyone I didn't want to be able to trace me when the time came. I told the feds I'd picked it out of the phone book, and when I showed them how many Kalases were listed for Boston, they let it go. For people whose job it is to be suspicious, they were surprisingly gullible.

The Amazon gave the apartment door a push. I backed up with the knob in my hand, letting her in.

"Nice to meet you," Jesse called after us. I saw him smirk as he trotted down the porch steps, revealing a pair of predatory canines.

"You want to watch yourself with that one," the Amazon said as I went into the bathroom to get dressed. "You'll be on your back with your panties on the floor before you know what hit you."

"Yeah?" I replied, curious. "Will I enjoy it?"

She made a disgusted noise. "How the hell should I know? I wouldn't touch him with a ten-foot pole."

Her eyes dropped to the two splotchy pink scars on my right side without changing, so she'd gotten at least that far into my file. I pulled on a T-shirt and checked my face in the mirror. It still looked the same.

"Who's Richard?" I asked, coming back into the kitchen.

She had coffee and filters out, and was filling a copper kettle at the porcelain sink. "My soon-to-be ex-husband. He's taking his time moving out, so you might run into him around the place. Don't let him give you any shit."

I got as comfortable as the chrome chairs at the dinette would let me. "Is he likely to offer me some?"

"He's likely to do any damned thing," the Amazon sighed, setting the kettle on the stove and lighting the gas. "Fortunately, it's not my problem anymore."

I wondered what her husband was like. Big guy. Rough around the edges, probably, to match her. "How long were you married?"

She waved it by, coming over to take the other chair. "Everything all right with the apartment?"

Some blood in the water there, I thought. Putting it on the back shelf to play with later, I replied, "I don't know—I haven't seen all of it yet. The door in the bedroom is locked, and the key you gave me doesn't open it."

"Yeah, that's my place," she said, leaning back and crossing her arms. "I split this floor into two units after Richard moved out."

I let my eyes drift around, and she pointed out dryly, "You're not gonna live here forever."

That reminded me. "There's only fifteen thousand in the bank account the feds set up. I was supposed to get fifty for the house in Bakersfield."

"The fifteen is for a car and living expenses until you can get a paycheck coming in," she said. "If you find a property you want to buy, let me know and I'll get what you need transferred down."

"Why can't I just have what they owe me, straight up?"

Her brown eyes jumped to my face, going sharp. "WIT-SEC's not in the business of giving habitual criminals big chunks of cash."

Again with the tone. I surveyed the backyard to give my temper time to settle. Jesse Reed was leaning against a small red pickup, talking urgently into a cell phone.

"Let's hear your backstory," the Amazon said, sounding dissatisfied. My lack of lip seemed to have thrown her off her game. Maybe she spent a lot of time with people who don't learn from their mistakes.

"I worked for your cousin Etta at her place in Roxbury," I recited, the words coming off my tongue like I'd been saying them all my life. "My marriage broke up last year, and you invited me down here to make a fresh start."

"What happened?"

I scowled at her, and she made a gesture with one hand. "I mean, what are you supposed to tell people happened?"

"Fuck if I know," I said. "I guess he ran off to Rio with his secretary or something."

"Pick a story and stick to it," she said, getting up to answer the whistling kettle. "People will ask you that—you'd be surprised."

Not as surprised as they'll be when I tell them to mind their own damned business, I thought, watching the Amazon pour. Her long hands were delicate on the kettle's porcelain handle, and there was something softly susceptible about the shape of her rounded arm, the angle of her head. I suddenly realized that she was pretty. You didn't notice it at first, with her professional gristle in the way.

"So how'd you win the federal babysitting lottery?" I asked her. "The locals don't give you enough business?"

"They can't keep an inspector down here," she said, watching the hot water sink through the coffee filter. "These kids from Washington show up thinking it's gonna be cowboys and Indians. They don't stay long."

"Why didn't they send me someplace with an active inspector?"

"You'll have to ask them, but I'm guessing it's at least partially because of my zero-tolerance policy for 'white power' crap in my jurisdiction." She brought the pot over to the table. "I'm kind of lame on some things, I admit it, but racist gangs?" She shook her head. "Homey, as they used to say, don't play that."

My radar homed in on her vehemence, and I wondered if there were something personal behind it. She didn't look like she had any color in her blood, but neither do I. "Why's that?"

She got a couple of heavy white mugs out of the cabinet, ignoring my question. "Your interview's at one, with Hector Guerra. In case the name doesn't make it obvious, he owns the place."

"You don't give a hell of a lot away for free, do you?"

She spooned a couple of sugars into her coffee and sat down, stirring it. She didn't say anything. It was starting to piss me off.

"Seriously," I said, "do I have to take this job?"

Her doe-lashed eyes flashed up at me, but she kept quiet. I gave her points for waiting out her temper this time.

"There's not a lot of work around here," she said when she finally spoke. Her voice was calm and even. "Hector's doing me a favor, giving you dibs on this bartending gig. I'm not gonna be very happy if you jerk him around."

"What if I want to do something for a living that I'm actually qualified for?"

"Like what, dealing guns and drugs?" A little crack in the calm and even.

I frowned at her. "We never dealt drugs."

"They're two ends of the same stick," she snapped. "You deal in one, you deal in the other."

I shut up and pulled my coffee over, just for something to do while she got a grip. A couple of minutes without talking, then she said, "Look, you helped your husband and father-in-law sell those black market pieces, and you laundered the profits through your construction books. That doesn't exactly inspire confidence in somebody responsible for the public safety." She tapped the Formica table with the tip of her index finger. Her nails were tastefully manicured, with a subtle pink polish. "You need to prove to me that you can be a law-abiding, responsible citizen. Holding down this job for a while is an easy first step."

"Helping the feds shut down that bunch of Ladders didn't buy me anything?"

She fixed her wise brown eyes on me. "Yeah, it bought you this chance. Don't fuck it up."

Before I could reply, she caught sight of her watch and got up, gulping her coffee. "I gotta go."

"Wait a minute," I said as she headed for the door. "How am I supposed to get downtown?"

"You can walk it in half an hour," she threw over her shoulder. "Make sure and give yourself enough time."

I waited until she was out of visual range to flip her the bird. Then I got up and poured out the coffee. I hate that shit.

IV

Around noon, I put my sneakers back on, wishing I had something a little nicer to wear. Hearing myself think that told me I was more stressed out than I'd realized. I've always been a pretty spectacular failure at femininity, what with the fat thing, the brain that won't shut up, and the obsession with machines and buildings; I'd successfully thrown in the towel after my torture-chamber puberty, and discovered that hauling plywood and Sheetrock instead of a purse didn't change anything except the way other people treated me. I only ever worry about how I look anymore when something else is bothering me. Right now, that included just about everything on the planet.

Chapped at having to think about it, I considered what to do with my hair. I'd worn it short and dyed dark since bailing out of Tucson for California after high school, but the feds had advised me to change my appearance as much as possible after going into protection, so I'd been letting it grow. It was past my shoulders now, an unruly pain in the ass with sprigs of gray silvering up its natural dead-grass color. I didn't mind the way it looked, but in this heat it was kind of like wearing a fur coat in hell, and putting it up required the kind of decision making I'd cut it off to avoid. I finally just twisted it up on the back of my head and clipped it there. It didn't exactly scream professionalism, but maybe failing my job interview would make it easier to talk some vocational sense into the Amazon.

On my way out, Jesse Reed popped into my memory, and I checked the stone foundation for basement windows. Sure enough, there they were, which I hadn't expected. Every now and then I'd come across a basement in Bakersfield, but they were rare because of the shallow frost depth, and I couldn't imagine that it got much colder here. I stopped to examine the house more closely. It was two stories with a steeply pitched roof—Victorian, if you held a gun to my head—easily a hundred years old or more. It was in pretty good shape, but needed a new roof and some repointing on the foundation masonry and chimneys. Looking at it made my hammer hand itch.

At the end of the driveway, I paused under a solitary tree to absorb some shade. Flat landscape covered in yellow grass spread almost treeless to that weird, low horizon in all directions, knuckling under to a sky so bright that it was almost white. The few buildings that dared stand up under it did so timidly, keeping low to the ground and far away from their neighbors. I could smell cows, but didn't see any. Up the road to my right, a sunburned Cadillac DeVille slanted off the pavement, bumper-deep in the weeds. To the left, toward town, the white clapboard church where we'd turned the night before stood to one side of a blockwide cemetery surrounded by a fence of heavy black chain slung between low granite piers. It seemed miles away.

I started walking along the gravel shoulder, wondering if the Amazon had warned my prospective employer that I'd be on foot, overdressed, and underqualified. Resentment stung the back of my throat again. I knew my way around a saloon, but not so well that you'd want to pay me for it. I'm good at reading people, and when Joe and Old Pete, his dad, had a buyer they weren't sure about, they'd stick me behind the bar so that I could observe on the down low. I'm not psychic or anything—just better than average at reading the unconscious, nonverbal information that every human being on earth throws out. It's a nice skill to have, but probably not worth its weight in actual bartending experience.

By the time I got to the church, I was giving serious thought to just telling Guerra, straight up, that I didn't want the job. The Amazon wouldn't like it, but what could she do? Tattle on me to WITSEC, I guess, but surely they'd prefer I not make an incompetent spectacle of myself. I was supposed to blend in.

A couple of the church's granite fence piers were in the shade, and I stopped to sit down and let some sweat dry. As I did so, the DeVille I'd seen parked in the ditch down the road from the Amazon's house appeared on the other side of the cemetery. It had dark-tinted windows, so I couldn't see who was driving. The back of my stomach went cold when it slowed and then stopped, watching me across the tombstones like a sheet-steel animal of prey.

My brain snapped off and I dropped into a high, cold land-scape of pure-body survival that slipped on like a familiar custom-made garment. The government shrinks had decided this was some kind of psychological damage from the shoot-ing, but it's a trick I've always had up my sleeve, and no way was I interested in being cured of something that's kept me alive for thirty-eight years and made me a damned successful criminal. The split seconds I save by not having to run everything through my prefrontal cortex are probably the reason I'm still here and Joe isn't.

I wasn't sure how long I sat there before the DeVille finally gunned its motor and sauntered insolently away, turning toward downtown on the other side of the church. It was still early afternoon, but it could have been a year later. I waited until my thought processes were working again, then got up and crossed the graveyard, putting some speed on it.

V

When I came into the northwest corner of the square about ten minutes later, the Cadillac was parked in front of a shopworn department store half a block straight ahead. I stayed on the sidewalk in the shade of a tall stone building on my right, keeping my eyes open while I decided what, if anything, to do.

In the daytime, the square looked almost monochromatic, most of its color bleached out by the hard white light. Some of the buildings had wood awnings that hung out over the sidewalk, but the sun seemed to blast right through them, sucking all the visual detail out of the window displays. The ones there were, anyway. I counted up the number of vacant properties: eighteen of twenty-four. Still showing signs of life were the department store, a corner store directly across the street from where I was standing, the courthouse, the bar, an indeterminate business a couple of doors down, and a large stone building diagonally across the intersection from that. Everything else seemed coated in graveyard dust, still and blank, like blind mice. The marquee above the theater on the other side of the courthouse still advertised a first-run matinee of *Pulp Fiction*, the plastic letters yellowed and crooked.

While I was thinking about Uma Thurman taking a needle in the chest, the old lady who'd talked to me at the fire the night before came out of the department store, a package under one arm. She got into the DeVille and drove off, in no hurry.

I stood there flat-footed for a minute, trying to decide whether I had something to worry about, or if I were overreacting to a normal level of local curiosity because of my circumstances. After ten minutes passed with the radar liking neither answer, I walked down and went into the department store. Bells hanging from the inside handle jangled as the door swung shut.

"I'm coming!" a faint voice called from somewhere out under the fluorescent lights.

The place smelled a thousand years old, even though it was probably only eighty or so. The mannequins in the front window were plaster, with hairstyles from the early '60s. I fingered a rack of blouses near me. They had a slick, plastic feel.

"Plus sizes are in the back," rasped the pint-size man in bow tie and horn-rims who materialized at my elbow. He was about the same age as the building, narrow-shouldered and wide-hipped, with strands of still-dark hair plastered back over his pale skull.

"Great, another segregationist," I muttered.

The old man scowled and withdrew his left hand from the pocket of his pleated gabardine pants. Only there wasn't any hand there, just the healed-over end of his wrist, which he shoved into my face. "This I lose to the worst racist in history so you can come in here calling me names?"

"I meant the clothes," I said, forcing myself not to flinch. "The bigger sizes are the same styles as all the other stuff, so why do they need their own section?"

He lifted his chin and examined me through the bottoms of his bifocals, pursing his lips. I paused to make sure he wasn't winding up to throw me out, then added, "Nobody likes being shoved to the back of the bus."

He stuck his wrist back in his pocket, still scowling. "Interesting pitch. What line are you with?"

"I'm not a sales rep," I said. "Just an easily annoyed fat broad who's done too much shopping."

He made a dismissive motion with one shoulder, eyeing me thoughtfully, then said, "What suburb of Los Angeles are you from?"

My stomach jumped. "What?"

The old man grinned, like he'd just done a magic trick, and tugged his right earlobe. "Still know my accents!"

"You might want to get a checkup," I told him. "I'm from Boston."

His expression turned skeptical, and I changed the subject before he could ask any more questions. "Listen, the lady who just left, Silvia something. Do you know her?"

Before I'd gotten my teeth back together, he sprang at the rack of clothes behind me, crying, "Those *gonif* kids!"

He yanked a satin slip off the rack, holding it out to show a long rip in the shiny pink fabric. It had clearly been slashed.

"That's the fourth one this week! What's the point of tearing up my goods and just leaving them here, will you tell me that?" He stalked over to the cash register by the front door, kvetching, "For their trouble, they could just steal the damned things."

"There's not much fence value in clothes," I said before I could stop myself.

He gave me a look, and I added quickly, "I'm a friend of Teresa Hallstedt's. I guess she's kind of rubbed off on me."

I thought it was pretty good for an extemporaneous fake, but his glare intensified, and he came back around the register. "Friends, are you? Then maybe you can make her see some sense."

I learned a long time ago that the best way to keep people talking is to give them room to do it. I showed him my best puzzled face and stayed quiet.

"I know she's against this downtown development project because it was Richard's idea, but we've gotta do something," the old guy said, waving his lone hand at his front window and the boarded-up storefronts beyond it. "People listen to her. If she keeps running it down, the whole thing will go kaput, and then I guess we can all go fly a kite."

My ear hair pricked upright. "What development project?"

"Oh, you know," he said, glancing around his faded business. "Tax incentives and whatnot. There was an article this morning—" He went back behind the register, throwing over his shoulder, "Silvia Molina's one of those Mexican witch doctors. Does her voodoo for the poor people down by the river."

"You mean she's a *curandera*?"

"Whatever," he grunted, rummaging under the counter. "Don't waste your money. We got a real doctor here, just like the rest of civilization."

The clock on the wall behind him warned that I was ten minutes late for my interview. I told him not to worry about finding the article, and made for the bar.

VI

Guerra's was the tallest building on its row, two stories with a nice old Metzger storefront. The big bay window on the second floor was mirrored in reverse on the first, and the recess in front of the door was paved with hexagonal black and white tile, '20s style.

The lights were off inside but the door was unlocked, and the familiar perfume of stale smoke and spilled liquor wafted up as I went in. A long serving top ran down the right side, with a row of short booths facing it across the worn board floor. At the far end of the high, narrow room was a small dance floor with a jukebox. To the right of this, a short hallway glowed with light.

"Hello?" I called.

I heard a chair creak, and a short, beefy figure appeared in the hall. As he ambled toward me, away from the light, I got a load of the details: long black hair, big dark eyes, Aztec nose, delicious mouth. The man was gorgeous.

"Sorry about that—the breaker went," he said, extending a hand about the size and shape of a bear's paw. His voice was rough and youthful sounding, with the full vowels and relaxed consonants of a native Spanish speaker. "I'm Hector Guerra. Come on back."

I followed him down into a hall about a third as big as the bar, all thoughts of throwing the interview evaporating.

A walk-in cooler faced the door, and a mismatched sofa and chairs were arranged around a low table in the center. In the far corner, a big black and white cat sprawled on the seat of a BMW motorcycle. The carburetor was lying in pieces on a mattress of stained newspapers underneath it, scenting the air with gasoline. There was a battered metal desk in the remaining corner, from which Guerra picked up a clipboard to hand me.

He stayed quiet as I took a chair, watching me frankly and without apparent self-consciousness. There was an uncanny calmness about him; he sat absolutely still, not even his eyes moving, as if rapt by some hypnotic internal mantra. My radar kept feeling around the edges of it, looking for a way in and not finding one.

I was halfway through the second page of the job application when I heard someone coming down the wood stairs we'd passed in the short hallway. A young Latino came around the door into the office. He was maybe twenty-five, with a shaved head and indigo prison tattoos spilling from the arms and neck of his snug white T-shirt. The only colored tag was a red crown on his left biceps, half hidden under the hem of his sleeve. The baggy chinos and illegible eyes told me the rest. If he wasn't a banger, he deserved an award for his impersonation of one.

"*¿Qué piensas?*" Guerra asked him, getting up.

The banger wiped his hands on a red shop rag. "*Lo puedo arreglar,*" he replied, his eyes taking a short trip in my direction. "It'll only be temporary, though, man. You probably need a new roof."

"*Está bien,*" I said. "*Hablo español.*"

Both men looked at me with their eyebrows up, and I explained, "In case you switched to English on my account."

The banger smiled a little. I occasionally have that effect on tough guys.

"What's a new roof gonna run?" Guerra asked him with a grimace. "You know how broke I am."

"Depends," the banger said. "There's a couple different kinds. A membrane roof would be best, but they ain't cheap."

"What's up there now?" I asked.

Again with the startled look, both of them.

"Tin," the banger said. "Why?"

"Sometimes on these old flat-roofed masonry places, the inside part of the building settles away from the exterior walls," I said, demonstrating by holding my hands out flat and dropping one a few inches. "That creates a dam at the drainage scuppers where water pools up. If that's what's going on, you can fix your leaks by enlarging the scupper openings."

I love it when guys look at me the way these two were looking at me right now—like I'd just grown a second, freakishly intelligent head.

"I'm not saying you don't need a new roof," I added deferentially, "but the scupper thing is something cheaper you can try first."

Guerra chuckled and gestured toward me. "Alex Méndez, Julia Kalas." He gave Alex an apologetic look. "Teresa didn't tell me she was a ringer."

"The scuppers are all plugged up with leaves and stuff," Alex challenged.

"Well, yeah," I said, glancing at Guerra. "That doesn't help. You gotta keep the roof clean."

Guerra seemed to be trying not to smile. I don't know why he bothered fighting it. All it did was make him prettier.

"Any roof will leak if it's got a swimming pool on top of it," I said.

Alex scratched the back of his neck with one finger, thinking. "Ya know, the scupper thing might work, now that I think about it."

"Lemme call you later, OK?" Guerra replied after a short pause. Alex nodded. The two men shook hands and Alex disappeared through the office door.

"Got any other secret superpowers I need to know about?" Guerra asked me, coming back over to his chair.

I considered telling him I bench-pressed my own body weight, but I wasn't sure I could anymore. Plus, I don't think that counts as a secret superpower. I hadn't been born doing it. I'd picked up weight training shortly after starting the construction business in Bakersfield, when it became clear that there wasn't a framing crew on earth who would take orders from someone who couldn't lift a sack of concrete by herself.

Guerra picked up the clipboard and put on a pair of spectacles that were lying on the low table. It was only then that I realized he was my age or older. I let my gaze slide casually across his left hand. No wedding ring, and no telltale crease of one recently removed. If he was single, the women in this town were slackers.

After reading over my application for a few minutes, he put the clipboard down on the table and sat back in his chair, but before he could say anything, a female voice called from the direction of the bar: "If you've got my DSM-four in there, you're a dead man!"

A young woman followed the warning in. She was small

and dark, with a cloud of springy hair that bounced off her shoulders as she hesitated to a stop in the doorway.

"Oh! Sorry!" she said, seeing me.

"My sister, Connie," Guerra said. I got up to shake hands and introduce myself.

When I told her my name, she said, "You're Teresa's friend, aren't you?"

I admitted I was, and I must have looked uncomfortable doing it, because she explained, "She let us know you were coming, last week. I wait tables for Hector part-time."

Her eyes had been darting around the room as she spoke, and now they homed in on a book lying open on the desk. She went over to get it, giving Guerra a light bonk on the head as she came back.

"How am I supposed to pass this practicum when you keep stealing all my field materials?" she complained.

"Maybe you shouldn't pass it," he groused, running a hand over the top of his hair.

"Oh, please. As if there were any danger of denting that thing."

The book she was holding appeared to be a twin to one the federal shrinks always had handy during my sessions. "Are you premed?" I asked her warily. The last thing I wanted in my life right now was another mental health care professional.

"No, social work," she said. "We all have to do a core in psychology. After I get my license, I'm hoping to go back to Guatemala and work with the indigenous populations down there."

Guerra cut in, "Can you start tonight?"

I balked, and Connie said, "Our bartender threatened to strike unless Hector hired some help by the end of October."

"I won't make you actually work," Guerra said to me. "We'll call it paid training. Drinks on the house."

"Paid how much?" I asked, feeling for the catch.

"Whatever it'll cost me to get you to start tonight," he said, his lazy smile threatening again.

I considered the offer. If he was really over a barrel, the thing to do was start the bidding high, but getting to look at him while I worked was worth a discount. I threw out a figure he couldn't refuse. Guerra dropped his big head forward and swung a hand toward me. "Sold."

Connie had turned toward the desk, reaching for the telephone. Hoping he wouldn't regret it, I said to Guerra, "What time do you want me?"

"I unlock the doors around four, but Mike won't be here until eight. Any time after that is fine."

VII

Back out on the front sidewalk, I stopped to feel my feet on the ground under the big sky. Guerra had got me thinking about my first meeting with Joe.

My cousin Norma and I had come out on the bus from Tucson and were doing the San Francisco waterfront—the seals, Ghirardelli Square, and all the rest—feeling like cosmopolitan grown-ups. We'd flipped a coin to decide which bar to drink in, and were under the influence of multiple rum and Cokes when Norma's eyes widened at something over my shoulder. I turned to see what had caught her attention, and got the thunderbolt. The tall, dark willow of a man sauntering toward us, eyes fixed on me, looked familiar even though I knew I'd never seen him before—I'd have remembered. He was wearing dark pants and a shirt with the top two buttons undone. The buttons were white mother-of-pearl. There was a silver ring on his right hand, and his hair was too long, curling down into his collar. Still infiltrating me with his eyes, he asked if we were from around here. I said no. It was the last time I ever said no to Joe Rizzoli.

The smell of something delicious wafting down from the corner, where a hand-painted sign advertised a café, brought me out of my reverie. I hadn't eaten breakfast, and maybe they'd know where I could get a newspaper, so that I could take a gander at the article the department store salesman had mentioned.

Old Town Kern, the historic center of Bakersfield, had devised a program where the city appraised properties they wanted renovated at or near zero, to entice developers. You couldn't get a loan on them, but if you had the cash—which, of course, the Rizzolis did—you could buy a place and fix it up without having to lay out the ten to twenty thousand for the property tax. If the old salesman was right and Azula was doing something similar, I wanted in, no matter what the Amazon said.

The café's floor plan was similar to Guerra's, with a serving counter along the inside wall, booths facing it on the other side. A dark-eyed teenager with a high puff of ponytail sat behind the cash register to the right of the front door, reading a vampire romance novel. She gave me a squinty look and told me I could have a seat anywhere.

I took a booth, noticing a couple of workmen near the back, puttying a new sheet of glass into one of the windows that faced the side street. A black guy of maybe thirty-five came out of the kitchen with a roll of silverware and a glass of water. "What'll you have, hon?"

I've never had a stranger call me "hon" before, and it made me grin. "What's that I smell?"

"Gumbo," he said. "It's been making all day."

He had bad skin but great teeth, and wore his hair in short, tight little knots that covered his head like cloves stuck into an orange. I thought the girl at the register resembled him, but he didn't look old enough to have a daughter her age.

"Let me have some of that," I said, "and some iced tea."

He nodded and went behind the counter to a stainless steel urn. When he came back with my tea, I pointed my eyes toward the workmen and said, "What happened?"

"My weekly brick," he deadpanned.

I gave him a look, and he waved a lazy hand. "I'm just playing. Last week it was a hammer."

My eyebrows flinched up. "So the old guy at the store across the square wasn't just trying to get a sympathy sale?"

"Mel," he said with a short, barking laugh. "That dude like to talk your ear off, give him half a chance." He squinted at me, increasing his resemblance to the girl at the register. "Where you from?"

The question wasn't bothering me anymore. "I just moved from Boston." I held a hand out. "Julia Kalas."

"Lavon Roberts," he replied, shaking it. He gave me a not-unfriendly visual exam, then gazed back out toward the square. "City council say this development thing gonna stop all the craziness been going on down here lately, but I ain't see how."

A *ding* from the serving counter called. He stepped over to the cash register and grabbed a newspaper from behind it. "Read all about it right there," he said, handing it my way as he went to pick up the order.

The half headline showing above the fold read DOWNTOWN REVITALIZATION PROJECT, and finished COMES UP FOR COUNCIL VOTE when I opened the paper. There was a photo—captioned "Project sponsor Dr. Richard Hallstedt meets with other members of the city council"—showing a colorless guy in starched khakis and a single-needle dress shirt centered in a group. He looked straight as a ruler, from his mainstream haircut to the tasseled loafers. Not at all what I'd envisioned as marriage material for the Amazon. I wondered what kind of doctor he was.

The article didn't say, but explained that Hallstedt, a second-term council member, was pushing a package of commercial property tax incentives, which he promised would bring new businesses to the square. This would in turn evict "the criminal element that has moved in over the last year."

When I got to the end of the article, I noticed that the brain had tweaked back to the Amazon's admission that she was "lame on some things." I didn't yet know what the connection was, but I bat about .750 on subconscious links. Something I hadn't noticed at the time was lodged in the underground gray matter. I knew from experience that trying to excavate it would be pointless. It would surface on its own schedule.

Lavon brought my lunch and I flipped to the classifieds while I ate. If I were going to go after this development thing, I'd have to be driving something I could park on a construction site without getting laughed at. Fifteen thousand wouldn't go far enough if I insisted on buying right off the assembly line. I needed a good used truck.

There were two likely options: a Chevy pickup and a Dodge. The Dodge was an '87, which meant it might still have a carburetor and was probably constructed mostly of steel. The ad said to "see Tova @ Bradshaw Arms." There was an e-mail address and phone number, but I preferred the direct approach option, if I could get there.

"Do you know where this is?" I asked Lavon when he brought my check, pointing out the ad.

He grinned and pointed at the side window with his eyes. I followed them over my shoulder to a light-colored stone building on the diagonal corner.

"If it was a snake, it woulda bit ya," he said.

VIII

The Arms had two pairs of etched glass doors—one fronting on the square and one on the side street—that fed into a corner lobby with a polychrome quarry tile floor and what had to be the original oak reception desk at the far end. A purple-haired Generation Xer sat behind this, staring at a laptop computer screen, her spine bowed out behind her in an impossible-looking curve.

I asked for Tova as instructed, and the clerk said, "What's your problem?"

She didn't sound belligerent, so it kind of stumped me. "What?"

"She's not consulting anymore, just filing paperwork," she said, a warning in her voice. I continued to boggle at her and the other shoe dropped. "You don't need legal advice?"

"Oh. No. I'm here about the truck that's for sale."

The clerk pressed her lips together, looking embarrassed, and picked up the desk phone. She told whoever answered what my mission was and then said I could "go on in," pointing down the hall to the right of the desk.

I passed a nicely restored old phone booth and turned into a blindingly bright room with a set of French doors opening onto a stone-paved courtyard. A pair of cockatoos was quietly cracking sunflower seeds in a large bamboo cage in one corner. Everything else in the room was white, or close to it—the carpet, the computer, the filing cabinets, even the desk and chair. After the opulence of the hotel's lobby, it felt a little like walking into an igloo.

The woman behind the desk was an eye-catching blonde, dressed to match the room in an expensive-looking linen pencil-skirt suit and nude pumps. Her platinum hair was done up in a French twist and her chilly blue eyes shoved me back in time to whispering high school cliques of perfumed rich girls, feminine and exotic in that way I could never pull off.

She got up as I came in, taking a set of keys out of the pencil drawer.

"It's out back," she said, coming around the desk. She had a bombshell figure and was proud of it, shoulders back, hips swinging.

"Who did the restoration on this place?" I asked, admiring some nice egg and dart crown molding as I followed her down the hall toward the back of the building. She threw a frown at me over one shoulder, and I said, "It's at least a hundred years old. There's no way it's lasted that long in shape this good without help."

She paused at the fire door. "Why do you want to know?"

"Just curious."

It takes some starch to ignore a throwaway like that, but she did it, pushing out into the alley without answering. My temper kicked, but I mashed it down until I knew for sure whether we'd have to haggle.

"What are you asking for the truck?" I said as we crunched across the gravel alley.

"Twelve thousand."

I made the shape of a whistle with my lips, but decided to keep quiet until I laid eyes on the merchandise. Maybe it had a solid gold steering wheel or something.

The blonde approached a corrugated steel warehouse and gave the big sliding door a push, revealing a pale yellow pickup, parked nose out. It wasn't encrusted with diamonds, but somebody had taken very good care of it.

"How many miles?" I asked, walking around to the side.

"Forty-seven thousand," she replied. I made a skeptical face, and she said, "It belonged to my father, who purchased it new and didn't drive it very often. He was an immigration lawyer, and his work took him out of the country frequently. It's always been kept in here when not being driven. I doubt that it's ever been parked outdoors for more than a few hours."

In contrast to her china-doll appearance, her voice was pitched low, and she spoke with a brisk, measured precision, as if holding back a tide of verbal energy that threatened to burst forth at any moment.

"How long since anybody drove it?" I asked.

"You're welcome to take it for a spin, if you like," she said, dangling the keys at me from one small white finger.

She gave a closed-lipped *Mona Lisa* smile as I got in and

cranked the ignition. The engine turned over on the first try, and from the sound of it, I knew that I'd probably be making her an offer. I eased out of the warehouse and went around the block, then took it up Main Street, which turned into a two-lane highway about half a mile out of town. It went up to eighty without complaint, riding stiff and choppy like a truck should.

When I turned back into the alley behind the hotel, the blonde was down at the far end, talking to a woman dressed in—yes, it was a crinoline, a short red one above a well-worn pair of tall black cowboy boots. Her bottle-black hair was tied up in a cotton bandanna, '40s-style, and she was tossing various items into a big green Dumpster from a water-stained cardboard box at her feet. I left the truck in the warehouse and walked down to them.

"Charlie, this is—" The blonde turned to me with an amused twinkle that felt calculated. "My goodness, how rude of me. I'm Tova Bradshaw."

"Julia Kalas," I said to both of them, shaking hands.

"Charlie Eames," the stranger said. She was what they used to call gawky, tall and narrow with more nose than chin, but her ostentatious outfit and theatrical makeup told me she didn't care. Something about her made me want to grin and tell a joke.

"Got a husband named Ray?" I cracked.

She winked at me. "No, I've got a girlfriend named Marie. Nice cultural reference, though."

So much for my gaydar. Casting around for something to cover the faux pas, I realized that the building next to us was the previous night's bonfire.

"Is this your place?" I asked, noticing that the bottles she was dropping into the Dumpster were caked with soot.

"It was," she said.

"You won't have to leave," Tova cut in with an air of picking up where she'd left off. "I'll make sure your policy pays out enough to rebuild."

Charlie made a face at the carcass of her business. "What's the point, Tova? You know as well as I do that we're all hanging on by a thread here. I didn't even make a hundred dollars last month."

I was only half listening, distracted by the building, which was trying to tell me something. They do that, the way some old north-country people used to say the sequoias talked to them, or beekeepers with their hives.

The place was two stories, all stone, and the sky showed through where some window glass had broken out on the top floor. The sashes up there were charred black at the top, but only marked with soot at the bottom. The lower-floor windows were still intact and didn't show any smoke or fire damage.

"At least Humphrey and Lauren are OK," Charlie said.

"Oh, my word," Tova breathed, putting a hand to her mouth. "I hadn't even thought." She turned to me. "Charlie has a pair of champion koi that have to be seen to be believed."

"Humphrey and Lauren are fish?" I said.

Charlie nodded, peering at me. "What's your animal?"

"My animal?"

"Yeah. Everybody has an animal totem that follows them through life."

I paused to think, then admitted, "I don't think I do."

"You have one," she said, and bent down for another load. "You just haven't noticed it yet."

Tova gave me an amused look over Charlie's head and said, "I've got all the records for the truck in my office. Charlie, I'll call the adjuster tomorrow and let you know what I find out, all right?"

Charlie gave an affirmative-sounding grunt, and Tova and I started back toward the hotel. As soon as we were out of earshot, she warned me in a low voice, "That girl gives the best manicure in the county, but trust me on this—don't let her touch your hair." She cut her eyes at my rapidly assembled updo and murmured, "If you care about that sort of thing."

The fire door from the hotel hall was one of the exit-only kind, so we had to walk around to the lobby doors on the street side to get back to her office, which gave my urge to slap her time to subside. Once inside, she went to the filing cabinet to get out a folder. "My brother is something of a motor head," she said, sitting down behind her desk. "He's been the truck's sole caretaker practically since the day Dad bought it."

"Is he a licensed mechanic?"

One corner of her coral mouth slipped upward. "No, but ask anyone in town what Hector Guerra knows about the internal combustion engine, and you'll get the same answer."

I twitched at the name, and she paused, giving me a quizzical look.

"I just took a job over at the bar," I said, unable to stop the doubtful once-over I was giving her. If this peaches-and-cream ice princess was related to the swarthy hunk who'd interviewed me, something had gone very wrong in the gene pool.

Her smile spread to the other corner. "Dad adopted Hector when I was three and Connie when I was nine."

There was a note of pride in her voice, and for a second I wondered if I'd been too quick to mark her down in the "entitled rich girl" column.

"My father was a softhearted man," she said. "After my mother died, he went a bit insane and started bringing home the children he found on the streets while working cases south of the border." The prideful note turned sardonic. "Fortunately, he passed away before it got out of hand."

It was only almost funny; I could feel some real resentment behind it. Tova seemed to notice, and changed the subject, going on the offensive again. "I'm happy to sell the truck to you if you can meet my price, but I must warn you that Hector may not be entirely happy about you purchasing it."

"Why's that?"

"He's been angling to buy it himself, but he can't afford to pay what I'm asking."

I started to join in on the joke, then realized that she was serious. I hesitated, wondering if I were unwittingly getting involved in some sort of family feud.

She snugged herself up against the edge of the desk, folding her delicate hands over the folder. "Would you want to finance, or pay the full amount in cash?"

"Maybe you'd better let me look at those records before we start talking money," I said, keeping my face neutral.

She leaned back in her oversize Naugahyde chair, sliding the folder toward me. "Of course."

Her white phone buzzed as I flipped the folder open. She picked up the receiver and said, "What is it, Kathleen?" She

listened, then made a face. "It can't be so dire that a few minutes will make any difference. Ask her to wait, please." I'd seen
enough to know that the truck was worth what she was asking.
"OK if I write you a personal check?"

She pursed her lips, studying me briefly, then said, "I
wouldn't normally, but Hector's instincts about people are pre-
ternaturally accurate. He wouldn't have hired you if you weren't
trustworthy."

I ducked my head so she wouldn't see me trying not to
laugh. When I came back up with my checkbook, composed,
she was watching me. She might trust her brother's instincts, but
she didn't trust her own.

IX

The feds hadn't let me drive myself anywhere during the trial,
and having wheels again took me back to the old life. Day trips
to the national forest, cruising Baker Street on Friday nights,
aimless runs to the coast when Joe was busy with clients and
wanted me out of the house. A low wave of sick agony roiled in
my gut as I remembered. I took a slow breath, refusing to sink
down into thinking about the past. He was gone. There was
nothing I could do about it.

Silvia Molina crawled back up into my head as I turned the
corner at the church. It occurred to me that she could have been
on her way home from somewhere on the other side of the
Amazon's place, and had just pulled over to pluck her eyebrows
or something. That didn't explain her stop at the graveyard to
look me over, but half an explanation was better than none.

I drove past my driveway turnoff and kept going. After a

couple of miles, the road sloped into a grove of trees, and the air began to smell of standing water. It was cooler down here, but the houses, half hidden in clumps of overgrown understory and sedentary farm equipment, were little more than dilapidated shacks anchoring worthless strips of floodplain. Rusted wire fences woven with spindly weeds ran around some of them, enclosing ragged-looking livestock.

None of it qualified as an obvious destination, but I knew that *curanderas* often paid house calls. Silvia might have been visiting a patient. Short of stopping to knock on doors, though, I had no way to find out for sure. Frustrated by not being able to put the issue definitively to bed, I looped back through the neighborhood to head home.

As I came to a four-way stop, one of three boys staked out on the corner raised a hand and stepped onto the asphalt. His face went deadpan when I pulled up. "Where you get this ride, lady?" he demanded with that soft, slightly belligerent cadence typical of the gangsta class.

He couldn't have been more than sixteen, and he was small for his age, dressed in a red tank top and a too-big black gimme cap set high and angled on his head to ensure that it was understood as a fashion statement. There was a red crown tattoo on the swell of his left shoulder, just like the one I'd spotted on Alex Méndez.

"Expecting Tova?" I said.

He pointed his brown chin at me. "You know her?"

"Sure," I said, stringing him along. "How am I gonna be driving her truck if I don't know her?"

"Maybe you boosted it."

The two other boys had crowded in behind him where he'd

stopped on the other side of the road. They stood listening, watching me with guarded eyes and pulling at their low-hanging pants. They were ten or eleven years old, tops; flying colors but without visible art.

"Maybe I did," I admitted. "If I'm stupid enough to clip a ringer like this, I'm probably stupid enough to drive it around town."

The point man lifted his chin higher, sucking his cheeks in. He reminded me a little of my cousin Joachim, who'd worked as a lookout for La Eme, one of the gangs trying to tear Bakersfield in half the year I hit town. I'd been fascinated and calmed by the simple, predictable rules of gang life—loyalty, revenge, and profit—the uncomplicated hierarchy, the clear link between action and consequence. Unfortunately, no matter how dark I dyed my hair or how much eyeliner I wore, nobody ever bought me as a *cholita*. I'd had to be satisfied on the fringes. Not that I'm complaining. Sometimes Edge City is a better learning experience than living downtown.

The baby Gs lost interest and turned to saunter back toward their shop. I pulled away, savoring the knowledge that the prim and proper Tova Bradshaw was a known quantity to the other end of the stick. I wondered what she was into. She was no crackhead or junkie. Weed or downers, probably. That would take the edge off the prim and proper when it got too sharp.

Back in town, I hooked a right at the courthouse, turning east. This took me through another neighborhood, more prosperous than the one I'd just visited but still pretty damned rustic. At a stop sign, my eye caught on a hand-painted wooden sign hanging from a mailbox a few houses down from the intersection: BOTÁNICA MOLINA.

I idled there, not completely sure why I wanted to drive down and go in. It reminded me of that weird fear you sometimes get up on something high, that you'll throw yourself off just to see what it feels like. The French have a word for the feeling, but I couldn't remember it.

Rationalizing that the chances of a geriatric Latina being connected to the Aryan Brotherhood were minimal, I made the turn and pulled up in front of the botanica. It was a small blue house with a pyramid-shaped metal roof and a corner porch. The painted white fence enclosed a minuscule patch of yard that had been manicured to within an inch of its life. A big yellow dog loped toward me as I approached the gate.

"He won' hurt you," I heard from the direction of the porch. I had to squint to see Silvia creaking up out of a rusty metal chair. The sunlight was so bright that it made the shade of the porch practically black in comparison.

"Come in, please," she said in her low, cordial voice.

The dog followed me up the narrow walk with his nose at my heels. Silvia pulled open the screen door and held it for me.

The front room was about the size of a king-size bed, with a small wood table in the center. The walls on either side were lined with floor-to-ceiling shelves crowded with votive candles, bottles, tins, and pasteboard boxes of all sizes, shapes, and colors, many with handwritten labels attached. It was dim and cool inside, with a faint smell of burnt matches. Through an arched opening in the back wall I could see a television and a chintz sofa in a larger room.

Silvia sat down at the table, drawing a deck of oversize cards toward her. She indicated the chair opposite, and I took it.

"*¿Hablas español?*" she asked, turning up one of the cards and laying it in the center of the table.

I nodded, and she laid out another card. I watched her, keeping quiet, until she'd constructed a large cross pattern with a vertical row of four cards running up the right side. She studied this arrangement, then flashed her bright little eyes at me and asked, in Spanish, "Do you have trouble sleeping?"

"Oh, you're going to warm me up first?" I said. "OK, yeah. Yeah, I've got terrible insomnia. I haven't slept in weeks."

She blew her breath out through her nose and shoved the cards back into a pile, looking disgusted. "There is a vibration around you," she tried next, lifting her hands, palms outward, toward me. She'd switched to English now. "Something dark. A sense of danger and loss."

"You're not very good at this," I told her.

"Then what are you doing here?" she asked quickly.

"Trying to find out why you've been following me around town."

I saw her consider denying it, then discard the idea in favor of something else. She got up, crooking a finger at me, and shuffled through the archway toward the back of the house. I wasn't getting anything scary off her, so I followed.

She was waiting for me in her dated but spotless kitchen, where she opened an unpainted board door and stepped down into a small chamber with a dirt floor. It was constructed of concrete block, with one high window and an old iron laundry sink. In the middle of the room, a body lay on a long table, covered with a white sheet.

Silvia went to the table and folded the sheet down, revealing the head and shoulders of an elderly Hispanic woman. The corpse was dressed in a freshly pressed high-necked blouse, her dead face skillfully painted with makeup.

"She looks good, don' she?" Silvia asked me, pride in her voice.

"Was she a friend of yours?"

"Anybody who can't afford to get buried right is a friend of mine," she said with a small, virtuous smile.

"OK," I said slowly, rotating my hand at her.

She passed a hand over the body. "My work takes me places ordinary people don' go, hearing things ordinary people don' hear."

Her peering black eyes checked my reaction, and I felt a little tickle around the bottom of my esophagus. I considered several responses, but didn't like any of them. Better to take the path of least resistance and just wait the story out of her.

That bought us five minutes of silent staring at each other, after which she emitted a small puff of breath and hiked up the concrete stairs into the kitchen. I followed her back to the front room, where she went over to one of the tall shelves and took down a pasteboard box and a small envelope. She shook out a quantity of dark yellow powder from the box into the envelope and made a note on the front with a pencil, then handed the envelope to me.

The label said WIDOW'S TEA.

My eyes jumped to her face. She gave me a solemn look and then her face creased into a wide grin. The glitter in her tiny black eyes was sure now.

"How much?" I heard myself say.

She motioned toward a stone plate on a stand next to the door, feigning surprise. "Whatever you wish."

The feds had prepped me for the possibility of blackmail, and I knew the protocol. I took a bill out of my wallet, laid it on the plate, and got the hell out of there.

X

The directory on the first floor of the courthouse told me that the police department was in the basement, which I'd have found funny if I hadn't been busy freaking out. I had to go back outside and down the wide limestone steps, walk around the building on a narrow concrete sidewalk, and down a sloped ramp to a single glass door at the rear.

Inside, the low room was sectioned off into nine cubes of space by a tic-tac-toe board of rough stone arches edged with red brick. In the quadrant immediately left of the door, a skinny brunette sat at a metal desk with an antiquated two-way radio console behind it. Her name patch said SCHERER.

"Is the chief in?" I asked her.

She shook her head. "What's the problem?"

I looked over at the clock hanging above a battered wood bench against the stone wall. It was three thirty. "What time do you expect her?"

"I don't, really," Scherer said with a hint of smile. I lifted my eyebrows, and she explained, "She does night shift, and she usually rolls out from home. She's in and out."

"How is anybody supposed to get hold of her?"

Scherer pointed at a phone next to the bench, and I remembered the Amazon giving me her card the previous night. I dug it out of my wallet and punched in the green-scribbled number on the back. The Amazon answered on the second ring with a short "Yeah?"

"Hey, it's Julia. I need to talk to you. It's about Etta. I ran into somebody who knows her." That was the WITSEC code drop to convey that my cover had been blown.

"This isn't a secure line," the Amazon warned, her voice going tense. "Keeping that in mind, what happened?"

"I went by to see Silvia Molina, the *curandera*?"

A burst of breath on the other end of the line cut me off. "What'd you do that for?"

I glanced over at Scherer, who'd gone back to reading the magazine on the blotter in front of her. Maybe twelve feet separated us. I lowered my voice and said into the phone, "She followed me downtown from your house."

"What do you mean, followed you?"

"What do you mean, what do I mean?" I hissed. "She was parked down the street when I left, and when I got to the church, she fucking stopped and watched me."

A uniform came in, and I paused to let him get out of hearing range before going on. "I went over there to see what the deal was, after my interview, and she tried to touch me."

"What, for money?"

"Yeah."

Another breath; then her voice came again, exasperated now. "That's not a cover bust. A cover bust is when somebody shoots at you, OK?"

"She knows I'm a widow," I said.

"She's a professional fortune-teller, Julia. She cold-reads people for a living."

"I had all my tells beaten out of me by the feds," I insisted. "There is no way in hell that I gave her that."

"Listen to me," the Amazon said, a brittle calmness coming into her voice. "If the Brotherhood knew where you were, you'd be ducking bullets, not talking to me on the phone."

"I know that. But if there's a leak somewhere, it's only a matter of time before it drips on the wrong people."

The Amazon's voice relaxed down another notch. "Look, I'll go talk to Silvia when I get back to town in a couple of hours, but trust me on this: you're OK. OK?"

She hung up without saying anything else, and I put the phone down, feeling stupid.

I closed my eyes to get a grip and run over everything I could remember about my brief interaction with the *curandera*. Maybe her knowing smirk at the fire had been a test of possible new meat for her fortune-telling business, and she was just turning up the heat with this following thing. My luggage in the backseat of the Amazon's car would have told her where I was staying, and she could have heard about my job interview on the small-town airwaves. It didn't explain the Widow's Tea, though.

"Everything all right?" Scherer asked. I opened my eyes and nodded, and she asked, "Are you the family friend from Boston?"

I couldn't help a wry smile, and her look went from professional to curious.

"I heard you took a job with Hector," she said.

"Yeah," I said, getting up. "Teresa put in a good word for me."

Scherer hesitated, skeptical; then her face creased into disbelief. "Really?"

"What, is the place haunted or something?"

The cop giggled, and I realized that she was younger than
she looked. "No, no. It's just—"

She shrugged, running her eyes down to my feet and then
back up. Maybe I didn't look sufficiently bartender-like, or she
was one of those people who thought that people who don't fit
into the "normal" range on those height/weight charts should all
take a walk in heavy traffic. I thought about pushing the question, but decided it probably wouldn't be worth it. Cops always
get more out of you than you get out of them, and I was already
as far into information debt to law enforcement as I cared to go.

XI

It was too early to show up at the bar, and I needed some time
to settle down anyway, so I drove around until I found a grocery store. I bought some staples, including a box of loose oolong
tea and a filter pot, and then headed back to the apartment.

On reflection, I decided it was probably a good thing that
the rest of my stuff—including my full wardrobe—hadn't arrived yet. I know a couple of things about men now that I didn't
when I was younger, and one of them is that you probably don't
want one you have to dress up for to catch. I don't dislike dressing up, but having it expected of you gets old fast.

I put some tea on to brew and took a cool bath, then went
online to see if Silvia Molina could have stumbled across my
true marital status there. The judge had blacked the press out

of the trial, but they'd been absolutely relentless everywhere his else. Maybe some juror had signed a tell-all book deal and was spilling his guts.

Entering my real name into the search engine yielded several news hits, but their Web sites all wanted me to register for access to the articles. I didn't want to leave an electronic trail, even with my new name, so I opened up another browser window and created a dummy e-mail account with one of the free services, under the name Margaret Ness.

Margaret was Elliot's fictional ex-wife, one of Joe's dad's creations. Despite being among the most feared of the West Coast capos back in the day—Old Pete was a small, trim man with one of those scary-calm faces that makes you wonder what executioners look like under their masks—he had a streak of ribald wackiness that made even people who were scared of him laugh out loud on a regular basis. Margaret's peccadilloes kept us entertained over many a family dinner, and prospective gun customers coming into the bar knew she was the one to ask for if they were interested in buying.

I got Margaret registered and took a look at the articles. None of them so much as mentioned the trial; most of them were about the restoration projects I'd done in California. I read through these wistfully, missing the clean sharp smell of aged pine and the way my shoulders ached after a long day of pulling nails and hanging trim.

I tried Joe's name next and got quite a few hits, which I clicked through gingerly. Most were safely general articles about his death and the arrest of the two skinheads. About half mentioned his wife, but not by name. I was a little afraid to do an image search, but managed it; there was only one, the ten-year-old headshot from his obituary.

An image search on both my maiden and married names yielded zip. "Julia Kalas" got me two hits, both in Finland. The feds had done a good job. The old me had ceased to exist, and the new me was a blank slate.

Which left me still in the dark on Silvia Molina. She'd never even addressed me by name, yet she'd managed to obtain a carefully hidden personal fact. OK, maybe I was paranoid, but I had good reason. I couldn't afford to believe that it was just a lucky guess.

I sat there cogitating unsuccessfully for maybe half an hour, then got up to make some dinner, feeling rough. There are downsides to this automatic pilot of mine, the primary one being that the brain often takes its sweet time clocking back in after the pressure's off. It usually brings some pretty good stuff with it, but it's a pain in the ass having to wait on it. In my next life, I want to be one of those fast thinkers. Being a fast feeler instead isn't much consolation.

XII

Hector was sitting next to the cash register with his feet up on the edge of the under-counter cooler when I came in, reading a book. There were two couples and a lone biker at the bar, and half a dozen other customers scattered out amongst the tables. I saw Jesse Reed slouched at the edge of the dance floor, watching a trio of young women undulating to some bass-heavy roadhouse blues. Near him, the purple-haired hotel clerk was sharing a pitcher with a small group.

Hector hopped up and slid his book under the register. "Mike's running late. You want a beer?"

I nodded and walked down around the curve in the bar, taking the stool in the corner formed by the serving top and the limestone wall. Joe had always referred to this as the "catbird seat"—the spot in a bar where you have full surveillance of the room and nobody behind you.

Hector got a frosted mug out of the refrigerator and filled it. Connie appeared at the wait station, which was situated halfway down the long side of the bar. Her springy hair lofted crazily around her shoulders as she moved, like a cloud of black birds rising from a field.

"Hey, Julia," she said; then, to Hector, "Can I get a couple of top-shelf martinis and a Shiner? Oh, and another peppermint schnapps for Marie."

The name caught my ear and I peeked over her shoulder at the booth she'd just come from. Sure enough, there was Charlie, still wearing her crinoline and boots. All I could see of her partner was the back of her head, which was covered in stringy hair that had been dyed blonde several times too many.

Hector frowned at Connie. "That's her fifth one."

"The judge took her license, remember?" Connie said. "She's not going to kill anybody."

"Just herself," Hector growled.

"Aren't you the one who's always saying that trying to control other people's behavior is insane? Just cut it with some tonic or something. She'll never know the difference."

Hector pressed his lips together, then started making up the order. Connie rolled her eyes, stage-whispering toward me, "Ethical bastard."

A wiry redhead came trotting through the front door. His auburn hair was clipped short, and he wore a small soul patch under his lower lip. His arms were roped with hard muscle, and his fashionably baggy clothes did little to conceal the fact that the rest of him probably was, too.

"Dr. Livingston, I presume," Hector said as the redhead came around and through the flip-top next to where I was sitting.

"Sorry, man," he said, getting a bar towel out from under the serving top and wrapping it hastily around his trim waist. "Where's the new meat? Tova said you hired somebody."

Hector nodded over toward me.

The man turned, eyes wide, and stuck his hand out. "Mike Hayes," he said.

"Ow," I answered involuntarily. His grip was brutal.

"Sorry," he said. "I beat people up for a living."

"Mike's a fighter," Hector explained to me. "He's finally trying to go professional this year, which is why I need you."

"Wow," I said. "I didn't know people still did that."

Mike's face went puzzled. "What?"

"Boxing. I thought it went out with communism."

He laughed and glanced at Hector, who lifted one of his long eyebrows and said, "You're not from around here, so we'll ignore that remark."

I waited a couple of seconds to see if they'd explain what the hell they were talking about. When they didn't, I moved on, asking Mike, "Where do you train?"

He gestured at Hector. "Grandpa Marx here insists we support our local sweat lodge. Tino's. It's down by the railroad tracks, on the east side." His amber eyes were darting over the part of my physique he could see, sizing me up. "Why?"

"I need to find a decent weight room. Something without a bunch of pink barbells and Nautilus machines."

"Don't see a lot of female powerlifters in these parts," Mike remarked.

"You're not seeing one now," I assured him. "Sometimes I just want to shove heavy things around."

"I know the feeling," he said, grinning. He paused to set up a couple of cocktail glasses, then asked, "You ever thought about training up to fight? The women's division down here is really slim."

I demurred, "I don't like people hitting me in the face. Especially on purpose."

Hector, who'd moved down past the ice well to take an order, snorted a commiserating laugh as he came back over to the cash register. "I hear that."

"Like you ever let a glove near that gorgeous mug, you vain bastard," Mike chuckled.

It didn't surprise me to learn that Hector had a past in the ring. With those shoulders, he easily made up in reach for what he lacked in height, and he looked about as easy to knock down as a Sherman tank.

He squeezed behind Mike, giving the bartender's head a good-natured shove. "Can you and Connie hold the fort while I give Julia the grand tour?"

"Yeah, no problem," Mike said.

Hector ducked under the flip-top and came to stand next to me, getting a flat yellow box out of his shirt pocket. He extracted a short cigarette and lit it.

"Did he just call you Grandpa Marx?" I asked.

"He's just yanking my chain," Hector said. "I'm a democratic

Socialist, not a Marxist." His voice was easy, and he let his gaze wander lazily around the bar as if not interested in my reaction, but I felt him waiting for it.

"So that's why people have been giving me funny looks all day," I said.

A flash of guilty amusement shot across Hector's face, and I realized that I'd been set up. It couldn't be easy for a pinko to find employees down here in the red state belt, so the Amazon had brought him an out-of-towner. I wondered what he'd done to earn the favor.

Hector cleared his throat and changed the subject. "OK, let's see. Well, I guess you can tell, I'm set up for two bartenders, which has been me and Mike up to now, but he's needing more time off to train, and I can't be around cigarette smoke for very long." He tapped his breastbone with a forefinger. "Asthma."

I looked pointedly at the smoldering cylinder between his fingers, and he explained, "These're herbal. I dunno what's in them, but if I smoke four or five a day, I don't need an inhaler. The local *curandera* makes them for me."

There couldn't be two in a town this size. "Are you talking about Silvia Molina?"

"Yeah," he said, sounding surprised.

"I met her at the fire last night," I said. "Teresa picked me up late, and she got the call just as we were coming into town."

Hector's long brows dropped, shading his eyes. "What was Silvia doing there?"

"Talking to the cops. They think it might be arson, and apparently she saw somebody run off."

"Son of a bitch," he muttered, his gaze sliding away from me. He seemed to be feeling for something just beyond his grasp, and the radar gave me a poke. Before I had time to focus the brain, Hector startled, looking down. The black and white cat that I'd seen at my interview was winding itself around his leg.

"Damn it, Lou, not again," Hector said, bending to pick it up. It gave me a friendly look, and I reached over to scrub behind its ears.

"Cat hair doesn't bother your lungs?" I said.

"Not in this place," Hector replied, his eyes running over the shiny floorboards. "No place for it to stick."

He motioned me to follow him, saying, "The only hard-and-fast rule here—besides don't rob me—is that Luigi stays upstairs or in the office when the bar's open."

I hopped down from the stool, smiling at the name. The cat did look cartoonishly Italian, with his big black mustache.

"I think he's figured out how to open my apartment door," Hector said as I followed him toward the office. "I haven't had time to fix the lock."

"What's wrong with it?"

Hector pushed the office door shut behind us. "Break-in last week. They stole some stuff and busted up the place. Cost me a damn fortune."

The last comment felt tacked on, obligatory. It wasn't the money that was bothering him.

"What did they take?" I asked.

"Nothing valuable. It was just destructive, mostly. Probably a bunch of kids gearing up for Halloween."

I watched him rummaging in the desk drawer, remembering a story Pete had told me about some West Coast wiseguys breaking into a mark's house and moving the furniture. The invasion of personal space produced results where more violent measures had failed.

"I can probably fix your lock, if you want," I offered.

Hector's slow grin started up. "Ah, yes, the secret superpowers. What else you got hiding under there?"

He'd come over from the desk, holding out a key, his otherworldly composure returning. A saucy response bubbled up into my mouth, but stayed there. I took the key mutely, and Hector gestured at the stacks of boxes against the stone wall.

"We keep beers and ales in the cooler, and hard liquor out here," he said. "There's no real system, just try not to cover up the labels. The most important thing—if you take the last case of something, mark it on the order sheet on the desk, so I'll know we're out."

I nodded, wondering what the hell was wrong with me. I haven't missed a flirtatious opening like that since my salad days.

"Hey, man," Mike's voice buzzed from the intercom. "Can you bring me a couple cases of Shiner longnecks? We're out up here."

Hector mashed the reply button and said, "Coming right up."

He went into the cooler and shouldered two beer boxes like they were meringues. As he came out, kicking the door shut behind him, an odd-shaped charm on a length of black cord swung out of his shirt, and I jumped at the chance to make up for lost opportunity.

"What is that thing?" I said, stepping over to take hold of the charm. Maybe I'd gone temporarily banterless, but there are other ways to gauge whether or not a man's attracted to you. Hector didn't retreat or adjust his posture as I moved into his personal space, and I felt a zing of satisfaction.

"It's a *chakana*," he said.

The charm was a gold square about an inch across, with zig-zag edges and a circular hole in the middle through which the string looped. I peered at it, stalling to stand there close to him as long as possible. He smelled warm and spicy, like leaf fires in the fall, and my body began to heat up like it had just had a shot of good whiskey.

"It's a pre-Columbian thing, symbolizes heaven and earth and the four directions," Hector explained, going a little breathless—probably from holding up the beer cases, but I let myself enjoy the fantasy that it was my physical proximity. "Get the door for me, will you?"

The club had filled up quite a bit while we'd been gone. There were a dozen couples on the dance floor now, and the air was thick with conversation and music. Mel, the one-handed department store salesman, was sitting on the first barstool in-side the front door, smoking a pipe and carrying on a lively conversation with another geezer in dusty overalls and a John Deere cap. Jesse Reed had moved to one of the booths and been joined there by a man who looked a lot like the picture of Richard Hallstedt I'd seen in the newspaper.

Kathleen's party eyed Hector hungrily as he hauled through the flip-top and dropped the beer cases in front of the ice well. Connie appeared at the wait station, and I went over and shouldered up next to her.

"Is that Teresa's husband over there?" I murmured, shifting my eyes toward the booth.

"Yeah. Teresa never introduced y'all?"

"I haven't seen her since she got married," I feinted. "He's a doctor, right?"

"Yeah. He runs the surgery program down at Memorial Hospital." Connie's eyes were focused on her hands while she counted change, but I felt her attention elsewhere.

I gave it a nudge. "He doesn't really seem like her type."

"Oh, there's nothing wrong with him that a decade or so of intensive therapy wouldn't fix," she said cheerfully, keeping her eyes on her money.

I looked over at Richard again. He and Jesse were leaning toward each other across the table, deep in conversation that didn't appear to be going well. I wondered what the two of them could possibly have to talk about. They were like aliens from different planets.

"What's your diagnosis?" I asked Connie.

She folded a slim stack of singles between her fingers, embarrassed. "Forget it. Richard and Teresa don't need me taking sides. Their divorce is acrimonious enough as it is."

I started to take another shot at it, but was distracted by a flash of bare skin. Hector's shirt had come unbuttoned, and bare skin showed all the way to his navel as he bent over the ice well.

"Am I supposed to be able to read this?" I heard Mike complain.

"Cuba libre," Connie's voice replied with a giggle in it. "Had your eyes checked lately?"

I came up for air and realized that the giggle was aimed at me. My face went hot. I like to think I've got more class than to ogle a man in front of his relatives.

"Oh, girl, don't even worry about it." Connie said in response to my obvious embarrassment. "Every woman in town has been through a Hector Guerra crush. It's a rite of passage around here." She picked up her tray. "Just don't let Teresa catch you at it."

I watched her swing back out onto the floor, the comment fizzling down into my consciousness. Now I understood that the funny looks I'd been getting on Hector's account had been about more than politics.

"Somebody just dropped an anvil on you, maybe?" Mel remarked on his way back from the men's room.

"Yeah, kind of," I said, putting a hand on his arm. "Why'd you act so surprised this morning, when I told you I was interviewing with Hector?"

Mel performed his old country shrug, black eyebrows appearing above the horn-rims. "Teresa gets her nose outta joint if Hector so much as stands downwind of a female under sixty, but she sends a tomato like you over here for a job?" He pursed his lips, his shoulders rising another delicate fraction of an inch. "Not that it's any of my business."

"So they're an item?"

"What, girlfriends don't talk about these things anymore?"

"For heaven's sake, Mel," a cool voice said, "the woman just moved here. Let her get her furniture arranged before you start winding her up with the local gossip, will you?" Tova Bradshaw was coming around the wait station, gazing archly in my informer's direction.

"Feh," he muttered, waving at her.

Mike came down the bar to meet her, and she slid a smartphone across the serving top at him, saying, "It was under the bed."

He hiked himself up and leaned toward her. I saw her eyes glint at me as she gave him a light kiss on the lips.

"I've got a thing tonight that's going to run late," she said in a low voice. "I'll see you tomorrow."

"What's up?" he said.

"Just business," she replied airily.

Mike seemed dissatisfied with this answer, but rolled his shoulders and said, "I gotta take Oscar in for some dogscaping in the morning anyway."

"When you gonna make an honest man of him, Tova?" Mel gibed at her.

Tova turned her cold blue eyes on him again. "As I've told you before, Mel, neither of us wants children and we're both financially independent. Marriage would be pointless."

"Doesn't want him getting his hands on her money, she means," Mel scoffed under his breath.

If Tova heard him, she gave no indication, and he made a tsking noise and went back to his seat at the far end of the bar.

Connie came back from delivering her last order, and Tova turned to her. "Bad tidings, I'm afraid. Herrera's offer on the Ranch fell through."

"Damn it!" Connie slapped her tray down on the serving top.

"Have you given any more thought to my suggestion to sub-divide?"

"I can't afford it, as you well know," Connie snapped, rubbing her forehead. "What the hell did I do in my last life to get saddled with this accursed piece of real estate?"

"You own a ranch?" I cut in.

"I wish," Connie said. "Maybe then somebody would buy the place."

"It's just twelve acres, west of town," Tova told me. "Dad always referred to it, with his typical levity, as 'the Ranch.'"

"Does it have a house on it?"

Both of them looked at me, momentarily speechless. Tova recovered first. "It's not habitable."

Now I was interested. It wasn't a commercial building, but it would get my foot in the local construction market door, and double as my place to live in the bargain.

"How old is it?" I asked.

Connie said, "The title lists the original building date as 1906. Dad fixed it up some before he died. Of course, that was ten years ago."

"What do you want for it?"

Connie put her outside hand on her hip and glowered. "If you're screwing with me, I swear to God, I will personally beat you senseless."

"It's appraised at fifty-one thousand," Tova said.

"No, I mean for the whole acreage."

"That *is* for the whole acreage."

My mouth didn't actually drop open, but I had to take a moment. In California, you'd be lucky to get an undersized vacant lot in a bad neighborhood for fifty thousand dollars.

"When can I see it?" I asked them.

"Any time you want," Connie said, sounding cautious.

"How about tomorrow morning?"

She grimaced, looking at Tova. "I'm in class all day."

"I'll be unavailable as well, I'm afraid," Tova said.

"You're welcome to go out there on your own," Connie offered. "Hector's got some stuff locked up in the barn, but the house is open. Take Fourth Street west for about eight miles, and you'll see the sign on the left, just before you cross the river."

The Amazon had come in and made a beeline for Richard and Jesse. Tova was watching them, and now she excused herself and joined them. Connie waited until she was out of earshot, then leaned toward me and said, "I've got tuition to pay. Make me an offer, it's yours."

Mike had set up her last couple of drinks, and she wound back out amongst the clientele to deliver them. Something in his demeanor pointed my attention at Tova again, who had taken the booth seat next to Jesse, facing Richard. The Amazon was rattling pointedly at her ex, leaning on the table. He made a short reply, then Teresa straightened up and stalked out. The remaining troika watched her go, then hunched toward each other like they might be dealing with the end of the world.

Watching them, I started to wonder what Richard was doing in here, considering what I'd just learned about Hector and Teresa. If the Amazon's divorce was proceeding as badly as Connie had suggested, I couldn't imagine that her husband was on good terms with her boyfriend.

XIII

Around eleven, the door behind Mel pushed open, and the young cashier from the café came in. I'd moved back to the catbird seat during a heavy rush around ten. Hector, serving customers at the far end of the bar, lifted his chin at her and headed for the bar register. "Ones and quarters?" he asked.

The cashier nodded, handing him a couple of bills.

"Y'all got anything left?" he said, opening the cash drawer.

"Some pork chops and potato salad," she said, with her squinty shy smile. "You want me to save some back for you?"

"Yes, please!" Hector replied.

Mike, who'd come down to fill some mugs at the beer taps to my left, chimed in, "Hey, I want in on that."

"Neffa, this is my new bartender, Julia," Hector said to the young cashier.

She smiled over at me and did a small wave.

"That's an interesting name," I said. "Is it short for something?"

She rolled her eyes, embarrassed. "Nefertiti."

"Queen of the Nile!" Mike crowed as Hector gave her a packet of bills and several coin rolls.

Neffa showed Mike her tongue with mature confidence, and he laughed. As she turned to go, Kathleen's table got her attention; she thanked Hector and joined them.

I went back to watching Mike and Hector work, which had been keeping me entertained for the last couple of hours. Mike was all nervous energy, moving constantly between customers, taps, and cash register, while Hector had a lazy man's efficiency, grouping tasks together so that he spent less time traveling. Mike's section of the bar turned over faster, but Hector sold more drinks—his slow ease put people in a relaxed and indulgent mood, keeping them pinned to their seats and their money flowing.

It was close to midnight when Connie came back to the wait station, plunking down her empty tray with a tired sigh. "If you guys are doing OK back there, I'm going to take a break."

"Go for it," Mike said. Hector was changing the keg spigots on his side of the ice well.

"Hand me my bag, will you?" Connie said to Mike.

While Mike rummaged under the register, a huge biker who'd taken the seat on this side of the wait station turned woozily toward Connie. "How yer doin' tonight, sugar?" he asked her. His voice was remarkably clear, considering he was barely managing to stay upright on the barstool.

"I'm fine," Connie said, raising an amused eyebrow in my direction. She got a set of keys and a pack of cigarettes out of her small tan shoulder bag, then gave it back to Mike.

The biker's head swiveled unsteadily around as she passed behind him. "Pretty hot for a beaner," he said, watching her make her way toward the office.

Hector's head snapped up, revealing a savage expression so intense that it seemed to blast-heat the air around him. "Hey, take that shit outside."

The biker swayed with indignation. "I was giving her a compliment, man! Don't you fucking wetbacks know when somebody's trying to be nice to ya?"

Hector had already pushed behind Mike and ducked under the flip-top. He turned rapidly around the curve in the bar and grabbed the biker's collar, lifting him bodily off the stool. Realizing he'd soon be on the sidewalk, the drunk emptied his cache of profanity into the bar as Hector dragged him toward the front.

"Wow," I said, watching the door close behind them. "Remind me never to piss him off."

Mike grinned at me. "We save a shitload of money on bouncers."

Through the storefront window, I saw Hector give the biker a shove that sent him stumbling toward the north. A cold fury radiated around my new boss, keeping the people on the sidewalk at a distance. The smell of bigotry in the air made my stomach hurt, reminding me of who I was hiding from.

Mel began to make leaving motions, and Mike went over to close out his tab. When he came back, he glanced out the front window, where Hector was now talking into a clamshell cell phone, and said, "Hey, I hate to put you to work, but would you mind getting me a couple bottles of Stoli from the back? There's an open case right next to the desk."

I nodded and slid off my stool. As I stepped into the mouth of the hall, I heard a sharp shriek from inside the office. A few fast steps, and there was Connie, standing against the rear wall next to the double doors, one leaf of which was standing open. She was breathing hard and had her hand pressed to her chest.

"Are you OK?" I asked, moving quickly around the sofa toward her.

She pointed at the floor. My eye followed her finger to a pale shape lying in the doorway.

It was a human hand.

FRIDAY, NOVEMBER 2

————————◆————————

1

"I stepped on it," Connie said, a shudder in her voice.

She moved in behind me as I crouched down to get a better look. A faint foul odor rose up, like dead fish soaked in paint thinner. This was no rubber Halloween prank. It was the real thing.

"Where—?" I started, but was interrupted by the office door crashing open. Hector plunged in, carrying a baseball bat.

"It's OK, Pops," Connie said, holding an open hand toward him. "We're both OK."

The wild look on his face froze as he came around the sofa. Connie pressed one hand gently against his chest, taking the baseball bat with the other. Hector receded back and deflated into the desk chair. She kept her hand on his shoulder while she picked up the phone and dialed.

"Benny? Hey, it's Connie. Could you and Teresa come over here? We just found something really creepy in the alley. Yeah. OK, thanks."

My head had gone silent as a church, and I could almost feel the blood scraping along the insides of my veins. One of the Brotherhood's classic tricks is leaving a family member's body parts at its enemies' homes or places of business. Kind of like the horse in *The Godfather*, only it's your mother's head. Pete would walk into the Pacific with his pockets full of rocks before playing ball with the feds, so I hadn't been surprised when he didn't join me in protection, and I hadn't worried too much about something happening to him, given his connections. Now I was wondering if I should have.

I willed my breath slow and steady as Connie put the phone down and slid her hand to Hector's wrist. His eyes wouldn't leave the thing on the floor.

"Would you do me a favor?" she said quietly to me. "Upstairs in the medicine cabinet there's a green bottle with some tablets in it—would you bring it down with a glass of water?"

I nodded and went around the sofa and out, glad for something to do besides stand there and try not to throw up. Mike was looking anxiously toward the office from behind the bar, where the flip-top stood open. I gave him the OK sign and turned up the stairs.

Hector's apartment was one big room with a stainless steel kitchen to the right of the front door. A rustic plank table stood in the center, and beyond it there was a sitting area with a sofa and side chairs, and a king-size bed half hidden behind a tall bookcase. Just like downstairs, a short hallway to my left led to a square back room, except up here it contained a laundry and dressing area. A shower, toilet, and sink backed up against the stairway wall.

Through the floor, I could hear a subterranean hum of

activity from downstairs that was oddly comforting, like a distant hive of friendly bees. I sat down on the toilet seat to wait for the brain to reboot. After a few minutes, it reminded me of what Teresa had said earlier that day: there was no payoff for the Brotherhood in wasting time trying to scare me. If they knew where I was, I'd be dead, not tripping over body parts.

Braced by this thought, I pulled the medicine cabinet open and found the green bottle. The name BOTÁNICA MOLINA was hand-printed in pencil at the top of the label, with a Latin plant name I didn't recognize written below. I filled a glass with water in the kitchen and went back downstairs. The Amazon had arrived and was standing just inside the double doors, looking at the hand while Connie talked. Benny was taking notes, an aluminum field case at his feet.

". . . had it propped open while I was in the alley," Connie was saying, "like I always do when I go out for a smoke."

"These doors swing out," the Amazon told her. "It couldn't have been there before you opened them, or it would have been pushed out into the alley."

I went over and handed the pill bottle and water to Hector. He took them without looking at me and set them on the desk.

"You're positive nobody came into the office while you were out there?" Benny prodded Connie.

"Listen, I'm telling you," she said, sounding irritated, "I was never more than a couple of feet from the door. I'd have seen anybody who got near it, inside or out."

"Why don't you show me where you were standing?" he replied with that patient tone cops use when they don't believe you. Connie got up with a sigh and they went out into the alley.

"Can I talk to you privately?" I said to the Amazon.

She glanced over at Hector, and I was surprised to catch an intensely hateful expression fleeing from his face as her eyes slid onto it. She looked quickly back at me and said, "It's OK. Hector knows your situation."

I stared at her for a baffled minute, then said, "God damn it."

"Not *who* you are," she said brusquely, "just that you're in protection. You'd want to know the same thing about a prospective employee."

I pressed my teeth together, holding on to my temper, and gestured at the hand on the floor. "I guess you missed gang day at orientation." The Amazon kept her poker face on, so I went ahead and spelled it out. "This is classic Aryan Brotherhood shit."

Before she could respond, Benny hurried back in, saying, "Couple of guys in the parking lot saw somebody on the roof about ten minutes ago."

He trotted past us toward the office door. The Amazon fell in behind him, her hand rising to the service pistol on her belt. They turned rapidly out of the room and we heard them moving fast up the stairs.

I gave Hector a puzzled look, and he explained, "The roof access is at the top of the stairs, on the landing."

The youthful buzz in his voice had aged, and he wouldn't look at me. Which was fine. I was feeling embarrassed, as if I'd tried to pass myself off to him as somehow better than I am and gotten caught at it.

Connie came back in, making her way gingerly around the thing on the floor. "Where'd Benny and Teresa go?"

"There might be somebody on the roof," I told her.

Her eyes widened. "You mean they threw it down while I was out there?"

Hector made a sudden, impatient movement. "How could they? We're the only place on the block with roof access that's open right now. We'd have seen them going up there."

"We've been pretty busy the last couple of hours, Pops," Connie said doubtfully. "We might not have noticed."

He moved his head in a nodding motion, but it didn't seem as if he'd heard her. Connie went over and leaned against the desk next to him. I paced around the office, trying to think, while we waited for the cops to return.

It was almost one-thirty when the Amazon came back in. Benny wasn't with her. "If anybody was on the roof, they were probably gone before we got here."

"But how'd they get down?" I said. "I was on my way back to the office when I heard Connie, and Hector came in right behind me. We'd have seen anybody coming out of the stairwell."

"I sent Benny to check the other buildings on the block," the Amazon said. "They could have found another access point." Her eyes flickered toward Hector, then back to Connie and me. "Y'all notice anyone acting weird this evening?"

"Hector threw a drunk out just before Connie went to the back," I said.

"Who?" Teresa asked him.

He shook his head. "Some biker. Not a regular. He made a nasty remark to Connie, so I took him outside and sent him on his way."

"To Connie?" the Amazon repeated, looking over at her.

She blanched and sank down onto the arm of the sofa again.

"You pissed anybody off recently?" Teresa asked her.

Connie paused and put a finger to her lips. The Amazon gestured, and Connie sighed reluctantly, "I turned Jesse Reed down for a date again last week. He wasn't very nice about it."

Teresa and Hector looked at each other, then back at her.

"Oh, come on," Connie protested. "Something like this really isn't Jesse's style. You know how he is. If he's going to be ugly, he'll be ugly to your face."

Mike's voice buzzed from the intercom. "Hey, what the hell's going on back there? I feel like a plague survivor up here."

"Oh, shoot!" Connie said, hopping up. "We left him by himself with all those customers." She trotted out, letting in a waft of club noise and smoke.

Teresa had gotten a digital camera out of the field case and gone over to take photos of the hand in situ. "Male, I'd say," she murmured, taking a few shots, then put the camera away and snapped on some latex gloves. She squatted and lifted it a few inches, peering at the wrist end. "That's a pretty clean cut. Might be surgical."

The brain, fully awake now, did a light-speed fact shuffle and told me that she'd just implicated her ex-husband.

She seemed to realize it, too, and pressed her lips together, inserting the hand into a plastic evidence bag. She peeled her gloves off and stood up. "I'll take this down to the lab in the morning," she said, reaching for a label. "If they can get me an ID, finding out where it came from should be pretty painless."

Hector didn't say anything, but the Amazon nodded toward

him as if he had, then picked up the field case and gestured at me to follow her into the alley.

A strip of garbage-stained asphalt ran between buildings to the left, forming a dark valley. The lots behind Guerra's and to the right were vacant. There was a collection of motorcycles parked there, their front wheels flopped sideways like sleeping birds.

I followed the Amazon as she stalked past them. She stopped about halfway to the street and turned, saying, "I don't need you questioning my competence in front of the locals." Her voice wasn't loud, but it stung like a whip. I kept my face quiet and waited.

"It's taken me years to establish my credibility here," she said. "Try to undermine me like that again, and I'll out you to the Brotherhood myself."

"I wasn't—," I started, but she cut me off.

"You get a whiff of this thing?" she snapped, lifting the field case in her hand. "It's been embalmed. It's not fresh meat off some gang carcass. OK? I know my turf. I know what goes on here and what doesn't." She jabbed a finger at me. "You don't."

I held my hands up, palms out. She continued to glare at me for a few seconds, then strode off, turning toward the square at the street. I let out a breath I didn't know I'd been holding.

As my midsection relaxed, the word "embalmed" reverberated up into my skull, and everything slid together like a bunch of flowers going into a vase: Silvia Molina. Hector must have let something slip about me when he was at the botanica picking up an order of cigarettes. That's how she'd found out I was a widow, and since I hadn't played ball on my visit, now she was upping the ante with some spare cadaver parts she had lying around.

I considered going after the Amazon, but decided it would probably be better to give her some cooling-off time. Letting Silvia cook until morning probably wouldn't bring on the apocalypse.

There was nobody in the office when I returned to it. I shut the back doors and made sure they latched before going up front.

II

The club was almost empty now, and Connie and Mike were standing at the serving top, talking quietly across the wait station. Mike had a sink full of hot, soapy water running, and he wrung out a rag as I came over.

"Is Hector still back there?" he asked me.

I shook my head. He and Connie exchanged a look that made the back of my stomach tickle.

"What?" I said.

"He must have gone upstairs," Mike replied as if it answered my question.

"God, what a night," Connie sighed, dropping her cigarettes and keys into her purse.

Mike started wiping down the serving top, cracking at her, "Hope the guy's head isn't waiting on your doorstep when you get home."

"Oh, you are just so friggin' funny," she mocked back, then tsked, "I don't know why Teresa thinks it has anything to do with me. The way things have been downtown lately, it's a wonder there aren't body parts littering the streets."

I was just about to ask her to elaborate when my eye caught

movement on the front sidewalk. Benny was standing outside the front door, his back to us, one hand braced against Richard Hallstedt's narrow chest to keep him from getting by. They were both talking at once, their voices escalating through the glass.

Mike followed my look. "Jesus Christ. What now?" He tossed his rag into the sink and came through the flip-top.

Connie motioned surreptitiously to me as he passed. "Let's go out the back. I've had enough drama for one night."

I nodded agreement, and we headed for the office. As we passed through, I noticed the bottle of pills and glass of water still on the desk, untouched.

"What are those tablets for?" I asked Connie.

"Oh, it's just an herbal sedative," she said, jingling her keys out of her pocket with a nervous gesture. "Come on, I'll walk you to your car."

She was a terrible liar. I remembered her deft, reassuring words to Hector as he'd come through the office door and seen the hand. His frozen expression; her fingers on his wrist.

"What's wrong with him?" I asked.

She paused, then said reluctantly, "Post-traumatic stress disorder."

"From what?"

"That's not usually the first question people ask," she said, eyeing me with curiosity.

"A couple of shrinks tried to convince a friend of mine that she had it," I said. It wasn't technically a lie. I consider myself a friend.

"Well," she said, taking a long breath, "he doesn't talk about it, so I don't know the details, but Dad found him living on the streets of Managua in '82, when he was in Nicaragua on a case. Apparently, Hector's family was killed in the civil war—you know, all that stuff with the Sandinistas and Somoza." She felt in her purse for a cigarette, then seemed to think better of it. "My guess is that he witnessed whatever happened to them."

The excruciating picture of Joe dropping to the pavement, half his beloved face gone, ripped through my memory. I resisted the urge to close my eyes.

"Things were pretty brutal even after the Sandinistas took over in '79, thanks to the Contras," Connie had gone on. "Sixty thousand people died, even more were 'disappeared.' People down there are still dealing with it psychologically. That's why I want to go back after I get my license."

I remembered our introduction. "Guatemala, right?"

She nodded. "Same song, second verse—government coup, civil war, all my relatives killed." Connie glanced down the alley over my shoulder, then fixed her eyes earnestly on my face. "Listen, keep this to yourself, will you? Everybody around here has always just assumed that we're Mexicans, and it's easier to let them think that. It keeps people from talking to Hector about stuff that's difficult for him to deal with."

A dishonorable satisfaction percolated down around my belly button. I wasn't the only one in town living a secret life. Knowing as much didn't do me any practical good at the moment, but it made up—a little—for the Amazon telling Hector about me.

I suddenly remembered his reaction to the drunk biker's remark. "Is he safe to be walking around loose?"

Connie frowned. "What do you mean?"

I described what I'd seen and she made a dismissive motion

with her head. "I dunno, you might do the same thing, if you had to listen to stuff like that all the time." She fidgeted, clearly ready to be done with the conversation. "Where are you parked?"

I gestured south, and we started down the alley.

The lights were still on at the café, and Lavon and Neffa were inside, doing their closing cleanup. Connie rapped on the window as we passed down the side street toward the square, and they both waved to us. We stopped on the corner, and I saw Richard and Benny get into Benny's cruiser, which was parked at the curb in front of the bar. I wondered if he'd driven it the couple of hundred feet from the courthouse.

"Damn it," Connie murmured as the crowd that had been observing the fireworks between Richard and Benny broke up and a young woman began weaving toward us.

She was under thirty, thin and pasty, with heavy dark brows making a lie of her blond hair, and a smear of bright lipstick sliding off her wide mouth. "Hey, girl, you gotcher car tonight?" she called in our direction.

"I can't, I'm going south," Connie replied as the woman approached us.

"You seen that cop cunt around?" she slurred, seeming to forget her request for a ride. "That bitch that ruined my life?"

Connie gave me a sidelong eye-roll and put an arm around her shoulders, guiding her off down the sidewalk. The drunk woman continued spewing incomprehensible venom all the way back to the bar.

I jaywalked the corner and made for the truck, which I'd parked in front of the burned-out salon. As I got in, I heard the unmistakable clatter of a BMW echoing away toward the north. I couldn't blame Hector. After a night like this, I felt like taking a drive myself.

III

When I got home about half an hour later, Hector's bike was parked under the oak tree next to Teresa's Pontiac. I felt a shiver of anticipation as I climbed the back stairs, but nobody was waiting. I went into the bedroom to drop my wallet and keys on the nightstand, and heard voices coming from the front apartment. I stopped still and listened. It was Hector and Teresa.

I couldn't tell what they were saying, but Teresa sounded like she was enjoying a good joke, and Hector was angry. I tiptoed over and pressed my ear to the locked door, but I couldn't make out any words, just the tone of the conversation.

After a couple of back-and-forths, her voice went serious; then his started getting louder, rising almost to a shout. There was a short silence, and then a door slammed. Hector's boots clomped across a wood floor, banged down some steps, and crunched onto the driveway gravel. A few seconds later, the BMW roared to life and gunned off toward the street. I could hear it almost all the way back to the square, out here in the silence. Then I heard the Pontiac starting up and rolling down the driveway. It, too, turned toward town. I looked at my little travel clock, glowing on the nightstand. It was three fifteen.

I remembered the hateful look I'd caught on Hector's face, and wondered if the affair was breaking up. Wishful thinking, maybe, but I've wished worse things.

I went back through the kitchen, peeling off my clothes, and started the bath running. It felt close to eighty inside the apartment, so I mixed the temperature to tepid and opened the windows. I took a long, cool soak, drank a big glass of ice water, and went to bed.

IV

A quiet scraping noise woke me some time later. I lay there listening intently into the dark. After a couple of minutes, I heard the noise again, coming from below the floor, and realized that someone was in the basement.

I looked over at the clock—ten minutes after four—then kneeled up on the bed to peer out the window. A rectangle of weak light lay on the narrow sidewalk below. I watched and listened for a little while, but sleep dragged me back down when it became clear that nothing very interesting was happening. Probably Richard, picking up the last of his stuff at a time when he knew he wouldn't run into Teresa. Maybe that was what she'd bitched him out for in the bar earlier.

I was awakened again after what seemed like only a few minutes, this time by a continuous banging on my apartment door. I got up and went to give whoever it was the piece of my mind that wasn't busy fantasizing about a good night's sleep in a cool room.

Richard Hallstedt demanded, "Where's Teresa?" almost before I got the door open. The gray light behind him told me it was near dawn.

"What the hell time is it?" I said, squinting past him through the porch screen.

"I don't know," he said, clearly unimpressed by the question. "Her car's gone, and she's not in her apartment."

His haughty tone was all the impetus I needed to shut the door in his face, but he set his foot against it before it latched. I pulled it open again and gave him an incredulous once-over. He wasn't a small man—just under six feet, maybe 170—but I'd taken down guys who made a lot more noise hitting the floor than he would. My heft comes in handy sometimes, and I'm strong as fuck when I can get to the gym on a regular basis.

"Get your foot out of my door, or I'll rip it off and feed it to you," I said.

His face went alarmed, and the foot flinched back. I shoved the door closed, locked it, and went back to bed.

I woke up again, pissed off and sweaty, just before noon. It took me a minute to remember Richard's visit, at which point I got up, shuffled into the kitchen, and looked out into the backyard. The Amazon's Pontiac wasn't there. I returned to the bedroom and dialed her cell, but it went direct to voice mail. I sat there holding the phone and waiting for inspiration until it was clear I wasn't going to get any, then went into the bathroom to get dressed.

V

The front door of the bar was unlocked, with the lights off inside except for the back hall, just like the day before. The office was closed and locked, so I went up the stairs and found Hector's apartment door cracked open. When I knocked on the frame, a muffled voice called, "Come on in!"

Hector was lying on the sofa, feet toward the door, up on

one elbow. He appeared to have been awake for only a few minutes. He was alone.

"Hey, there," he said in a thick, slurry voice. "I thought you were Mike."

He was shirtless and barefoot, his midsection covered by a red and black blanket. As he sat up, it slipped to his hips and I realized that he was naked underneath.

"Christ, I feel like hell," he said, wiping his hands down over his face.

I forced myself to stop wishing for X-ray vision and noticed the gray stains under his bloodshot eyes. He made a motion as if to get up, and seemed only then to realize the show I'd get if he did. Spotting a crumpled pair of jeans lying on the floor nearby, he reached unsteadily for them and said, "You want some coffee?"

"No," I said, "but I'll make you some. You look like you need it."

He nodded, pulling the jeans up under the blanket. Disappointed by his modesty, I went into the kitchen and filled up the stainless steel kettle sitting next to the sink.

"Must have been quite a bender," I said, lighting the stove.

Hector, decent and partially vertical now, reached for the box of cigarettes on the coffee table. He gave me a blank look, then asked, "You come by to quit?"

"No, I wanted to talk to Teresa."

He didn't say anything. The silence turned thick as I rummaged through the cabinets above the sink, finally finding a French press.

"Listen," I said, putting it down on the counter, "if I'm going to have to run interference on your personal life, maybe you'd better fill me in on what you want me to tell who."

He squinted over at me, his expression perplexed.

"Richard Hallstedt woke me up at the crack of dawn this morning, looking for her," I said.

"What's that got to do with me?"

"You're telling me she didn't follow you over here after your argument last night?"

He started to answer, and then his expression fuzzed over and he leaned forward and pinched the bridge of his nose.

"I'm in the apartment behind her," I told him. "I could hear you guys when I got home."

Hector examined his cigarette, not saying anything. The kettle whistled, and I reached to turn it off. "Coffee's in the freezer," he said.

I found it and reduced a handful of beans to a fine grit with the grinder, noticing an empty wine bottle and two glasses on the drainboard, with the cork still on the screw next to them. So that was why Hector seemed so out of it. I've consumed way more than half a bottle of wine without paying for it the next day, but people's tolerances vary. I smiled at the irony of a bar owner being a cheap drunk.

Hector stayed quiet, smoking, until I went over to the sofa and handed him a steaming mug. He took it without looking at me and set it on the low table in front of him.

"What were Teresa and I arguing about?" he said, tapping ash into a small brass tray on the side table.

"Don't you know?" I asked, surprised, then realized that he was feeling me out to see what I'd overheard. I started to tell him that he had nothing to worry about, then decided to see what would happen if I didn't.

When it became clear that he wasn't going to break out in a rash from the silence, I said, "So, are you named in the divorce papers?"

A muscle at the back of his arm tensed, and his face went murderous, like it had with the drunk biker the night before. A flash of genuine fear sprinted across the back of my neck.

"Teresa and I have known each other since sixth grade," he said. I could feel him holding his temper down. "If her husband wants to make more out of that than it is, let him answer for the consequences."

I noticed that it wasn't an actual answer to my question, and waited to see if he'd notice it, too. He drank some of his coffee and smoked in silence for a minute, then said more gently, "Richard's a pretty damaged individual. I don't know how she put up with him as long as she did."

"He can't be that bad," I said, despite the bedside manner at my door that morning. "I saw in the paper that he's a city council member. Don't they have to get elected?"

Hector made a wry face. "He's related to half the county. Plus, you know what they say about books and their covers." He looked over at me. "I'd never have guessed you were involved with the Aryan Brotherhood, for instance."

"I wasn't," I said, recoiling from the idea. "They're the ones who killed my husband."

He didn't say anything, just gazed dumbstruck at me with those melted-obsidian eyes of his. A quiver of nausea passed over me. "You didn't know I was a widow?"

He shook his head. "All Teresa told me was that you dodged a weapons indictment by going into protection."

So much for Hector's being the source of Silvia Molina's knowing my real marital status. He couldn't have told her something he didn't know.

"I'm sorry," he said in a soft voice. "Why'd they kill him?"

"I can't tell you," I replied quickly, in a hurry to ask, "What *do* you know about my marriage?"

He made a negligent motion with one shoulder. "Nothing, 'til just now."

Even in its agitated state, the brain took a millisecond to register that he hadn't known I was single until just now, either.

"Was he Latino?" Hector asked. "You speak pretty good Spanish, and those Aryan guys don't usually kill their own kind."

"Listen, if I could tell you the whole story, I would. It's just not safe."

"Hey, no, it's fine," he said, leaning forward to crush out his cigarette.

A step sounded on the landing, and Mike Hayes appeared. He was dressed in sweatpants and a T-shirt, and bounced into the room on sneakered feet, punching at the air. He didn't seem surprised to see me. "Hey, Julia, what's up?"

"Just working the boss over for a raise," I cracked, vacating my chair.

"Damn, you don't waste any time, do ya?" he cracked. "Find any more body parts on your way home?"

"Jesus, Mike," Hector said, dragging himself forward off the sofa. Mike stood back, hands up, and Hector padded by, muttering, "I'll be ready in a second."

Mike watched him disappear into the back, his hands still raised as if I were about to demand his wallet. "What's with him?"

I pointed a look at the empty wine bottle, and Mike dropped his hands. "Naw, naw. Man is not a drinker. Still treats himself like he's training for a belt." He tucked up one corner of his mouth with a mock shudder. "Maybe that creepy-ass shit last night kept him awake, like it did me."

"Did the cops figure out how the guy got on and off the roof?"

He made a face. "Benny got that guy-on-the-roof story from the drunk Hector threw out. Pink elephants, you ask me."

"So how'd the hand get there?"

Mike shrugged and glanced toward the back, cracking his knuckles. He seemed nervous, maybe about having to make small talk with a relative stranger. It's funny how those high-energy gregarious types aren't always so comfortable one-on-one. I'd given up banal chatter along with the rest of my girl suit, and after a strained silence, he threw out, "I hear you and Teresa go back."

"Sort of," I allowed. "I worked for her aunt in Boston for a while."

"I guess it's been a long time since you've seen her, then," he said. "I don't think she's taken a vacation for a decade, at least."

"Hector says he's known her since grade school," I parried, to distract him from digging any deeper into my personal history.

"Yeah, we all used to run around together. He started school a couple of years behind and didn't speak very good English, so naturally the other kids treated him like a freak. Teresa was always getting picked on for her weight, and I was, like, a walking target. We formed a kind of loser coalition."

I let out a little chuckle of recognition. "How'd you qualify?"

"Hey, I wasn't always the Adonis you see before you." He flashed his brisk grin again, holding his arms wide. "Truly tragic orthodontics and a bad case of acne. Plus, ya know, I didn't even make five-six until I was twenty-one."

"And look at him now," Hector said, coming back dressed in shorts and a T-shirt. I made a point of not admiring his muscular legs as he sat down to put on his gym shoes. I had it bad enough already.

"Oh," Hector said to me, straightening up. "Can you come in at six tonight? Mike's gotta go to San Antonio after we work out."

"Sure," I said. "I might be a little rusty, though."

"Friday-night immersion learning'll get you back up to speed plenty quick," Hector assured me, hopping up.

"You coming with us?" Mike asked as we clomped downstairs.

"I don't have my gear with me," I hedged. The thing with Silvia was drilling into the brain again, and I wanted to talk to the Amazon before it hit an artery.

VI

Teresa's Pontiac hadn't returned to its parking spot under the tree behind the house, so I dialed her cell, but she didn't answer. I tried again after half an hour, then once more around four, at which point I finally snapped to the fact that she was screening my calls. Probably trying to teach me a lesson for mouthing off at her the previous night. I left her a message full of gory details and told her to come see me at the bar after six if she didn't want me reciting any more sensitive information on her unsecured line.

Then, just to give her a taste of her own medicine, I decided to make myself scarce for a while.

VII

A faded FOR SALE sign appeared approximately where Connie had told me it would, just past a dry creek bed some eight miles from town. A driveway paved with chalky white gravel ran away from it down a long, bare hill. I stopped and got out to take a look before turning in, not ready to bust an axle on my new ride just yet.

About a football field away, down and off to the right, stood a small house with an open shed connected to it by a wire-fenced yard. It didn't look like much, and it stood perilously close to the low-water crossing just beyond it.

Satisfied that the driveway was navigable, I turned in. About halfway down, a bigger house, tall and narrow, came into view on the left, and I realized that the two smaller buildings must be what Connie had referred to as "the barn."

The bigger house backed up to a stand of cottonwood trees, leaning uphill slightly as if digging in its heels. I parked on a bare patch of ground next to it and got out.

It was one room deep, with a long veranda across the facade facing the river. It didn't look like it had been painted since the day they nailed it together. Inside, the wallpaper hung off muslined wallboards in long, dusty arcs. The pine floor was covered with old tile mastic and carpet furring. There was no kitchen, and a modern bathroom had been installed in the back part of the main hall, the fixtures long gone. I didn't trust the stairs, but from what I could see of it, the second floor was a twin of the first, minus the bathroom.

I went back outside and stuck my head into the open crawl space. The house sat atop a forest of stripped tree trunks, none of which seemed to be rotted. I scooped down into the powdery dirt around the one closest to me and found the wood pier sound as far as I could dig.

The wiring was 1930s knob and tube in remarkably good shape, then sat down on the porch steps to think. A hot breeze came up from across the river, bringing a perfume of dry grass and cows. The sun slanting along the lumpy ground was turning yellow with the afternoon, and I heard myself wondering why anyone would sell the place. That's when I knew I was going to buy it.

As I sat there, a movement down near the barn caught my attention. A small brown donkey was trotting toward me, followed by a girl dressed in jeans and a red T-shirt. She was calling after the animal, which appeared to be making a beeline for the porch I was sitting on.

"Can you grab him, please?" she yelled to me. As she got closer, I saw that it was Neffa.

I went down the steps and waited for the donkey to reach me, then put out a hand and took hold of the woven bridle. He seemed to expect it and stopped, twitching his ears back at his pursuer.

"I'm sorry," she panted, hiking over. "He got through our dang busted-ass fence again." The donkey was shoving his nose down around my pockets, and she laughed. "The people who lived here before used to give them apples and stuff. They're always trying to get over here."

"I guess I'll have to stock up on donkey treats."

"You gonna buy the place?"

"I'm thinking about it," I admitted.

"We're just across the river, there." She tossed her head toward the rolling brown pasture on the other side. "What you gonna put on it? It ain't good for nothing but goats." She seemed more sure of herself out here under the sky, stroking the donkey's big nose, and I smiled, remembering Charlie's animal quiz. Neffa had a horsy, outdoorsy quality that I hadn't noticed in the café, and her squint looked natural in the hard sunlight.

"I don't have any immediate plans," I hedged.

She nodded, saying, "Daddy'll lease some acres from you, if you got a mind."

"I may take him up on that," I said. It would be a way to get something extra coming in while I was waiting to win the lottery.

"All right, then." She gave me her shy smile, tugging at the donkey's head. "We'll see you later on."

The animal gave in reluctantly, and they scrunched off away through the dry grass.

VIII

I did some grocery shopping, then went back to the apartment to eat and make sure Connie and Tova hadn't been winding me up about the property appraisal. Happily, the county tax assessor's office had been modern-minded enough to get all its records online, but as I opened the search window, I realized that I didn't know Connie's last name. Since Hector didn't go by Bradshaw, I doubted that she did either, but I typed in "Connie Bradshaw" anyway, just in case. No direct hits, but there was a record for a "C. Bradshaw."

When I opened it, though, the name was Christine Tova Bradshaw. I scrolled down to see if maybe there were a title document or something that referred to the other inheritors, but stopped as this year's appraisal slid by. The lavishly restored hotel and its triple lot were valued at only $68,600. Misprint, I told myself, but the previous year's appraisal, listed directly underneath the current one, was $67,450.

I hesitated, not wanting to get drawn off track, but a nascent buzz was kicking up behind my eyeballs. I returned to the property search page and typed in what I figured would be the next address on Third Street: the vacant theater. When it came up similarly undervalued, the buzz got stronger. Half a dozen more addresses on the square and I sat back, gobsmacked. I'd apparently died and gone to real estate heaven.

I hate to admit that I believe in a concept as hackneyed as the Criminal Mind, but I can remember having thoughts like the ones I was having now as far back as my memory goes. On the night Joe died, Pete had been holding $120,000 in cash from my laundry account, in preparation for a buying trip the next day. We were all going to drive down to L.A. for the pickup together—look at some movie stars, have a little fun beforehand. Joe and I had put in half of that $120K, and I couldn't imagine that Pete had gone through with the buy after what happened. Even if he had, he was the kind of guy who'd want to get square.

I had my federal fifty coming, which would cover the Ranch, nice and legal. An additional sixty would buy at least one of the vacant square buildings with enough left over to rehab it and put myself back in the construction business more or less immediately. I'd been assuming instead that my only option was to get there the hard way: building up my reputation with small projects until I could get hired on for larger ones, dodging the Amazon the whole time.

The problem wasn't making my books look straight after I spent the money—I wouldn't be where I was without my master chops on that score—it was how to get it here without the feds or the Brotherhood smelling me out. Pete could easily hide a big withdrawal—hell, the cash might still be sitting in the bar safe, for all I knew—but as soon as it hit my bank account, I'd be back in Langley handcuffed to Kang and Buford, or worse. Cashier's check, wire transfer, online payment— same thing. There's only one untraceable way to transfer money anymore, and the only time I'd ever seen anybody successfully pull it off long-distance, the event had been so remarkable that we'd named it.

You know how the post office always warns you not to mail cash? It's not because they're worried about you getting ripped off. It's because they know that if they told people it was safe, there'd be so much currency leaving the country the mint wouldn't be able to print replacements fast enough. Pete had once taken advantage of that little-known fact by using twenty thousand in small bills as packing material around an "antique" lamp. We'd sat at his kitchen table in the house on Oregon Street, crumpling money and drinking cold hard cider until well past midnight. Everybody assumed Pete was nuts; I think a couple of guys even made book on it. But when the cash arrived in Chicago without a dollar missing, Pete became the proud inventor of the Bakersfield Transfer. Sixty thousand was a lot more to lose, but I was willing to risk it if he was.

I got a pen and scrolled down to the owner's contact details on the vacant theater. It was something called Milestone Properties, Inc., with a post-office box address. I wrote it down and brought up the next record, which I remembered as a narrow one-story brick storefront on the other side of the salon. It also had Milestone listed as the owner. When the third property came up under the same name, my excitement went wary. Milestone might be a community holding corporation, set up as a tax shelter until the downtown incentives went through, like they'd done in Bakersfield. However, those appraisals had been set at or near zero, so that property taxes would be nonexistent while the redevelopment plans were finalized. These numbers were too high for that. Plus, I couldn't find any information online about Milestone, and it hadn't been mentioned in the newspaper article I'd read. Community development needs publicity to succeed; nobody tries to hide that stuff. Whoever Milestone was, they had beaten me to the punch. Which, when you think about it, is hardly surprising. It's not like I invented real estate profiteering. There were much better criminals than me out there making a good living at it.

Unfortunately, the idea of recovering my sixty thousand bucks wouldn't go back in the bag. The square buildings weren't the only real estate in town.

I cleaned up, changed clothes, and drove downtown, remembering the corner store across from where I'd stopped to watch Silvia Molina's DeVille. Inside, the place looked like it had once been a grocery, with the old painted wooden shelves still in place, now holding the usual quick-stop fare. I found a writing pad and an overpriced box of envelopes and took them to the register.

"Where's the closest post office?" I asked the cashier as he rang me up.

He was a middle-aged Asian guy, tall and slightly stooped. "Mm, other side of the river," he said, pointing east.

I laid a five on the counter, and nearly jumped out of my skin when I realized that the miniature canine figurine sitting there amongst the lottery ticket displays, gum boxes, and cigarette lighters was panting.

"Wow," I said. "That's the smallest dog I've ever seen."

"Ah, watchdog!" the cashier replied, touching the tiny brown and black head with his forefinger. The wee beastie smiled up at him, showing a flicker of pink tongue.

"Yeah, she looks like she'd take my leg right off," I cracked.

The post office was a lone building out in the middle of the nowhere Teresa and I had driven through my first night in town, adrift on a sea of fallow black dirt turned under for the winter. It had a freshly poured, nearly empty concrete parking lot in front. I turned off the motor and rolled down the windows, getting out the pad and a pen.

I wrote the date and *Dear Pete*—then my hand stopped. How would he react to hearing from me? The feds had come to me in the hospital, before I'd been allowed any visitors, and I'd seized their deal immediately, my hatred of the punks who'd put me there throbbing almost as painfully as the bullet holes in my side. I'd effectively gone over the wall, leaving Pete behind to grieve alone. I'd never have to explain to a friend or customer what had happened, never have to find an old photo in a drawer, never be reminded of a touch or a look or a kiss when returning to a familiar place. Would Pete hold that against me?

Deciding that if he did, he could shred the letter and forget it, I made it short and to the point, not wasting anything on making nice. When I finished, I read over it and added Margaret's e-mail address. I was using snail mail precisely because it was safer than digital communication, but if some details needed to be confirmed, we both knew how to do that online without bringing out the cavalry. I folded up the single sheet, sealed it in an envelope, and addressed it. I cogitated briefly, then put *Luigi Guerra* in the upper left corner and the bar's address underneath. I'd let Hector know that anything arriving for the cat was mine. If he got curious, I'd tell him it was top secret WITSEC stuff.

I went into the post office, bought a book of stamps out of the machine, and stuck one on the letter. As I dropped it into the mail slot, I caught myself smiling.

IX

The row of motorcycles parked outside Guerra's was longer tonight, and the crew milling on the sidewalk in front as I walked up was making good progress toward abject inebriation. People trickled all the way down to the café, which also seemed to be doing a brisk business.

Inside the bar, the jukebox was blasting Hank Williams, and there were so many people standing in the aisle between the serving top and the booths that I couldn't even see the end of the bar, much less get to it. I caught a glimpse of Hector between bodies. Connie was out on the floor with a tray full of drinks, her slim hips swinging around the tables.

I turned to the young woman sitting on the barstool just inside the door. She was wearing a red spandex dress so short it didn't deserve the name, and a pair of stiletto heels that made my feet hurt just looking at them.

"Would you mind getting up a second?" I said.

She gave me an unfriendly once-over.

"There's a free drink in it for you," I told her.

Her look didn't get any friendlier. "What good's that going to do me if I have to drink it standing up?"

I leaned in and pointed down the bar at Hector. "How about if I get him to bring it to you?"

She smiled and slid off the stool. I hoisted myself up onto the serving top and swung my legs across into the pit. Hector spotted me and lifted his chin in my direction, busy with an order.

"What would you like?" I asked the young woman, who'd scrambled back onto her stool before anybody else could snag it.

"Margarita on the rocks, no salt," she said, still smiling.

I nodded and went down to Hector. "Want me to spell you for a while?"

"Halle-freakin'-lujah," he breathed.

"Before you go, the lady by the door would like a margarita rocks, no salt, and probably your phone number," I said.

He shot a look down the bar, then back at me. For a minute I thought he was going to give me a piece; then his face relaxed and he pushed past me, sighing.

I started taking orders at the flip-top and worked my way

around the curve, a little creaky at first, but feeling a rhythm start to kick in after a few setups. When I got to the wait station, Hector was there, having served his admirer and moved north.

"This rush should calm down in a little while," he said, his hands busy. "I'll back you up until then."

His voice was going raspy, and I replied, "You do realize that if you drop dead, it's just going to be more work for me, don't you?"

Connie appeared at the wait station, consulting her order pad. "OK, who wants it?"

"Hit me," I said before Hector could answer.

She tore a sheet off and handed it over. "Give me the top two orders now. I'll come back for the rest."

I cracked three longnecks and set them up with cold mugs, then mixed a Long Island Iced Tea and a Kamikaze while Connie added up the tab.

"I went out to look at your place this afternoon," I told her, taking the two twenties she held out. "Are there any deed restrictions on it?"

She shook her head, looking wary.

"How about floodplain?"

"It's mostly on Lavon's side," she said as I went over to the cash register. "The barn's been under once or twice, but never the house."

I came back to the wait station. "Thirty-eight thousand," I said, passing her the change.

She pursed her lips, then said, "I'll have to think it over."

That's the response you want. If your seller accepts right away, you've offered too high; if they tell you to fuck off, you're too low. Wanting time to consider means you've hit the sweet spot. I nodded without letting myself smile and went back to work.

X

As soon as I wasn't using all my time listening to customers, I started nagging Hector to get out of the smoke. He didn't put up much of a fight.

"I'll be in the back if y'all need me," he croaked, and headed for the office.

Connie reappeared at the wait station, tray empty, fronds of her wild hair lying damp around the perimeter of her face. "OK," she said to me with an air of finality. "If you're serious, you've got yourself a deal."

I reached across the bar and shook her hand. We both broke into wide grins, and she did a little celebratory shimmy, getting the attention of several male customers.

"Tova's already done the title search, from that offer that just fell through," she said, glancing up at the clock. It was a little after eleven, and I felt a flash of anger at the Amazon. Did she really think the silent treatment was going to improve our relationship?

"The survey's only six months old," Connie continued. "Just let me know when you want to close, and I'll get Tova to update the paperwork."

There was a moist wind kicking up outside, and the eastern horizon had been pulsing with oncoming lightning for the last hour or so. Now an enormous clap of thunder sounded, and a sudden splatter of big raindrops slapped against the front windows, like the sky had sneezed. Then the lights shut off.

"Damn it," I heard Connie say. A groan rose from the crowd, and she called out, "Everybody, please, take it easy, OK? I don't want to have to scrape any of you off the floor. Make love, not war!"

This was greeted with whoops and whistles. As my eyes adjusted, I saw the people near the front door trickling onto the sidewalk, although it was just as dark out there. It looked like the whole square had lost power.

"I got it, you guys!" Hector called faintly from the back.

"Hey, will you go let him know it's not the breaker?" Connie asked me, coming into the serving pit and feeling around under the bar. She handed me one of two hurricane flashlights; I switched it on and went back to the office.

The double door was open, and I heard Hector scuffling around in the alley. I went outside and pointed the flashlight toward the noise. He appeared from behind a slimy-looking green Dumpster, his hands, shirt, and jeans covered with something black.

"Aw, man!" He grimaced, looking down and holding his long arms out away from his body.

"It's not the breaker," I said.

"No shit." He looked at my flashlight, then at his filthy hands. "Shine me upstairs, will you, so I can change?"

Back in the office, I saw that Connie had the other flashlight going in the bar. The place was almost empty. I followed Hector up the stairs, aiming my flashlight a couple of steps ahead of us.

A plaintive *meow* came from the direction of the sofa as we went into the apartment, and Luigi trotted over to thread himself around our legs. Hector laughed. "He's afraid of the dark. You believe that?"

"I'll keep him company," I promised, pointing the flashlight back toward the bathroom. I held it down the short hall until Hector disappeared around the corner, then set it on the floor. It gave enough ambient light that way for him to see what he was doing, and for me to find my way back up front, where Luigi was waiting on the kitchen table.

I picked him up and carried him over to the big bay window. The wind, which had been gusting hard, suddenly stopped, and the rain dumped down like a dam had failed somewhere. Oddly, the cat didn't seem to mind this, and sat placidly in my arms looking out the window at the weather with a philosophical air.

"Man, it is really coming down," Hector said behind me.

I jumped, and Luigi sprang to the floor. "Jesus, make a noise or something, will you?"

"Hey, I can't help it if you're deaf."

I'd turned toward him with my hand pressed to my chest, my heart pounding from the scare he'd given me. His lips were parted, his teeth showing pearly in the darkness, and he was standing way too close to me. There was no way I was missing my opening this time; I leaned forward and kissed him. For a stunned fraction of a second, he didn't move. Then his arms came up around and pulled me in.

Not only was he as good a kisser as a man with his looks should be; our bodies fit together like a continent split by an ancient ocean. Joe had been tall, which always required some adjustments. Hector and I measured up like we'd been made as a matching set. I had just starting thinking about how far it was to the bed when the lights came on again. We flinched apart, and he said quietly, "Damn it."

At first, I thought it was about what we were doing, but then I saw that he was looking past me, toward the sofa. The stone wall behind it was running with dirty yellow water. We shoved the furniture out of harm's way, and then Hector started toward the apartment door.

"I never went up to clear out those scupper drains," he admitted shamefacedly.

"You're going to do it now?" I said. The plaintive note in my voice drew a smile from him across the kitchen table.

"Hey, you've got nobody to blame but yourself." He grinned, his eyes dropping to my mouth. "I won't be long."

I watched him clamber up a track of two-by-fours nailed to the landing wall and disappear above the door frame, then went over and joined Luigi on the sofa, trying to think cool, abstract thoughts.

It had been almost three years since I'd done anything more serious than flirt with a man—I'd forgotten how that hot energy comes up through you, turning you half crazy until you burn it off the way nature intended. I know it's just a hormonal trick to keep the species going, but right then I was wishing it had an "off" switch.

The longest fifteen minutes in history passed. Then I couldn't take it anymore. I left the cat on guard duty and climbed up the ladder to the roof hatch, which was open. It was the old kind, a separate lid that just lifted off a built-up curb. I got high enough to stick my head up and look out.

The roof sloped from a low peak in the middle to the parapet on either side, forming gutters that led to the scuppers at the rear. Hector was squatting with his back to me, about halfway between the hatch and the alley end of the building. Beyond him, a dark mass of stuff was bunched up in the southwest corner of the roof, blocking the scupper there.

"You need a hand?" I called.

He rotated on the balls of his feet, half rising. "Don't come out here!"

His movement revealed the pale shape of a human face among the junk at the scupper. My overheated body went suddenly cold. Hector duck-walked rapidly over to me, getting hold of me under the arms as I lost my grip on the ladder.

"Is—is that—?"

"It's Teresa," he said. "She's dead."

SATURDAY, NOVEMBER 3

1

"What's she doing up here?" My voice felt funny sliding out of my throat. It sounded like it was coming from somewhere else.

Hector shook his head mutely. He'd hauled me out of the hatch, and I was half sitting, half lying against him. I pushed myself away and got up. He tried to hold on to me, but I slithered out of his grasp and stumbled toward Teresa.

She was lying faceup, her dark hair wadded against the scupper opening. A shallow pool of water had formed around her, and a wood-handled kitchen knife jutted from just below her left collarbone, a white corsage of maggots writhing at the wound. Her eyes were open, clouded over and looking at the sky. They still weren't friendly.

I felt someone pulling at me. "Come on, we have to go call the cops," Hector said.

We were back down in the apartment and Hector had hung up after dialing 911 before I realized that we were both soaking wet. I noticed then that he was having trouble breathing.

He dropped into one of the chairs alongside the plank table and pointed toward the hallway, panting, "Inhaler."

I remembered seeing one in the medicine cabinet, and ran back to get it. When I returned to the kitchen, Hector was sitting with his elbows on his knees, head down, fighting for air. He took two hits off the inhaler, then sat up and tilted his head back, eyes closed. His brown sugar skin had gone bluish, and he gulped at the air for a tense few seconds. Then the wheezing faded, and he started pinking back up.

The jukebox downstairs went off, and several people could be heard coming rapidly up the stairs. Benny was the first to appear on the landing. He took one step into the apartment, his eyes wild.

"She's on the roof," Hector said, still breathless.

Scherer appeared behind Benny with another cop, a chubby strawberry blond with spots of color high on his pale cheeks. Benny said something to them that I couldn't hear, then climbed up the ladder. The blond came into the apartment. Scherer stayed on the landing.

The blond, whose name patch said DAVIS, asked us, "What happened?"

"I went up to clear the roof scuppers and found her," Hector said.

Davis eyed my wet clothes. "You go up there, too?"

I nodded but didn't feel moved to say anything. My head was so empty I felt like I was understanding language by cellular osmosis.

A skinny kid in his twenties with bleached spiked hair appeared on the landing and looked in. He was wearing a navy blue raincoat and carrying a field case like the one Benny had brought over the night before. Scherer said something to him, and they stood there and watched us, waiting.

Benny reappeared, and the three of them held a short conference in the doorway; then Benny came over to the kitchen table. His face looked like it had been chipped out of gray rock. "Was she in the bar tonight?" he asked, feeling for his notebook. His hand stumbled, but his voice was steady.

Hector and I shook our heads in unison.

"When's the last time either of y'all saw her?"

"Last night," Hector said, "when you two came over here about that hand business."

My eyes jumped to his face. Benny noticed, and I covered quickly, "Same for me." It wasn't really a lie. Technically, I'd only heard Teresa on Thursday night, not seen her.

"So neither of you had any contact with her today?" Benny asked us. We both shook our heads again.

Scherer and the kid on the landing took a step back, and a lanky man in a tan felt cowboy hat appeared. He was tall and pale, fifty or better, with a high stoop that made him look like he spent a lot of time reading in bad light. The wire-framed spectacles across the top half of his face reinforced this impression, but the rest of him made me doubt he perused anything more complex than the livestock section. He ambled into the room in his round-toed boots, as if joining a party he didn't really want to attend.

"Sheriff," said Benny, his voice brisk and unhappy.

"Did I hear the call right?" The newcomer's voice was a mild, quiet drawl, spectacular in its absolute lack of inflection.

Benny nodded grimly, and the sheriff turned to me. The eyes behind his lenses were a faded teal, almost as colorless as the rest of him. He looked me over for a full thirty seconds, then said, "John Maines."

The context told me it was an introduction; otherwise I'd have thought he was simply pronouncing his name out loud to hear how it sounded. He didn't offer to shake my hand, just looked at me until I told him who I was. After I'd done it, the wet-stone eyes slid down my face, then back up. "Friend of hers, weren't you?"

A pigeon-shaped woman in a wrinkled white lab coat puffed up onto the landing, carrying a black leather case. The sheriff saw my eyes move toward her, and he turned. Benny started for the door, but Maines put a hand out.

"I'll take it from here, Ramírez."

The cop's bullet head whipped around, his face contorting. "The hell you will!"

"You know the drill," the sheriff said, his drawl almost apologetic. "I don't want nobody getting off on this thing saying her loyal crew messed with the evidence to get a conviction."

"You'd rather whoever killed her got off on a nepotism charge?" Benny shot back.

The sheriff started for the apartment door as if Benny hadn't spoken. Benny made a disgusted noise and pushed past, gesturing at Davis and Scherer, who followed him down the stairs.

Maines talked to the doctor and the spiky-haired kid briefly, then motioned down the stairwell. A tan-uniformed deputy came up and into the apartment with him. The two medicos started up the ladder for the roof.

"Either of you washed or changed clothes since coming back down here?" Maines asked me and Hector.

"No," I said.

It took Hector a couple of seconds to shake his head.

"Touch the body, either of you?"

"I did," Hector said after a short pause. "I couldn't . . . I didn't . . ." His voice trailed off.

Maines watched him, silently. He let almost a full minute of silence tick by before he asked, "Anybody go anywhere besides this room?"

"I went to the back for the inhaler," I said, gesturing at the canister lying on the table. "Hector had an attack after we came down."

The sheriff absorbed this for some seconds, seeming to be thinking about something else. "Show me," he said finally.

I didn't know what he expected to find, but I led him down the short hall to the bathroom and pointed at the medicine cabinet, which was still standing open. He stepped over to it and peered in. He didn't touch anything, but studied the contents closely, taking his time. He struck me as the kind of guy who'd take his time dodging a runaway train.

A hollow clunk told us someone was coming down from the roof. Maines moved toward me, indicating that I should precede him back out into the apartment.

I held still and said, "I'm a federal witness, in protection. Teresa was acting as my WITSEC contact."

At first, I didn't think he'd heard me. His face remained as expressionless as if I were the wind blowing. I was starting to wonder if he were some kind of idiot savant.

"Ah, right," he said after a long pause. His eyes did their frank slide again, down, then up. "Aryan Brotherhood killed your husband, right?"

I huffed, rattled. "Jesus, is there anybody she didn't tell?"

The sheriff's sandy eyebrows rose, showing above his wire frames. "Your identity's been compromised?"

"I'm not sure," I said, and gave him a synopsis of my interaction with Silvia Molina, including my suspicion that she might be responsible for the embalmed hand we'd found the previous night. "Teresa told Hector I was in protection, but that's all. I don't know how Silvia found out that I'm a widow."

Maines's flat lenses glinted. He stood there for what seemed an eternity, then gestured toward the hallway with his head. A fence of fine vertical lines had appeared between his eyebrows.

Back in the front room, the spiky-haired kid was conferring quietly with the doctor on the landing, and the deputy was standing in the kitchen, arms folded across his beefy chest. Maines had a few words with the medical team, then brought the kid with him to the table and addressed me and Hector.

"Page here will need to take y'all's clothes, fingerprints, and a cheek swab," he said. "You both OK with that?"

I nodded, but Hector was far away, barely responding to his environment. Maines squinted at him, then called over his shoulder. "Liz, would you come in here, please?"

The doctor, who'd been putting some instruments back into her case, straightened up and strode toward us. Maines nodded wordlessly at Hector, and she went around the table, reaching for his wrist. He jumped up out of his chair and backed away, fists at the ready.

The deputy hustled over, but the doctor motioned him back, speaking to Hector in a soothing voice. "It's Doc Harman, Hector. I'm not gonna hurt you."

The animal gleam died in Hector's eyes. "Sorry," he said, swallowing and wiping his palms down over his jeans. "Sorry."

"It's all right," she said, her warm voice patient. "This is a hell of a thing."

Page murmured to me, "You got some other clothes to change into?" I shook my head and he said, "Let me have your keys and I'll send one of the guys over to your place."

There was no way I was letting an unsupervised cop dig around in my stuff. "I'll find something here," I told the kid.

Page looked at the sheriff, who dropped his head forward a fraction of an inch. The kid gestured me to follow him into the bathroom.

I submitted to his cool-handed ministrations without complaint. He was deft and cheerful, exuding a nerdy pleasure as he combed out my hair, scraped under my nails, and bagged up my clothes. The forensics people on Joe's case had been the same way. Something about the profession seems to draw the upbeat type. I guess you don't get much guff from the clients.

After he'd finished, I started for the chest of drawers in the corner, but he held up a latex-gloved hand. The brain was still cold, dry, and silent, but a vague understanding elbowed its way into my consciousness.

"I didn't kill her," I said.

"Hey, don't tell me," Page said, nodding toward the front room. "Tell him."

11

The doctor had left and Maines was standing at the table talking to Hector, who still looked pretty shell-shocked, but was back on the planet again.

". . . access to the roof?"

Hector lifted one hand toward the landing. "Anybody who wants to can get up there, from the bar."

The sheriff had his long, bony arms crossed over his chest, and was watching the floor while he listened. The hat cast a deep shadow over the top of his face, but from the side I saw his eyes moving behind his glasses, scanning for something.

"I'm ready for Hector now," Page said.

"Forensics will need the building for at least a couple of hours," Maines told Hector as he got up. "You got another place to stay tonight?"

"I'm sure Tova can find room for me."

Hector's eyes slid over to me, then quickly away. As he and Page disappeared down the hall, Maines curled a finger at me, moving toward the apartment door. I followed him, not asking where we were going.

Two deputies were standing guard at the foot of the stairs, and Maines stopped to give them some instructions. I peered out into the bar. The place was empty.

"This way," Maines said, indicating the office door.

We went through to the alley. Parked there was a tan four-door with cherries on top and a county insignia on the driver's side door. I went around and got in the other side, trying not to think about what might be sticking to my bare feet. Maines slid in behind the wheel. "Teresa has a secure line in her office," he said. "I'll call the Marshal's office from there tomorrow morning and find out what to do about your situation."

The rain had made the night air heavy, and a smell of ripe garbage wafted from the alley. I nodded, and the sheriff let another lengthy pause go by before saying, "What do you know about her relationship with Guerra?"

I couldn't see his face in the dark, but I was pretty sure it was expressionless anyway. "You can't seriously suspect him."

"Why can't I?" The sheriff's voice was mild and curious.

"The man's a basket case," I said. "Let's see you fake an asthma attack and shock."

Maines put his elbow on the window ledge, not saying anything. The closed interior of the car amplified the sound of his breathing and his odor of grocery store soap, and I had a sudden, unpleasant sense of intimacy.

"She's been up there at least twelve hours," I added, impatient with his silence. "There were maggots on her, and her scleras were cloudy. Why would he leave her all that time, and then practically lead me to the body?"

Maines gave me a leisurely visual examination. "I guess you got a little forensics training on your husband's case."

I shrugged. I didn't really want to tell him how many dead bodies I've seen.

"Doc gives me twenty-four hours ago as a preliminary time of death," Maines said, looking at the dashboard clock, which glowed 3:48. Right around the time I'd heard Teresa arguing with Hector. I knew I should tell Maines about it, but I wasn't all that inspired by what he was doing with the information he already had.

The sheriff rubbed his chin with a long hand, narrow across the knuckles and meaty at the heel. It made a dry, sandpapery noise. "What did the chief think about this business with Silvia Molina?"

"When I talked to her about it on Friday, she didn't think it was any big deal. She told me she'd go over and see her, but I don't know if she ever got around to it."

Maines shifted in his seat, a slow fidget. I listened to his breath bouncing off the windshield for almost a full minute, and then he got out of the car and stepped over to the fire doors, which he'd left open a crack, and stuck his head in. He called a muffled name, and one of the deputies appeared. The two men came back over to the car, and Maines leaned down into the door opening. "I want you to come and see me first thing when you get up tomorrow. Samuels here will keep an eye on you until then."

The deputy got behind the wheel before I could say yea or nay. Maines peeled off and went back into the bar, letting the metal door fall shut behind him with a quiet clank.

Samuels drove me the block and half to my truck, then followed me home to Teresa's. I felt a twinge of conscience that the guy would have to spend the night parked alongside the driveway, but it hadn't been my idea.

III

I was again awakened, too early, by someone banging on my apartment door. This time it was Jesse Reed. He looked scared. "Is it true?" he breathed at me through the screen.

I nodded. His fashionable pallor intensified, and afraid he might pass out, I gestured him in. He went over to the dinette and dropped into a chair. I got the kettle off the drainboard and filled it.

"Did Richard do it?" he asked.

I threw a surprised look at him.

He swallowed audibly and said, "The other night I came home late—like, five in the morning—and I saw the basement door standing open—"

"You mean Friday morning?" I cut in, remembering the noises I'd heard.

Jesse nodded and went on. "So I go over to check it out, and Richard comes driving up, sees me, and pitches a complete fit. I tell him I found it open, and he goes tearing upstairs, hollering for Teresa."

The brain flashed on it; if he'd killed her, why was he looking for her two hours later? "For Teresa? Why?"

"I dunno." Jesse shrugged. "She was letting him hold on to her key until he got all of his stuff out of there, and the other day she told him if he didn't step lively, she'd change the lock and put it all out on the curb. I guess he thought she was making good on it."

The kettle started to boil, and I flicked off the gas and spooned some loose tea into the pot, the radar squirming. Richard could have been making a production so that Jesse would remember it later and give him an alibi. "Have you talked to the sheriff about this?"

"Like Maines'd do anything," Jesse snorted.

I remembered Benny's nepotism remark. "Is he related to Teresa somehow?"

Jesse shook his head. "Richard. They're cousins or something."

I counted to sixty, removed the strainer, and took the pot over to the table. Jesse seemed puzzled as he watched me pour him a finger of tea. "What am I supposed to do with this?" he said, glaring at the almost-empty cup.

"I like it strong," I explained. "That's for you to taste and make sure you want more."

He lifted it with a wry smirk, sticking out his pinkie.

"Yes, yes, very amusing," I snarked in reply. It felt oddly comforting to be shuffling around a morning kitchen, defending my gastronomic quirks to a man again. I brought the sugar over and sat down. "Are they close enough that Maines would try to pin Teresa's death on somebody else, if he thought Richard had done it?"

Jesse leaned back in his chair, considering, then made a face. "I doubt he's smart enough for something like that."

"Can't say that I was liking him for a Pulitzer," I admitted.

"Couple of weeks ago"—Jesse grinned, coming forward again and propping his elbows on the table—"an alarm goes off in one of my square buildings. Middle of the night. Benny goes over there, and it's *Maines*. Just walked in to take a look around, he said." Jesse laughed, shaking his head. "County sheriff, unclear on the concept of breaking and entering."

The caffeine had barely begun making its way into my central nervous system, but the brain jumped at what he'd just said. "One of your square buildings?"

He hesitated, sizing me up through his long lashes, then said, "Yeah. On Main, next door to the bar."

"You're Milestone Properties?"

I could tell immediately that he didn't like me knowing it, but he wasn't scared, just nettled. He showed me his snaky grin again, this time with fangs. "Well, look at you, just getting right up to speed on all the local news."

I flickered over his faded T-shirt and scuffed high-tops. "Do you have a trust fund or something?"

"Like I'd gamble with my own money," he scoffed, still watching me with wary ease.

"What's the buy-in?"

He lifted his fingertips off the table, dropping his head forward in a gesture of polite refusal.

"Come on," I said. "Another sixty thousand wouldn't do you any good?"

"Capital isn't a problem for us," he insisted. He hadn't even blinked at the amount; he must be working with a lot more zeros.

"Who's the 'us'?" I tried.

He made a derisive noise. "Why do you think we incorporated? This downtown thing isn't popular with everybody. Some of my investors would rather their name isn't, ya know, printed on the letterhead."

"What's unpopular about it?"

"You'll have to ask your boss. He's the pinko leading that particular revolution."

That surprised me. Government-sponsored development seemed like something that would be pretty tasty to a socialist. Obviously, I didn't know as much about politics as I thought I did.

A heavy sliding sensation, like tectonic plates shifting behind my eyes, shut off the buzz in my stomach. The brain had caught up.

"Did you hear about that cadaver hand we found behind the bar the other night?" I asked Jesse.

"Uh, yeah," he replied as if I'd just asked him what year it was. "Who didn't?"

"The cops think somebody threw it off the roof."

He cocked his head like a dog with an itchy ear. "And?"

I smiled at him, and he got it. "Hector wouldn't sell me his place if I left an entire dead body at his door." I twitched, and his expression went apologetic. "Sorry. Going off on all this other stuff, I forgot about Teresa."

And I'd forgotten that I was supposed to be in mourning for the Amazon. Worried that my face might talk, I got up to go back over to the stove and noticed the brain out in left field playing with the idea that the cadaver hand had something to do with Hector's past.

This radar of mine can be a double-edged sword; it essentially picks up everything, and I have to depend on my slower-moving gray matter to sift out what's valuable. By the time the brain has assembled my random impressions into actual facts, the original source of those impressions is often long forgotten. This idea was one of those. It felt like it had been caught in the works for a while, so I didn't think the conversation with Jesse had spawned it, but I couldn't put my finger on what had.

"I hope I'm wrong about Richard," Jesse said behind me. "This downtown thing is dead in the water if he gets mixed up in this mess."

Almost automatically, I asked, "Is Richard one of your investors?"

"Nice try." Jesse smirked. "City council members aren't allowed to own any property—or interest in any property—in the development district. The one guy who does, they don't let him vote."

"He can lobby, though, right?"

"Well, sure. I mean, everybody with a stake is trying to

swing the thing their way, including me. I'm not buying Richard drinks because I like him."

I gave him room to keep talking, but he got up and said, "I'd better get going." He went over to the apartment door and paused with his hand on the knob. "You doing OK with all of this?"

I wasn't sure of the answer to that question yet, but he wasn't really asking. I gave him the brave nod he was looking for, and he said, "If you need anything, I'm right upstairs."

The words were meant to be kind, but he wasn't looking at me like a philanthropist.

IV

I followed Samuels in my new truck, not wanting to get stuck someplace out in the boondocks with no way to leave, but my worry was wasted. He led me to the courthouse and pointed me into the police station. Davis was on duty. He told me Maines was in Teresa's office and pointed toward an open door at the back.

The sheriff was sitting with his boots up on the corner of a big oak desk, his hat tipped forward. Behind him, three high windows gave a worm's-eye view of Main Street. Water pipes gurgled somewhere overhead. It was like being in the hold of a big stone ship.

"Did you talk to the feds?" I asked by way of checking if he was awake.

The boots came down one at a time, and he poked back his hat, creaking forward in the chair. "We're playing phone tag.

This secure-line business is a pain in the ass." He pulled a manila folder lying on the blotter toward him. "Got the coroner's report this morning."

"That was fast," I said.

The sheriff's eyes moved languidly behind his flat lenses. "It's just preliminary." He flipped the folder open and, to my surprise, read aloud:

"Time of death, between three and five a.m., Friday, November second. Victim ingested an undetermined amount of"—Maines paused to peer at the page, enunciating slowly—"*flunitrazepam*, approximately forty minutes prior to death. Cause of death was exsanguination due to a single stab wound to the upper left thorax. Knife had Guerra's prints on it."

I took the side chair next to the desk, not asking why he was letting me in on the case facts. "Fluni-what's-it—that's roofies, isn't it? Was she raped?"

"There was semen present. Doc says no signs of forcible intercourse. But there wouldn't be, since she was drugged. Nothing on the roof. Nothing on the body or weapon. Rain took care of that." He made a noise halfway between a sigh and a grunt, closing the folder. "Not that I need any more evidence. There were traces of the dope in a wine bottle in Guerra's kitchen. We also found her blood in several places inside his apartment."

He waited, watching for my reaction. I didn't give him one. I was busy trying to make sense of what I'd just heard.

"Any idea why she was on the roof?" I asked him.

Maines twisted his head from side to side, once. "No concrete evidence of a reason, anyway."

"But you've got theories?"

The corners of his mouth twitched again. "I don't do theories."

As if I'd never heard it from dozens of other cops. Just the facts, ma'am. We don't care why you did it, we just want to know if you did it. Tell me what you saw, not what you think.

"I'd like to verify some information," Maines was saying, looking down at a legal pad that he'd dragged over. There was a chronological list of events on it, with gaps. "What time was it when she left the bar on Thursday night? After this hand business?"

"Right around two."

Maines placed a check mark next to an item on his list. He held the pencil down close to the point, like a first grader. "And what time'd you get home?"

"A little after three."

Another check. "You're in the efficiency. Behind the chief's apartment. Right?"

I nodded. He took it in without looking up. "Did you hear her come home?"

I shook my head. Another technical truth.

"What time'd you go to bed?"

"Right after I got in."

"Sleep through the night?"

"Why wouldn't I?"

Maines's head came up. "That right there is what we call an evasion." His eyes seemed to float to the surface of his glasses, pressing through them at me.

"I heard some noise in the basement around four," I admitted without any dramatics. "I looked out the window, saw the light on, figured it was Teresa's husband picking up some of his stuff, and went back to sleep."

Maines looked down at his pad again, setting the tip of the pencil against a line below a big blank spot. "Couldn't have been. Richard was with Benny Ramírez at four."

I remembered the two of them getting into Benny's cruiser in front of the bar as Connie and I had come around from the alley. "Doing what?"

"Lost his keys," Maines said, sitting back. "Got to his car after y'all closed and realized he didn't have 'em. Benny helped him hunt around the square awhile. Then drove him out to his place up north to get his spare set. Took 'em half an hour to get out there, then they had to deal with Richard's security system. Couple of hours with the locksmith. Benny dropped him off back here around four forty to pick up his car."

"That's a pretty good alibi," I said, "but it still gives him twenty minutes to kill her."

"Doesn't track with the roofies," Maines said.

"The lock on Hector's apartment is broken," I told him. "Richard was in the bar that night. He could have slipped up there anytime and spiked the bottle."

"How'd he know she'd be the one to drink it?"

"She and Hector were having a thing," I said. "Maybe he knew they made a habit of sharing a bottle of wine after closing time. Knocking both of them out would be pretty handy if he wanted to kill her and pin it on Hector."

Maines made a dismissive gesture. "She was on the clock. Wouldn't so much as read the newspaper on city time. That's how she was."

"The harder they come, the harder they fall," I said. "You can take that to the bank."

A minute glimmer swam across the sheriff's colorless eyes. He had one of those mouths that cut straight across, with the corners fading off dead parallel to the ground. I watched them to see if they'd twitch again. They didn't. He looked back at his pad and skimmed down a few more lines. "Guerra says you came by the next day. Around one. What was that about?"

"Richard woke me up at the crack of dawn, looking for Teresa. Her car wasn't at the house, so I figured that she'd spent the night at Hector's. I wanted to tell her to put a leash on her ex."

Maines's wet-stone eyes had come up, interested. "What time'd Richard wake you?"

I gave him Jesse's timeline and calculated, "Jesse says he got home around five, so it would have been shortly after that." Maines kept looking at me. I gave him a minute, then made it simple for him: "Richard made sure his appearance was memorable."

The sheriff didn't nettle easily, I'll give him that. He watched me with the impassive curiosity of a scientist observing a new species, then went back to his pad. "What was Guerra wearing? When you stopped by on Friday?"

"Nothing." I grinned, remembering. Maines appeared interested, and I realized that it was evidence. "His jeans from the night before were right there on the floor, and they were clean. No bloodstains."

"Shirt? Shoes?"

I shook my head.

Maines made a couple of notes, then sat back and asked, "Why are you so quick to lie for someone you've known less than forty-eight hours?"

"What am I lying about?" I said, galled.

"Don't know yet," he replied. "Something."

"You shouldn't even be on this case," I snapped. "You and Richard are related."

Maines flicked a finger back and forth between the two of us. "So are we, if you go back far enough."

"How do you explain Hector leaving her body up there, if he killed her?" I said, his deadpan humor wearing a sore spot on my patience.

"The chief was a big woman. Not easy to move in the best of circumstances. Even for him."

"So—what?" I guffawed, turning my palms up. "He was going to wait for her to mummify? Let the buzzards eat her? Turn her into a rooftop planter?"

The sheriff kept his eyes on my face, silent.

My logic was biting into his certainty. I kept talking. "If he was waiting for some future opportunity to move the body, why'd he go up there while I was with him?"

Maines's jaw moved, and he looked away. He let the air settle for a second, then said, "What were the two of you doing, just before?"

I started to tell him it was none of his damned business, but then I saw the snare lying there, waiting. "Look, he's either an evil genius or an idiot," I said. "He can't be both."

"You'd be surprised," Maines answered, something light touching his pale face.

The son of a bitch was enjoying himself. It wasn't the standard cop enjoyment of being the designated authority figure; there was something else—a sense that I was entertaining him somehow. Maybe he had a sadistic streak. A lot of them do.

"Are we done?" I asked, getting up.

"No," he said.

It was polite, but there was no way I was sitting back down. I folded my arms and waited for him to get on with it.

"I haven't had a chance to talk to Silvia Molina yet," he said. "I don't want to go over there until I've gotten hold of the Marshal's office. I'm not sure how safe you are to be running around loose."

"I'll be careful," I promised.

He paused, then said, "I want to put you in protective custody until I get this thing sorted out."

I felt my eyes widen. "You are seriously confused if you think I'm going to willingly let anybody lock me up after what I did to avoid it."

Maines had sat back in the low banker's chair and was examining me again. "That doesn't make any sense." His voice was mild and toneless, as usual, but had a note of curiosity in it.

"Then it ought to feel right at home between your ears," I said, and left.

V

As I stopped at the truck to get out my keys, I heard my name and looked up to see Tova Bradshaw motioning to me from the front door of the hotel.

"What on earth happened last night?" she asked as I walked over. "No one will tell us anything except that Teresa was killed."

"You haven't talked to Hector?"

"He hasn't been home."

My stomach blipped. "I thought he stayed here last night."

Tova shook her head. A couple of Harleys roared by on

Main. She made a face and said, "Come inside for a few minutes, will you?"

I nodded and followed her into the lobby. Instead of going to her office, though, she turned at the main corridor and pressed the elevator call button. The purple-haired clerk watched us, curious.

"Hector and I found her on his roof," I said once we were inside the elevator car and rising. "She'd been stabbed."

Tova covered her mouth, then asked in a hushed, incredulous voice, "What was she doing on his roof?"

I shrugged.

"How was Hector when you left him?"

"Better than when we first found her," I admitted. She looked away from me, her composure hardening back into place, and I added, "Connie told me about his PTSD."

Her eyes came back at me, but she didn't say anything. The elevator opened, and I followed her down a thickly carpeted corridor to a suite at the back of the building, on the street side. This consisted of a tall sitting room with a queen-size bed hidden in a damask-draped nook, a small kitchenette opposite, and an open door showing a white bathroom with a big walk-in closet. Connie was sitting on one of the twin velour sofas in front of an arch-top window, smoking a cigarette. She looked like she hadn't gotten much sleep. "Julia," she said, sitting up. "Are you OK?"

"She was stabbed on Hector's roof," Tova said to her.

"I'm fine," I replied to Connie's question.

Tova balked, looking annoyed, then went on. "Julia doesn't know where Hector is, either."

Connie leaned forward for the ashtray, sighing. "For God's sake, Tova, would you let it go?"

"He needs to be around people at a time like this," her sister snapped back at her.

"No, *you* would need to be around people at a time like this," Connie returned, her voice brittle with enforced calm. "*He* needs to be by himself."

"Because *you* keep filling his head with all that politically correct nonsense about 'psychocultural differences'! If you'd—"

"The sheriff thinks Hector killed her," I cut in before they could get up to warp speed.

Two pairs of eyes jumped toward my face. Tova made an impatient motion and said, "That's absurd. Hector's no more capable of killing someone than I am."

"Everyone's capable under the right circumstances," I said.

"Oh, *please*," Tova said, rolling her eyes and turning to hunt for something on the kitchenette counter. "You're as bad as she is."

Connie said something under her breath that I couldn't hear and got up. "I need some air."

Tova had found a cell phone and was punching angrily at the buttons, muttering, "John Maines is going to rue the day he decided to visit his incompetence on one of *my* relatives."

I got up, too. The only thing I hate worse than having a telephone conversation is listening to someone else's.

In the corridor, as we walked to the elevators, Connie told me, "She's got every lawyer in the state on speed dial. Dad's contact list was almost as valuable as the money he left."

I pressed the elevator call button, looking pointedly around the opulent hallway. "It must have been quite a pile."

"Oh, it was," she said, then corrected herself. "Is. A couple of million, from what I've heard."

"From what you've heard?"

"Tova doesn't want me and Hector to know exactly how much. Dad never got around to legally adopting us, so Tova got everything when he died. She gave me the Ranch and Hector the bar and called it even." As we got on the elevator, she caught a look at my face and cracked, "Not that I'm bitter or anything."

Her self-deprecating tone made me laugh.

She gave me a smiling, questioning look and said, "You seem to be coping OK."

"I didn't know Teresa that well," I told her, feeling as though I'd been saying it constantly.

She gave a shaky sigh as we started to drop toward the lobby. "I didn't either, but it still just feels—unreal. I can't imagine how it must be hitting Hector."

I nodded and said, "I wonder where he is."

"Enchanted Rock, probably. That's been his retreat of choice lately. It's usually pretty deserted this time of year." Connie paused to sigh again, then added, almost apologetically, "Tova means well—she just doesn't understand that Hector's social persona was already pretty fully formed when he came to us. He's never going to do things the way she was always taught is the right way."

"Do you remember anything from before you came to the States?" I asked her, curious.

"Oh, no. I wasn't even a year old." Connie paused, then mused, "I'm not sure why Tova and I are so different."

The elevator dinged open, and we stepped out into the wide corridor. Kathleen got Connie's attention as we passed the desk, and Connie said she'd see me later.

I stopped on the sidewalk in front of the theater to fish out my keys and heard a low crunching noise to the right. A couple of guys were walking over the top of a full roll-off in front of the salon, mashing down a mound of charred construction debris in preparation for hauling it away. Charlie was watching them from the sidewalk, drinking a take-out coffee.

"How's the cleanup going?" I asked as I walked up, smiling at her outfit of yellow satin capri pants, pink ballet flats, and off-the-shoulder black blouse.

"Faster than I expected," she replied. "I didn't expect to see you out and about today."

Having to explain my lack of visible grief on Teresa's behalf was getting old, but I went ahead and trotted out the standard disclaimer.

Charlie waited a decent interval, then said, "I warned that idiot sheriff that Richard Hallstedt was dangerous, but he wouldn't take me seriously."

I lifted my eyebrows at her, and she said, "Why did Teresa ask you to come down here?"

She obviously had a theory, so I just shrugged.

"She needed help," Charlie said. "Help that she couldn't ask any of us for."

"What do you mean?"

"I mean Richard. He was abusing her."

"Oh, come on," I scoffed. "She could have broken him in half."

One of the workmen came around the Dumpster, and Charlie stepped back, lowering her voice. "Last April, right after Richard proposed this downtown development thing, I saw him slap her, right out there on the courthouse lawn, and she just took it. Didn't say a word, just turned and walked off."

"I wouldn't exactly call one slap a pattern."

"How many times does a man have to hit a woman for it to matter?" she shot back. "A dozen? A hundred?"

"They're in the middle of a divorce," I reminded her. "I'm guessing their marriage wasn't all rose petals and candle-lit baths."

Charlie made an exasperated motion with her coffee cup. "Yeah, I guess. Still."

"Want to give me the grand tour?" I said, leaning toward the building.

"Sure, if you're up for it."

I took a look around the square before we went in, then remembered I didn't have to worry about Teresa catching me anymore. Something started to flutter under my breastbone at the thought, but Charlie and I were coming to the top of the stairs, and the lack of anything between us and the big sky overhead was getting all my attention.

"They couldn't save any of the roof framing?" I said, stepping out onto the scorched wood floor.

"It was all down," Charlie said. "The rafters, the ceiling, everything."

I walked toward the rear, examining the limestone walls. They were black with soot, and some of the mortar had crumbled out of the joints near the top, where the char was darkest. The smell of burned timber was still strong, even with the roof gone.

"It was all just storage up here," Charlie was saying. "I thought about making it into an apartment, like Hector's place, but never could afford to do it." She rolled her eyes at the sky. "Thank God. I really *would* be screwed if this had been my living quarters."

I was looking at the top of the wall where the joists had sat. There were still some remnants of the wood bearing plate, but most of it had burned away. "Not much of an arsonist," I said.

Charlie quirked at me, and I said, "It looks like the fire started on the roof."

She nodded. "The fire marshal said that they found accelerant up there."

"That doesn't make much sense, if whoever torched the place wanted it to burn to the ground."

"You know, I thought the same thing," she said, her pointy face animating. "Why go to the trouble to climb all the way up there, when they could have just broken the back window, thrown in some gasoline, and lit a match?"

I got that weird sense of heavy things sliding together between my ears again, like cargo shifting across the deck of a rolling ship. I held still, waiting, and after a second the brain sent up a flare.

"Did you say the development project started up last April?" I asked. Charlie nodded, and I said, "Mel told me this downtown crime wave has been going on for about a year."

"Yeah, something like that," she said, looking puzzled. "Why?"

"I saw an article in the newspaper that said Richard proposed the development project in response to increased crime on the square. But if it kicked off last April, and the crime wave didn't start until November, that doesn't add up."

Charlie frowned, then shook it off. "I must be remembering the dates wrong."

I walked to the front of the building and scanned the vacant properties on the square. None of them looked like they'd been touched since the businesses closed. All the vandalism I'd heard about had been on occupied buildings, the ones that Milestone didn't own yet. It was too definite a correlation to be a coincidence.

I took a breath, trying to pop the bubble of suspicion I felt rising. Even if I was right, and Jesse had created the crime wave to soften up the owners of properties he wanted to buy, so what? It's a long run from petty vandalism to murder, and I couldn't see where killing Teresa would advance Milestone's agenda any.

"Has anyone approached you recently to try and buy this place?" I asked Charlie.

"I wish," she snorted. "Richard keeps telling me I should sell out, but he's not allowed to buy it, so I don't know why he keeps going on about it. It's probably not worth much now."

Now it started to tighten up. Jesse was paying Richard to make sure the bond package passed. That's why they were always in each other's pockets. Considering how much money I suspected was involved, I could easily see the two of them offing Teresa, if she'd gotten wind.

I noticed that Charlie was gazing at my head. "You know, if you want, we could barter some salon services."

"Yeah, maybe," I said hedgingly, starting for the stairs. "I'll get back to you in a day or two."

It wasn't entirely a dodge; I was remembering an office renovation I'd done for a small company in Bakersfield. They'd neglected to pay me, and to file the mechanic's lien, I'd had to get copies of the company's incorporation instruments, which hadn't been difficult to obtain. Surely something similar existed for Milestone, and I wanted to lay my hands on it as soon as I could figure out how.

VI

The directory in the courthouse didn't list a county clerk's office, so I stepped into the nearest door and asked the receptionist sitting there where it was.

"Johnson City, forty miles north," she told me. "Went up there when they moved the county seat."

My eyes flicked involuntarily around at the building I was standing in, and she laughed one of those big, raucous laughs that most women try to suppress. "You ain't from around here, are ya?"

I couldn't help grinning back at her. She was mid-fifties, frankly dyed blond, with lots of makeup, but there was something rough and Western about her that her grooming didn't touch.

"We're the only county in Texas with two historic courthouses," she told me. "Ya think we'd have more money."

"How'd that happen?"

She waved a French manicure at the past. "Oh, some political thing, way back. There's a plaque up there if you really wanna know."

"Thanks," I said, and ducked out.

I got into the truck and drove north, passing into a forest of new-looking subdivisions after about half an hour. The houses were bloated and ugly, set too close together in the vastness of the surrounding landscape, and I found myself wondering if this was Richard's neighborhood. It struck me as ironic that someone who publicly championed revitalizing a small town's business district might be part of the lifestyle that was killing it to begin with.

That kept me busy until I hit open road again, at which point I couldn't hide anymore from the question of what the hell I thought I was doing. I tried "righting a wrong that was about to be perpetrated on an innocent man," but the notion didn't offer to shake my paw. After chewing around for a while, I finally got down to the bone: publicly hoisting the idiot Maines on his own petard was too good to pass up. Law enforcement loves to play ethical watchdog, as if they're the only people in the world with honor. It gives me a pain.

A brown and white road sign reading ENCHANTED ROCK STATE NATURAL AREA flashed by, pointing down a turnoff toward the west. Maybe I'd go out there on my way home and see if Hector would explain to me why we weren't telling anybody about his argument with Teresa on Thursday night. That sharp flutter of sensation jabbed up under my ribs again. It wasn't jealousy or scorn or any of the other familiar emotions I was used to feeling about other people's lives; it was something meeker and less noisy. I couldn't identify it.

Houses were starting to appear alongside the highway again now, and I passed a sign welcoming me to the Johnson City limits. Just beyond this came a wider stretch of road that had been cutesied up to within an inch of its life with corny-looking restaurants and antique stores. Another sign pointed discreetly off this main drag to the HISTORIC CENTRAL BUSINESS DISTRICT.

This turned out to be a square very much like the one in

Azula—only here the buildings surrounding the nicely re-stored courthouse all seemed to house operating businesses. I parked at the low curb in front of what appeared to be a pool hall and crossed the dusty street. The building directory at the top of the courthouse stairs advised me that the clerk's office was to the right, through a pair of pine doors with a transom at the top. Inside, modern modular office furniture the color of dried puke divided a big room into cubicles, with a small coun-ter at the front. The gray top of a grandmotherly head showed just above it.

"Melp you?" the woman asked, keeping her eyes on her computer screen. She was stringy and dry-looking, like a har-vested stalk of corn.

"Yes, I'd like to see some incorporation instruments."

"What's the name?"

I told her, and spelled it, as requested. She tapped it into the computer and said, "They're sealed."

"Sealed?" I repeated, both irritated and gratified. Irritated because my telephone phobia had cost me the drive; gratified because the sealed records meant Milestone had something to hide.

"It's a private corporation. They don't gotta make their com-pany information public if they don't want to."

"What if I suspect they're doing something illegal?" I asked.

"Get yourself a lawyer," she advised, seeming slightly more interested. "You gotta have a court order to look at these."

I thought for a minute. "Do you keep a log of court orders?"

She gave me the eye. "Yeah? . . ."

"Can I take a look at that?"

She started to resist, but then got up and brought over a green-bound ledger. She set it on the counter in front of me and resumed her seat at the computer.

I flipped through until I found the current entries, then went back a few pages and found what I hoped might be there: T. Hallstedt had obtained a copy of the incorporation instruments for Milestone Properties on October 27, by order of the Honorable Melrose J. Smith. She'd had Milestone's records for less than a week before she'd been killed.

VII

My first impulse was to drive straight back to Azula and wave it in Maines's face, but I wanted to synchronize with Hector first. Naturally, it had occurred to me that he was keeping his argument with Teresa quiet because he'd killed her, but every time the thought crossed my mind, every cell in my body rebelled. It just wasn't possible. Maines, shackled to mere logic, would never get that. He'd never understand that what matters when figuring people out isn't looking at them, it's looking at yourself. If you've been tuned right by life—if you've had to depend on successfully identifying someone else's half conscious preferences and repressed motives to survive—listening to your own reactions will tell you what the person in front of you is really made of.

The thought suddenly turned around and bit me. While I was mostly sure that Hector wasn't a killer, he still tied my stomach in knots, and not entirely in a good way. It was that weird stillness of his, the way he went vicious in an instant. I'd told myself it was a PTSD thing, but what if I were just making excuses for his behavior because he blew my skirt up?

The turnoff to Enchanted Rock put me on another two-lane road with no shoulder. A mile or so in, a patch of pink appeared in the dirty brown landscape off to my left, growing gradually larger until it dipped out of sight when I turned onto a gravel drive at the direction of yet another sign. This stopped at a small guardhouse with a gate, on which was hung a sign that said PARK CLOSED FOR REPAIRS UNTIL DECEMBER 1.

Remembering Connie's remark about Hector's liking to have the place to himself, I pulled up and shut the motor off. There was a deserted parking area about fifty yards beyond the gate, but a gravel path, wide enough to drive a motorcycle on, led farther into the park. I walked along it until I came out from under the trees, and got a close-up of the pink bulb I'd seen on the way in. It was huge, curving up from the ground like a giant egg pushing through the earth's crust. I wouldn't have called it "enchanted," exactly, but it was pretty impressive.

The park map tacked to the guardhouse wall showed that the trail went all the way around the monadnock's base, with several camping areas along it. The sun was starting to go down, turning the white light yellow. Even at my fastest clip, I'd never make the loop before it got dark. I decided instead to climb up top and see what I could see from there.

The low slope was relatively easy to navigate, but it took longer than I expected. The sunset was well under way as I walked around the rock's crown without seeing any signs of life along the trail below. I sat down to enjoy the evening and think about how to proceed. No point in wasting the light show.

That peculiar reverse vertigo that I'd felt coming out of the bus station on my first night in town hit me again. I lay back on the scurfy granite, looking up into the sky, which had gone a deep indigo blue. I floated up into it, swimming through the air back toward town. People were out, some of them on the rooftops of the buildings, looking up at me. Teresa was among them, her dead eyes a cold white beam that dragged at me, sucking me back toward the earth. I woke up just before I crashed down on top of her.

VIII

It's weird how the atmosphere of some dreams lingers over into your waking time as if they were real occurrences. I couldn't shake off the sensation of having descended into a place very far away, with languages and rituals that I didn't understand; Azula but not Azula, like some hallucinated parallel universe. That alien strangeness rode shotgun with me all the way back to the apartment.

It was almost seven, but I called the police station to see if Maines was there. Scherer advised that he wouldn't be back until tomorrow morning. I thought about asking for his home number but decided to give fate a chance. Maybe I'd run into Hector somewhere before the next day.

Just sitting around the house with this stuff on my mind was out of the question, so I threw some workout clothes into my gym bag and went to see if the place Mike had told me about was open late. It was: the only one of the old brick factory buildings facing the railroad tracks with lights on. A big overhead door stood open on the loading dock, through which I saw several boxing rings set up inside. I parked on the gravel, got my bag out of the truck bed, and went up the concrete steps.

The place was huge inside, maybe half the size of a football field, with exposed steel beams and columns holding up the distant ceiling. A faint odor of creosote and sawdust still hovered in the air. The weight pile was against the back wall, directly in front of me, spread out on a large rubber mat. There was a squat rack, two benches with uprights, and a bar and plates collection fit for an Olympic squad.

A plastic sign bragging OFFICE was tacked to a hollow-core door on my right. I opened it and went in, and found myself in somebody's living room. The somebody was sitting on the sofa, watching television.

"Sorry," I said, giving the door sign the hairy eyeball.

"No problem," he said, getting up. "What can I do for you?" He was close to sixty, with a big black pompadour and mustache, and a military bearing that made him look a little bit like Stalin. A fighter's physique with forty years on top of it.

"I'd like to use your weights," I said.

He picked up the remote on the coffee table and clicked off the television. "You wanna join the boxing club?" he asked doubtfully.

"I'll join, if that's how you're set up, but I'm not a fighter."

He was looking me over, trying not to appear skeptical. "It's nothing but guys here. I don't got no sauna or nothing."

"All I need is a lock on the bathroom door," I told him.

He pushed his lips forward, making the mustache bristle, then said, "How about ten bucks a month?"

I got out my checkbook, not looking the gift horse in the mouth. "You make money at those rates?"

"I ain't in this to make money," he replied. "I'm trying to keep these boys outta trouble so I don't gotta call the cops on 'em later."

"That seems a little fatalistic," I remarked, tearing off my check.

He made a dimissive gesture at me. "Ah, you women never get it. When that testosterone hits, it makes you crazy. You been playing with teddy bears and Legos for ten, fifteen years, then alla the sudden you just want to tear shit up. At least here, they can channel it into something that won't land 'em in jail."

That took me back to California, sitting on my aunt's back steps, watching Joachim and a couple of his homeys blowing up tree stumps with some black powder they'd run across while robbing a sporting goods store. I don't understand it any better now than I did then, but it had never occurred to me that there might be more at work than just sheer stupidity.

Lifting in the vast warehouse felt a little public after the minuscule weight room at the Pacific Street gym, but after some warm-ups, I forgot anyone else was there. I did the full monty—dead lifts, squats, presses, and curls—and was resting on the bench when one of the fighters from the center ring came my way and stopped at the edge of the mat, taking off his headgear. It was Mike Hayes.

"What the hell did you tell the cops?" he snarled at me in a low voice.

I was too stoned on endorphins to answer right away, so I just looked at him and waited for the rest of it.

"Maines is on the warpath for Hector," he said, still puffing a little from his own workout. "It ain't bad enough, one of his oldest friends killed like that, now he's gotta deal with the law thinking he did it?"

"Hey, Maines came up with that all by himself," I said, getting up to unload the preacher bar. "I didn't help him get there."

"What did you tell him?" Mike insisted. His scattergun energy was all aimed at me now, and the sensation wasn't pleasant.

"Do you get a lot of results with that approach?" I asked him. "Because all it's doing over here is pissing me off."

He looked away, clenching his jaw. "What is your problem? It's a simple question. Just answer it."

I took the plates off the bar and carried them to the rack, muttering mildly, "Fuck you."

Instead of being gone when I turned around to come back, he was still standing there—only he was smirking now. "You know how I pick out glass heads? They're the ones that get all mouthy and hard when you lean on 'em."

"I guess we're both a couple of lightweights, then."

He didn't care much for that, but he couldn't argue with it. He started unwinding his hand wraps. "Hope the sheriff's life insurance is paid up."

He wasn't looking at my face, so I said, "You might not want to go around saying shit like that out loud."

Mike's head came up, eyes sharp.

"Has Hector always had that fire-bomb temper?" I asked him.

"Of course," Mike said. "It's what made him so great in the ring. He had this"—Mike searched for the word—"*fury* that would come over him at the bell. It was like watching some kinda natural disaster in progress—horrible and beautiful at the same time."

"What does he do with that fury now that he's retired?"

"Takes it out on me, mostly." Mike grinned, refusing to be goaded. I shrugged it off, turning back to my cleanup, and heard him add, "He ain't violent, if that's what you're getting at."

"That drunk he threw out Thursday night might disagree."

Our eyes met, and I saw the humor drain from his.

I started talking before he could. "He and Teresa fought a lot, didn't they?"

"They *always* did. If he was gonna kill her in a fit of rage, he'd have done it twenty years ago."

"Maybe it took twenty years to light the fuse."

Mike sighed again, turning to head for the showers. "Lady, I wish you'd figure out whose side you're fucking on."

Mine, I thought, watching him disappear.

IX

I swung by the bar again on my way home and saw that there was a light on upstairs now. I parked quickly and went in. The door to the apartment was standing open, but there was nobody inside. I listened for a minute, then went over to the mouth of the hall and called "Hector?" back toward the bathroom. There was no answer.

Getting a chance to search the living quarters of somebody who's exercising my radar doesn't happen all that often, so I took it without asking questions. I'd locked the bar behind me, so if Hector came in from wherever he'd gone, I'd hear him in time to desist before he came upstairs. The half curtains across the bay window were drawn, so I didn't feel exposed as I went over to the desk.

The pencil drawer held the usual pencil-drawer stuff—feral paper clips and rubber bands, even some pencils. I looked through more of the same in the side drawer, then moved on to the files below. Bank statements, the building title, medical records—none of these told me anything I didn't already know, except that Hector's cholesterol was a little high and that he hadn't been kidding about being broke.

Toward the back I found an unlabeled folder with a couple of photos in it. One was a full-sheet promo shot of a young fighter in a pair of satin boxing trunks, posed in about-to-kick-your-ass mode. It took me a minute to realize that the boxer was Hector. His hair was cropped short and the fringe falling over his forehead, as well as the thousand-yard stare in his dark eyes, made him look like a different person. The second photo was a snapshot of this same curiously different Hector at maybe sixteen, with a big, sixtyish blond man and two little girls, which I took to be a family photo with Connie, Tova, and her father. They were all smiling except for Connie, who was holding Hector's hand and looking at the camera with the gravity that only children of that age can muster.

My radar was simmering, and after a pause I saw what it was pointing at: everything in the desk, except the two photographs, was recent and impersonal. No old letters, clippings, or memorabilia; none of the banal minutiae that congeal around a life in progress. It reminded me of my apartment at Teresa's.

It occurred to me that Hector might also be in protection, but that didn't track with his independently verified history in

Azula, and I doubted that the feds would send two clients to the same pin-dot tiny Texas town. Maybe he purposely avoided keeping anything that reminded him of his past, because of whatever had happened to him, but surely that didn't preclude more recent keepsakes. If anything, those would have served to replace the old memories.

More curious than ever now, I booted up the computer, where I found the same lack of history. Even his Internet bookmarks were nondescript. His e-mail folders were all empty, and I didn't have the know-how to recover stuff he might have thrown out. Even if I did, though, I was willing to bet I wouldn't find anything informative. I knew what living anonymously looked like. The question was why Hector Guerra was doing it.

I checked the bottoms and backs of the desk drawers and the hidden surfaces of the desk carcass. Then I went over and took a look at the bookshelf next to the bed. The top shelf was mostly political texts whose authors I didn't recognize. Lower down was mixed Latin American fiction—Borges, Pablo Neruda, Isabel Allende, and others—a few English-language classics, some prosaic things like a Chilton's for the truck and an Audubon bird guide, and a smattering of pre-Columbian history. I didn't want to take the time to go through them all, but I fanned a couple at random just to see if anything fell out from between the pages. No luck.

Nothing under the sheets, the mattress, or the bed frame; same for the sofa and chairs. The kitchen cabinets held only groceries and dishes, no wads of money or classified documents. In the bathroom I frisked the dresser, then started going through the pockets of the hanging clothes. About halfway down the rod, my knuckles raked across a smooth spot in the rough stone behind them. It was a wall safe, empty, with the door closed but unlocked. Since it wasn't contemporary with the building, I theorized that Hector had installed it when he inherited the place, which meant that he had something he wanted to keep inside it. I wondered if the recent burglars had gotten to it. Breaking a safe isn't something you just walk into a place and do—if that's what had happened, they had come prepared. That meant they knew ahead of time what was in the safe and that they wanted it.

When I backed out of the clothes, Luigi was sitting in the bathroom doorway, watching me. He looked suspicious.

"Any idea what was in there?" I asked him.

The cat did a slow blink—the feline equivalent of a shrug, I guess. He didn't say anything.

The rest of the bathroom was unremarkable. Luigi escorted me back to the kitchen and showed me where the cat food was. I duly filled his bowl and stepped out onto the landing, shutting the door behind me.

A couple of Harleys were going by on Main, and it took me a second to realize that the reason they sounded so loud was that the noise was raining down from overhead. I peered up into the darkness. After a minute for my eyes to adjust, I saw that the roof hatch was open.

My radar flashed alarm, but the brain cut in to assure me that the forensics people had probably just forgotten to close it. I climbed up to do it, but halfway there my morbid curiosity got the better of me, sending me out onto the roof.

The floodlights from the courthouse filtered over, almost bright enough to read by. A pale stain marked where Teresa's body had lain in its shallow pool. The scupper was clear, and I wondered if the forensics squad had collected all the water and trash to take back to the lab. What a job.

Not sure exactly why I'd come up in the first place, I turned to go back downstairs, and caught sight of a bright spot to the south. The hatch at the café building, two roofs over, was also open, its rim illuminated from within.

I froze, trying to remember if those lights had been on when I drove up. Then the brain reminded me of Hector's burglary again, and I sidled over to the parapet along the alley to look down. No car waiting in the dark with the motor running and the lights off. I watched and listened for a while; the light coming from the rear window of the café building didn't flicker, and nothing stirred but the occasional rumble of a passing vehicle and a lonely dog on night duty off in the distance. Unless somebody was over there taking a nap, I was up here alone.

My pulse had slowed down a little, and the brain started to percolate. If Milestone owned the café building, Richard or Jesse could have stashed the cadaver hand there, then picked his moment on Wednesday night to run down the block, go upstairs, cross over to Hector's roof, and throw it off. By the time Benny and Teresa arrived, he'd have been back down on the street, innocently mingling with the bar patrons. Granted, it didn't prove anything, but the fact that Richard and Jesse might have had a second access point to the roof where Teresa died was at least interesting.

I stepped over to the parapet to check out the two intervening building roofs. They were a story lower than the bar, but there was an old iron service ladder running down to them about halfway along the parapet. The café building showed maybe six feet of wall above its adjoining roof—it would be easy enough to hop down from there, cross over the flat roofs between, and take the ladder up here. I couldn't tell from this distance, though, whether it would be possible to climb back up the café building wall. I made use of the service ladder and went to find out.

Up close, the wall proved to be rough-cut stone with plenty of voids in the old mortar. I took a shot at climbing it, and found it almost as easy as walking over had been.

The café building's hatch was the same type as Hector's, a lift-off cap with no lock or latch. I peered down into the second floor, empty except for an old wooden desk and a long painter's ladder propped against the wall next to it. What looked like an enclosed stair led down to the alley from the back corner.

The radar wasn't giving me any grief, so I swung my legs over the hatch curb and in, getting a good overhand grip. Then I lowered myself until my arms were straight and let go, making sure to bend my knees as my feet hit the floor. It didn't hurt—much—but it made a lot of noise, and I crouched there for several minutes, listening, before straightening up and going over to the desk.

There was nothing in it but a single manila folder in the pencil drawer, with the name MILESTONE PROPERTIES scribbled on the tab in Teresa's signature green ballpoint. I stared, not quite believing what I was seeing, then reached down and opened it. I had just finished reading "Instruments of Incorporation, Milestone Properties" on the title page when I heard a creak. I turned my head, and my check ran into something hard and cold.

"Don't move," Richard Hallstedt said.

SUNDAY, NOVEMBER 4

1

"Gonna rip my arm off and feed it to me?" Richard asked with soft mockery, backing up.

I turned to face him. He was smiling, which wasn't a pretty sight. Neither was the Smith & Wesson nine-millimeter he was holding, the same kind of gun that had killed Joe. It had a silencer affixed to the end of the barrel, which made it look huge. The door into the stairwell behind him was standing open. He had been behind it, waiting.

Considering their ubiquity in my life, I've always had a relatively dispassionate relationship with guns, classifying them as no more than small machines useful for certain purposes. Now, though, facing one for the first time since taking two bullets in the side and watching a third rip my husband's head in half, I felt a sharp jab of disgust and outrage punched into me. The urge to lunge forward and shove the pistol down Richard's throat was almost irresistible.

"Here's what we're going to do," he was saying. "My car's

parked in the alley. It's open. If you do anything but walk straight down the stairs and get in, I'll shoot you. Got it?"

I nodded, my palms itching. His yellow-brown eyes ran down my body with a sort of prissy lewdness, as if he'd undressed me with his eyes and didn't approve of what he saw. I noticed that he was wearing athletic shoes now, instead of the tasseled dress loafers that had tried to insert themselves into my doorway on Friday morning. The rest of his apparel was the same: pressed khakis, polo shirt, smug expression.

He stepped out of my path, flicking the gun toward the stairs. It was a clumsy, unpracticed motion, made by a man unused to handling a firearm. I started down with him following behind, toward the pale side of a car showing through the open door at the bottom.

"Stop," Richard said after we'd covered about half the distance.

He stood there breathing for a little while, probably thinking the same thing that I was: passing through the door into the alley was going to be tricky. I could easily lunge left or right and get the car between us before he could do anything about it. He was going to have to go by me on the narrow staircase. I waited for him to make the mistake all beginning captors make. They usually make it only once.

"Face the wall," he said.

I did it. As he started to rustle past, I pushed myself back, fast and hard. Richard's slack, reedy body slammed into the opposite wall, the gun clacking against the plaster. I turned toward the top of the stairs and swung my far elbow at the back of his head. It connected, but my foot landed on something pliable and moving, and I went down, landing on my right side against the wooden risers.

Richard scrambled to his feet above me. "You fucking bitch," he panted.

All I could pay attention to at the moment was the pain in my back and side. I was lying against the bottom three steps, on my stomach, my right hand flat on the tread above me.

Richard stepped down, putting his weight on it, and pressed the muzzle of the gun against my forehead. "Listen. I don't want to kill you, but I will." His scratchy tenor had risen a notch, and he sounded scared.

I believed him, but my left hand had already made the trip up along my side and grabbed hold of his ankle. I yanked, and the Smith & Wesson went flying as he cartwheeled down and slammed against the doorjamb. The gun clattered out into the alley.

My right side stabbed sharply as I came vertical, and in the split second I paused to wince, Richard lunged and got an arm around my neck. He levered me back against him, arching my spine. It felt like someone had run me through with a spear. My scream was silent, because Richard's arms were scissoring my throat. He had the strength of desperation, and I was cramped by pain. The last thing I remembered was the sound of his breathless grunts against the side of my face.

11

I came to in the backseat of a moving car. My hands were clasped between my knees and tied to my lower legs, which were bound at the knees and ankles, keeping me in a com-

pressed fetal position. The car was running steadily, not starting and stopping, and it was featurelessly dark outside. We
weren't in town anymore.

My right side stabbed with every breath. Silently, I con-
gratulated Richard on learning from his mistake: disable a
captive before attempting to move them. An unrestrained, able-
bodied person will always fight. It's hard-wired in the human
brain. It is in mine, anyway.

The car stopped. Keys jingled out of the ignition and fabric
moved across leather as Richard got out. He crunched away,
and I heard the unmistakable drum of a guy taking an al fresco
leak.

My best chance would be when he came back to drag
me out. If I stayed motionless, he might think I was still unconscious, which would give me an advantage. I waited, listening. Nothing happened for perhaps five minutes; then I
heard another vehicle approaching. It stopped near where I'd
heard Richard peeing. A car door opened and closed, and
then there were voices. I'd just started thinking about taking
a peek when I heard them coming my way. I held still, eyes
closed.

The man who wasn't Richard said, "Whattya mean, you got
a job for me? You ain't paid us for the last one, man."

That rangy Texas twang was starting to sound normal to my
ears. They were standing just outside the car, above my head.

"My cash is tied up just now," Richard replied with what
I realized now was his usual undertone of annoyed conde-
scension.

"I ain't come all the way out here for nothing," the newcomer complained.

A key chunked into the driver's-side door lock. "You'll get paid, don't worry about it. Right now, I need you to—"

There was a rustle and a faint metallic click, followed by a brief silence. Then I heard Richard's voice, tense and placating. "Take it easy."

"Who d'ya think yer messing with, man? Get the fuck over there."

Silence for an instant, then footsteps crunching away. I waited for the sound of a gunshot, but it didn't come. Instead, I heard car doors slam, at which point I jerked myself up to look out, just in time to see the faint shape of a dark four-door gunning off from under a low tree about fifteen feet away.

I watched the taillights fade into the distance for an incredulous minute, then rocked myself up to sitting, biting down against the pain in my side. Richard could be telling the guy about me right now. I had to work fast.

The rope was nylon cord, tied in an almost comical series of complicated knots down near my feet. I could wiggle my fingers but not my hands. I wormed forward and wedged my shoulder between the front seats. It took a couple of tries, and I jammed my already damaged side painfully against the parking brake in the process, but I finally slithered through to the front.

Working my index fingers out from between my legs as far as I could, I pressed my knees against the dashboard, pushing the cigarette lighter in. When it popped out, I fumbled it around and pressed the hot end against the length of rope across my knees. It took a couple of passes, and I burned the crap out of my right index finger, but the rope eventually melted apart, and I wriggled free.

I got out on the passenger side and started walking fast along the gravel shoulder, keeping my ears open. There was wire fence on both sides of the two-lane road, almost hidden in the long grass of the ditches, with pasture and cattle beyond. Up ahead, maybe two miles, I saw a pole light hovering above a small house.

I'd gone about fifty feet when I remembered the Milestone folder. I turned back, telling myself that if a car appeared, I could dive into the ditch and hide myself in the overgrown grass.

As I came up on Richard's champagne-colored Lexus, I saw a shadow at the driver's-side door handle and realized that it was his keys, hanging from the lock. I didn't waste any time searching the car. I just got in and started driving.

III

It was about three fifteen when I got back to town. I pulled into the lot behind Guerra's and tossed the Lexus, without finding the Milestone folder. Then I took Richard's keys and walked down to the café. The alley door was standing open and the lights were still on—he must have been in a hurry to get out of there, with me hog-tied in the backseat. I gave him silent props for getting me trussed and lifted into the car without help and without being seen. He was stronger than he looked.

The folder wasn't in the desk. There wasn't a good hiding place elsewhere in the bare room, and what would be the point? Either Richard wanted it or he didn't, which meant he'd have taken it with him, or left it where it was. He wouldn't have wasted time hiding it. He must have had it with him when his irate associate had taken him away.

I stood there making up stories about how Richard had gotten into what must have been Teresa's private records stash, and what the hell he was trying to pull now. The setup with the open attic hatches had obviously been a trap for Hector, but why? Richard couldn't seriously believe that he'd get away with kidnapping or killing his rival that blatantly.

I gave the brain a few more minutes, then went back down the stairs. At the bottom, the radar told me to try Richard's keys in the alley door. One of them fit the lock.

IV

A cop I didn't recognize, a weedy youngish Latino, was at the duty desk in the police station. His name patch said NORIEGA.

"Can you get hold of Sheriff Maines for me?" I asked him. "I know it's late, but it's important."

"You can get hold of him yourself," he said, jerking a thumb toward Teresa's office with a disgusted look.

"You're kidding."

Noriega grimaced. "Dude is like a fungus."

Maines was sitting in exactly the same position he'd been in the last time I'd come to see him: hat on, head down, heels on the edge of the desk. I was beginning to wonder if the fringe of sandy hair showing around the perimeter of the battered Stetson was all he had, but he hadn't struck me as smart enough to be vain.

"Richard Hallstedt just tried to kill me," I said.

I waited the obligatory ten seconds while Maines assumed

an upright position and got his words in order. "What do you mean, tried to kill you?"

I gave him a rundown of the evening's activities, starting with my trip up to Hector's roof. He didn't need to know that I'd searched the apartment.

Maines digested briefly, then said, "In Texas, it's legal to use lethal force against someone you perceive as a threat to your life or property."

"I wasn't the one with the gun."

Maines dropped his head forward, examining the front right corner of the desk. "Richard was sole inheritor of his wife's estate."

I boggled at him silently for a second; then it came together. "Teresa owned the café building?" The sheriff nodded, watching me. "I thought council members were prohibited from owning square property."

"She came to the marriage with it. Kept it in her name. He didn't even know about it until they read the will."

I felt the brain grappling, but pulled myself up short. There would be time for that later. Right now, I needed to penetrate the thick skull in front of me.

"OK, fine, I entered the building illegally," I said, "but this life and property thing can't possibly cover tying me up and driving me out to the boonies for God knows what."

Maines pursed his lips. "Technically, perceived threat persists into and beyond the legal right of way. Under certain circumstances."

I pressed my back teeth together and put my hands on the edge of the desk, leaning toward him. "Listen. This guy that picked Richard up? Richard hired him to do something shifty—maybe kill his wife. If you don't send somebody out after them, you're going to have another dead body on your hands shortly."

Maines remained motionless, looking at me with no change in expression. I waited a few minutes, giving it plenty of time to sink in. Then he said, "Richard's kinda weird. I'll give you that. But he idn't a killer. Hired or otherwise."

I was getting exasperated. "OK, then it was Jesse Reed. Same difference. This guy is still going to do some damage to Richard unless you stop him."

"Jesse?" Maines said, frowning. "What in hell does Jesse have to do with it?"

It amazed me that the man could manage to dress himself every morning. Speaking slowly, I explained, "Teresa got a copy of Milestone Properties' incorporation instruments last week—that's what that folder in the desk was. Milestone is Jesse's real estate company. He and Richard are working together to scare property owners on the square into selling out, by manufacturing this downtown crime wave. Teresa must have found out somehow, and one or both of them killed her for it."

Maines creaked back in the chair, folding his long hands over his midsection. "If that were the case, Richard'd hardly file a legal document linking him to Milestone."

"Then why did Teresa want those records?" I challenged him.

"She was chief of police. It was her job to be interested in what all went on around town."

"So it's just a coincidence that she was killed a couple of days after she got them?"

"Me and my team have been through all of her stuff with a

fine-toothed comb. Including the contents of that building. If she had proof of anything funny going on, we'd have found it."

"Was that folder up there when you looked?"

Maines came forward onto his elbows again, ignoring my question. "Look. Chief Hallstedt would have smelled this thing you're talking about coming out of the oven. They'd never have gotten off the ground. Much less carried on for however long."

"She knew," I insisted.

"There was nothing to know," Maines pushed back. I made a frustrated noise, and he said, "Let's say you're right. Let's say Richard and Jesse are in cahoots, and something in those instruments somehow proves it. They're public record. Killing her for getting them'd be stupid. It'd just bring attention where it wasn't wanted."

"If there was a cop on the case with half a brain, it would," I snapped.

This seemed to bother him for an instant; then his face went blank again. "I ain't gonna waste my limited time and resources tearing around after some half-assed story from a professional liar."

My temper kicked again, harder now. "You think I'm making this up?"

His mild gaze remained aimed at my face, but he didn't reply. Blind frustration was making me dizzy. I leaned back off the desk and took a short walk around the office to clear my head.

"The full forensics report came back this afternoon," Maines said after I'd finished. "The semen was Guerra's. Arrest warrant should come through some time tomorrow."

I looked at him wordlessly for a few minutes, then said, "It's amazing. You're actually dumber than you look."

"I ain't thinking with my gonads," he replied.

There was no heat in his calm, affable face, not the slightest tremor of emotion. I felt like a veritable volcano in comparison. Maybe that was the intent. I got up and headed for the door.

"Oh, by the way," Maines sent after me, "I finally got hold of the Marshal's office. WITSEC is formally terminating their agreement with you. Because of your involvement in Chief Hallstedt's case."

The sensation of rug yanking out from under me was so strong that I nearly stumbled. I turned back to look at Maines, stunned.

"You'll be able to keep your new identity and everything, but they want you off their books," he said. That pale, bloodless glimmer came at me from behind his spectacles again. "You've become a bad risk."

"I haven't done anything!"

Maines replied evenly, "That remains to be seen."

A choking fury surged up, and the room dimmed. It quickly cleared, leaving a chill resolution in its wake.

"You son of a bitch," I said. My voice sounded calm, even friendly, but something in the sheriff's face went wary. I turned and left.

V

I didn't sleep well, and woke earlier than I should have. A front had come in during the night, and the air in my shoe-box bedroom was cool despite the bright sunlight flashing through the window.

Getting out of bed was an interesting endeavor. You don't realize how many muscles you use to perform the simple act of sitting up until you've had them slammed around a little.

I went into the bathroom and took a look at my side. A purple stripe about two inches wide ran diagonally from my right armpit to the front of my right hip, through a field of mottled red, yellow, and blue. My ribs were sore, but I didn't think they were broken. My throat wasn't bad, just a patch of red across the front, and the blister on my finger had broken during the night, leaving the tip crusted and oozing. I put a Band-Aid on it and looked in the mirror.

Something strange had happened to my face while I slept. I looked uneasy, almost troubled, which I never look, even when uneasy or troubled. It wasn't just a residual expression or the result of a restless night; the bones under the skin seemed to have shifted. For some reason, it made me think back to the younger, almost unrecognizable picture of Hector I'd found in his apartment.

After I got some tea water going, I turned on my laptop, but after it had booted up, I just sat there watching the screen saver, not sure what to do. My head was as thick and quiet as a pool of molasses.

Going through the ritual motions of making tea helped some of the muck ooze away, and I realized then that it was possible—even probable—that Maines was just fucking with me. Whatever I did next, if anything, knowing for sure whether I was really in or out with WITSEC struck me as critical.

I went back to the computer and looked up the address of the regional Marshal's office, which was in Austin. There was an e-mail address and phone number listed, but I knew neither of them were secure enough to handle the information I needed. Fortunately, I could drive the distance in about an hour and a half.

VI

Austin reminded me a little bit of San Francisco. It had the same grid of one-way streets dicing up a thick cake of multistory buildings at its center, and the same vaguely insubordinate air, like a conscientious objector forced into uniform.

The Marshal's office was on the fifth floor of a concrete box with an armed guard in the glassy lobby who got friendly with a scanner wand and made me sign in. There were a couple of guys in the beige waiting room when I got upstairs, and I tried to keep things nonspecific with the receptionist, who slid her heavy glass window open as I walked up.

"I need to see someone about a federal witness," I told her.

"What time is your appointment?"

"I don't have one," I said. "It's kind of an emergency."

"Did you contact the person's WITSEC liaison?"

I glanced over at the two guys, one of whom was almost certainly a plainclothes cop. "She's not available right now."

The receptionist started to ask another question, and I pointed at the heavy steel access door to one side of her reception window. "I could explain this a lot more easily with some privacy. Can I come in there?"

She gave me as much of a once-over as her window would allow. "No way."

The cop's companion, a blond kid with a street tan and an

untrustworthy look that he'd probably never get rid of, had been watching me, and now he grinned.

"Look," I said to the receptionist, "just give me the next available appointment with somebody I can talk to privately, all right?"

She tapped her computer, then drawled, "I've got an eight o'clock on December twenty-first."

I didn't even bother to scoff. I just turned and walked out.

Frustration caught up with me at the truck, which I'd parked in a meter space across from the building entrance. I got in, but didn't start the motor; I was thinking too seriously about turning the lobby into a drive-through.

While I sat there waiting to cool off, a carillon sounded somewhere, signaling the start of the lunch hour. People began to stream out of the building I'd just left, among them a crew-cut black guy in a tan polyester Western suit. His odor of cop reached me all the way across the street.

I got out of the truck and angled over to meet him at the intersection. I wasn't trying to be sneaky about it, and he clocked me almost as soon as I crossed the street, his eyes moving rapidly down around my hands. I kept them visible and said, "Do you know Teresa Hallstedt?"

He clearly didn't like the look of me, but he didn't get any more interested in the gun under his arm, either. "You got something you want to tell me about her?"

It was a broad, deep voice, used to command. I replied, "She was my WITSEC contact."

His scowl hardened. "You're a private citizen now, Ms. Kalas."

The light changed, and he started across the intersection. I fell into step beside him, careful not to get too close.

"Look, this guy Maines, he doesn't know what the hell he's doing. I didn't have anything to do with her being killed."

The Marshal's eyes slid my way. "You know how many times a day I hear variations on that theme?"

I should have known better. He was law all the way through, just like the rest of them.

We were halfway down the block, people swarming past us on either side. He stopped and turned to face me. "Let me give you some advice, girl. If you've really gone straight, act the part and you'll probably survive. Start following me around, you probably won't. You read me?"

I could tell he was done. There wasn't another inch of tolerance in that impassive face. He turned and left me standing there on the sidewalk. I didn't try to follow him.

VII

Driving back to Azula, I considered my options. If I had any sense, I'd take the Marshal's advice—keep my head down and let Maines do whatever the hell it was he had in mind. With Tova's connections, Hector probably wouldn't spend a lot of time in prison, and if Richard turned up dead—well, it wasn't my fault.

I tried to talk myself into it and couldn't. Yeah, I still liked the idea of seeing Maines swinging in the wind, but I realized now that it wasn't what was really driving me.

Most people have some variety of reality filter, an ability to ignore the ugly truths of life enough that they can sleep at night, hold down a job, raise their kids. Mine is broken; this radar doesn't have an off switch. The only way I can live with that and not go insane is the trade-off it gives me of being one step ahead. If the stuff I was picking up wasn't accurate anymore—if something had broken down between here and California, disintegrated under the weight of Joe's death—I needed to know.

Now that I didn't have to play by WITSEC's rules, finding out would be considerably easier. I decided to start with shaking down Silvia Molina. If she'd just taken a lucky read on me, as the Amazon had insisted, I could probably risk the local notoriety. But if I was right and she had inside knowledge somehow, all bets were off.

The primary difficulty would be cutting through her shrewd avarice—going in point-blank would just lead to another round of Pin the Tail on the Mark. I'd need a persuader, and getting one legally wasn't an option for me anymore. My social security numbers, both old and new, were almost certainly flagged in every database in the country. Fortunately, I knew how to get around that better than probably anyone else in the world.

Back in Azula, I cut through the square and headed out past Teresa's to the run-down neighborhood along the river. The three baby gangsters were once again staked out at their stop sign. I pulled up and waited. The older boy came over, chin high.

"I need to buy a pocket piece," I said, getting my wallet out of the glove compartment. "A nine or better."

"Gun shop up the road," he said.

"I know it," I told him. "I can't pass the background check."

I have the kind of face that makes people believe me when I say things like that. I made sure he got a good look at it.

His eyes slid down to the stack of bills in my wallet. "You got a phone number?"

"No, I'm off the grid."

"Hold on," he said, and moved off away from the truck, getting his cell out of a low-riding pocket.

I cut the motor. The two younger boys were leaning on the truck on either side of the driver's-side window, observing the proceedings with a languid interest.

"You guys ever tangle with the Aryan Brotherhood?" I asked them.

The older one, whose voice hadn't changed yet, turned his head and spit into the ditch. "Them *maricones* know better than to come over here. Us country boys kick they ass."

I resisted the urge to grin, feeling a prick of sorrow at knowing that this kid, young enough that I could be his mother, had likely traded the unpredictable care of an impaired parent for this more stable life of casual violence, just like I had. Of course, I'd been thirteen to his eight or nine, and I hadn't actually succeeded. Not completely, anyway.

"Are you guys People or Folk Nation?" I asked him, making conversation until the point man returned.

"Independent," he said, throwing up a sign with his left hand. "Texas Kings don't bitch for nobody."

No independent gang could successfully defend its territory against an organization like the Brotherhood, if the Brotherhood wanted it. There probably wasn't enough of value in this backwater community to make it worth their while.

The point man returned, telling me, "Be back here in an

hour." He slipped his phone into his baggy pants. "Don't bring nobody with you."

"I know the drill," I assured him. "How much?"

"Nickel," he said.

I nodded, and the two younger boys leaned back off the truck as I started the motor.

VIII

I found my bank in a small red-brick building two blocks off the square, and withdrew six hundred in cash. This took only about fifteen minutes, so I left the truck where it was and walked over to the café to get something to eat while I killed the rest of the hour.

The place was unexpectedly packed. Neffa and her father were both on duty, neither of them reading books. Lavon gave me a curious look when he brought my silverware and water over, murmuring, "Sorry to hear about Teresa."

"Thanks." It was starting to feel natural.

"She was something, that girl," he said. "I can't hardly believe it."

I nodded, not saying anything.

"Did I hear she was on Hector's roof?" he asked.

"Yeah."

"Lord. I knew that mess was gonna turn out bad." He looked over at Neffa. "Her mama used to run around on me. I like to kill the woman myself once or twice, before she run off for good."

I tried to ignore my reaction, but couldn't. "Can I ask you something? This guy Maines, what's his story?"

"How do you mean?"

"You're the third person today who's suggested that Richard killed his wife, but he likes Hector for it."

"Well, him and Richard family. You know he's gonna look at everybody else first."

"But, I mean—if it came down to it, would he break the rules to get Richard off?"

Lavon held up both hands. "I ain't the person to ask about white cops." His eyes flickered at me. "No offense."

"None taken," I murmured, distracted. Something about what he'd said was tweaking the radar.

"We got catfish po'boys today," he offered after a short pause.

"Sounds good," I nodded, and he headed back to the kitchen.

I looked out the window at the side of the hotel, waiting for the itch at the base of my solar plexus to either subside or morph into a conscious thought. It did the latter after a few minutes, telling me that all the surviving businesses on the square were owned or operated by minorities—Latino, Jewish, black, Korean, gay, disabled, elderly, female. Not a single straight, able-bodied white man in the bunch. Was that just a coincidence, or did it point to something?

Lavon's voice cut through my thoughts. "I hear we're gonna be neighbors," he said, setting down a heavy white plate with my sandwich on it.

Before I could get a response out, he continued, "You ever want to sell off any of that place, you talk to me first, hear? My forty acres and a mule ain't enough to run a restaurant on. One of these days everything I serve gonna be home-grown. Vegetables, meat, everything." He nodded down at my plate. "Caught them catfish my own self, right out of the river here."

The brain was sliding around between my ears like a semi on an icy road, and I found myself gaping at him, unable to speak.

He waited, then said, "I told the girl she oughta split it up, but she didn't want to fool with that."

I continued to look at him, mute. I knew what I wanted to say, but the words just wouldn't penetrate the high, quiet buzz inside my head.

After a minute, Lavon did a small shrug and returned to the kitchen.

I looked down at my sandwich, forcing myself to breathe slowly. What had the shrinks called this, again? I couldn't remember, but it was clear to me now that my failure to banter with Hector on my first night at work might not have been just a one-off. Of course, it had happened right after my scare with Silvia, and the heads had warned me that stress could bring this on. I wasn't feeling particularly edgy at the moment, but maybe it was a delayed reaction to getting yanked from protection, or even Teresa's death. Most people would be curled up in the fetal position if they'd lived through what had happened to me over the last couple of days.

Joe had always warned me that I leaned too hard on my tough-broad persona, that someday it would crumble and drop me right on my ass. I'd patiently explained that it wasn't an act, that the hypersensitive, solemn kid my mother had sent daily to her sister's house so that she could drink the demons away in peace had actually evolved into the indestructible woman he'd married. He never bought it, spending our eleven years together constantly trying to squeeze something soft out of me. It got to be a joke between us after a while. Now it was crawling under my skin.

I squelched the wave of memories I felt coming and scarfed my sandwich, then made a point of having a completely coherent conversation with Neffa while I paid my bill. By the time I hit the sidewalk, I was feeling bulletproof again.

IX

Cutting through the alley on my way back to the truck, I saw that Richard's Lexus was still parked where I'd left it in the vacant lot behind Guerra's. Fucking Maines. Where I come from, you don't take people's money to do a job and then not do it, not without experiencing repercussions. A Bakersfield cop who tried it would find his snitches closing down shop, or anonymous evidence of his ounce-a-week coke habit showing up on his supervisor's desk.

OK, I wasn't the most trustworthy citizen on earth, but Maines couldn't seriously believe that I was fabricating what I'd tried to tell him about Richard and Jesse. I mean, if I was going to devise something to get Hector off the hook, it damn sure wouldn't be something that convoluted. I could have just said that we spent Thursday night together. The only person who could say it wasn't true was dead.

Of course, if Maines really was in Richard's pocket, he was going to shoot down anything involving his cousin. Which meant that I'd have to find something definitive to prove this Milestone thing, something Maines couldn't sweep under the rug.

Maybe Jesse or Richard would be willing to roll over on the other guy in exchange for immunity, if I could make them believe that discovery of their scheme was imminent. Richard's attempt to kidnap me suggested that he at least was getting desperate.

As I got into the truck, I wondered if he was even still alive. It was theoretically possible that he'd made peace with his disgruntled associate and gone home without picking up his car, since I still had his keys. Maybe I'd go by his place after I finished with Silvia, assuming that whatever she revealed didn't send me down a hole. If he'd made it back in one piece, we could have a nice little chat about what he'd had in mind for me the last time we met.

X

It was just the point man waiting for me when I got back to the river-bottom neighborhood. I pulled onto the dirt shoulder and shut off the motor, but before we could speak, his cell phone rang, and he showed me the palm of his hand, stepping away as before.

It was a longer conversation this time, and he came back to the truck with an aggrieved expression. "You gotta come in the house."

I looked at the destroyed box leaning into the sunset behind him. "What am I, stupid?"

"My man say he knows you."

I put it together pretty quickly and got out, locking up the cab.

Alex Méndez, the roofer I'd met during my job interview

with Hector, was sitting on the edge of a decaying sofa in what had once been a cozy living room. There were three pistols lying on the scarred wood floor in front of him: a Tomcat, a Kel-Tec, and a Kahr. An odd, dizzy nausea passed over me, and it took a second to realize that it wasn't a reaction to seeing Alex. It was the guns. Clearly, it was going to take some time for me to get used to being around them again.

"What's your story?" Alex asked, his voice hard.

"No story," I said. "I've got a record. If I'd known you were dealing, I wouldn't have bothered your middlemen."

"You were friends with the police chief," he said, his flavorless eyes searching me up and down.

"I worked for her aunt for a while," I said. "It's not like we were joined at the hip."

My naturally iffy vibe was doing its thing; the suspicion in his eyes was slipping away.

"Lemme see your money," he said.

I opened my wallet and handed over ten of the fifties I'd withdrawn from the bank. He put them to his nose, and I couldn't help smiling.

"I can smell that marking stuff they use," he told me, not smiling back.

I went ahead and laughed then. "Come on, man."

He stretched one leg out in front of him and slid the bills into his pocket, then got up, collecting the pistols. "I'ma have to check you out with my Inca. Tomorrow night you come see him, around nine. Everything's good, your piece'll be waiting for you there."

I sighed, looking off to one side. "What's the address?"

Alex recited it; then he and his associates sloped out of the house with my five hundred bucks.

XI

When I got back to the apartment, there was a cardboard box with Luigi's name on it leaning against the door, inside the screen. Hector had accepted my mailing arrangement without comment, and must have come by to drop it off while I was out. Considering that he hadn't returned any of the numerous calls I'd made to the bar and his cell, it was beginning to look like he was avoiding me. I was disappointed, but when you're barely five feet tall and wear a size 16, you get used to these things. A lot of men don't seem to know what the hell to do when they find themselves attracted to me; it's like they woke up on Mars.

I carried the box inside and slit the clear tape with a kitchen knife. A framed lithograph snuggled into a nest of crisply wrinkled currency. It was the print of Cochise's son Naiche that had hung in the front foyer of our house on Avenue B, the one possession I'd regretted leaving behind. The paper was mostly twenties, with some tens and fifties mixed in. Good old Pete.

The Internet told me that Richard lived about an hour's drive northwest. I went into the bedroom to get his keys off the bedside table where I'd dropped them last night, and then thought about where to hide the box of money while I was gone. Before I'd decided, the phone rang. I grabbed it up, hoping to hear Hector's voice. Instead, it was Tova. "Connie can close any evening after six," she said. "What works for you?"

So much had happened since making the offer on the Ranch that it took me a second to remember doing it. "Sorry, Tova," I said. The sixty thousand was now my running stash, until I sussed out my new circumstances. "I'm going to have to bow out of the deal. After all this stuff with Teresa, I'm not sure I'll be staying in town."

She made an outraged noise. "You might have mentioned that when we spoke the other day."

"It wasn't the main thing on my mind at the time," I said, amazed that it required saying.

"I've already spent several hours compiling the paperwork for the sale. My time is valuable."

I wanted to tell her what I'd been doing for the last two days, just to see what it would take to interest her in something besides herself. Instead I asked, "Have you heard from Hector?"

"No," she said. "Why?"

"I haven't been able to catch him at home or get him on the phone since we found Teresa, and he wasn't at Enchanted Rock when I went out there yesterday."

"Went out there?" There was a catch in Tova's voice. She paused to clear her throat, then said dryly, "It's a shame Hector can't bottle his sex appeal and sell it. None of us would ever have to worry about money again."

"I needed to talk to him about something."

"I'm sure you did."

Her kitten-with-a-whip tone was actively repelling me now. "Something funny is going on with this downtown development thing. It might be connected to Teresa's death."

I thought Tova had hung up, so total was the silence on the

other end of the line. Then a snide snicker crackled in my ear. "Well, thank heaven you're on the case, Miss Marple."

"What, you're OK with this pinhead Maines trying to put your brother in prison?"

Tova tsked. "Hector's not going to go to prison."

"Look, you're not going to be able to hide his PTSD from the lawyers, and even if the defense can spin it into an insanity plea—"

"I've been related to Hector for almost thirty years," Tova cut in. "If he were dangerous, I would certainly be aware of the fact. When he finds himself in stressful situations from which he can't remove himself, he simply zones out. He doesn't grab a knife and start stabbing people."

I tried to wade back in, but she wasn't having it. "I'd prefer not to have to be the one to tell Connie, once again, that a prospective buyer has backed out. Please make a point of speaking with her directly."

Before I could reply, she hung up.

I'm not sure how long I sat there, feeling unsettled, before I heard a low burble of something that sounded like people talking. I stood up, listening, and realized that it was coming from the basement. I hustled out of the apartment and down the porch steps. The basement door was closed, but flew open when I yanked on it.

"Who's down here?" I called into the musty darkness.

There was no answer, and I didn't hear the voices now. Cautiously, I stepped in and pulled the string on the single lightbulb next to the door. It lit up a low, wide room with a concrete mud slab and a forest of stone piers holding up the massive pine beams of the house overhead. A collection of cardboard boxes and furniture was stacked neatly in the center, away from the exterior walls.

I strained my ears, but didn't hear a car dying off in the distance, nor had I seen one leaving on my way down here. Apparently I was hearing things in addition to losing my ability to speak.

I turned to go back upstairs, and caught sight of the doorjamb. It was worn with age but intact, and so was the lock.

Leaning out of the light, I bent down to take a closer look. Except for some wear at the bottom where the door leaf scraped over the sidewalk, the entrance was undamaged. I straightened up, stomach tickling, and went around to check the six high windows, all glazed with wired glass. Each one was painted securely shut.

Nobody had broken in here. Not in the last decade.

A certainty began to blossom in my belly like ink meeting water. Richard hadn't lost his keys. Someone had taken them, with or without his knowledge, for the express purpose of getting in here. On the same night, and around the same time, that Teresa had been killed.

As usual, I had to do a mental backtrack to figure out how my gut had gotten there. If the keys had really been lost, a finder probably wouldn't have known immediately that they were Richard's. Even if they had, the odds of the finder also knowing that they included the only key to Teresa's basement, and said finder also having a reason to want to get in here, were astronomical. Those keys had to have changed hands purposely. Whether that had anything to do with Teresa's death, I declined to decide. I've erroneously assigned meaning to coincidence enough times in my life to be wary of doing it again.

Just the same, I went over and had a look inside the cardboard boxes that weren't completely buried. Clothes neatly folded into plastic vacuum bags, books organized by size, Christmas decorations heaped into a minty-smelling box with a festive green stain at the bottom, knickknacks and kitchen gadgets encased in Bubble Wrap. Nothing worth killing over.

What if Richard had stashed something down here that was, though? Maybe something that proved his collusion with Jesse on the Milestone deal. Stashed it down here, thinking it was the last place Teresa would ever look, and then she'd outguessed him. Palmed his keys Thursday night in the bar and gotten her proof before Richard noticed that they were missing. That would explain why he'd been so frantic to find her when Jesse had told him he'd found the door open. I briefly considered digging out the boxes underneath the ones I'd already looked in, but realized immediately that whatever the proof had been, it was almost certainly long gone by now.

XII

Predictably, Richard's subdivision was a gated community, a plastic approximation of some English country estate that had never existed outside a Jane Austen novel. It appeared to be engaged in a campaign, armed with Astroturf and man-made water features, to exterminate any inkling its inhabitants may have had that they lived in Central Texas. Everything was brightly lit in the early evening twilight, as if it were some sort of movie set. I could practically hear the fevered spinning of countless electric meters as I stopped at the gate.

A uniformed person of indeterminate age and gender leaned

out of a glowing glass booth and asked me what my business was. I considered saying I was casing the place for a break-in later, just to see what s/he'd do. Instead, I said I had an appointment at the Hallstedt residence, and I was issued a pass and let in. I wondered what the point was.

Richard's house was a stone-clad monstrosity big enough to play football in, with a semicircular driveway in front. I parked under the porte cochere and got out. As I came around toward the door, it opened, and a uniformed maid stepped out onto the stoop.

"May I help you?" she asked, suspicious. She looked familiar, and I realized it was the young woman Connie and I had run into on the sidewalk in front of the bar, on our way out Thursday night. She wasn't drunk now, but she had the shrunken hips and nervous hands of someone who soon would be. Again.

"I'm here to see Richard."

She ran her eyes down to my feet, then back up, not impressed. "Are you a patient?"

"That's a pretty personal question."

She gave me a disapproving look. "He's not here."

"Do you know when he'll be back?"

"What's this regarding?" she snapped.

Her unprovoked animosity was making my radar tickle. It wasn't just a bad hangover. "Has he been home since yesterday?"

"What business is that of yours?"

We were going in circles, so I shut up and just stood there, waiting for her to come around the track again.

"Did something happen?" she asked after a minute.

"Yes," I said.

When I didn't explain, she muttered, "I'm calling the police," and slammed the door.

I silently wished her better luck than I'd had, and started back around the truck. Halfway, I remembered my original pretext, and made a return trip to drop Richard's keys through the mail slot.

XIII

It actually took some time for my eyes to readjust to the darkness again after I turned out of the glaring subdivision—I blame this for the fact that, forty-five minutes later, I had to admit to myself that I was lost. I have a lousy sense of direction, and without a map or visible landmarks to navigate by, it's usually just a matter of time. When I realized that the road wasn't even remotely familiar, I reversed direction, but whatever wrong turn I'd taken ran both ways.

After winding around for what felt like hours in almost pitch darkness, a weak flicker of light appeared up ahead on the right. Relieved, I gave the gas a nudge, and was rewarded with a bump so hard my head hit the cab roof. I stamped the brake, and the engine light came on. Swearing, I pulled over onto the grass verge and got out to check below. Even in the dark I could see a fast drip of viscous fluid falling from the undercarriage.

The lights weren't far, so I got my wallet, locked up, and started walking. A few hundred yards later, the pale outline of a couple of small houses materialized out of the darkness. The road continued sloping down toward them, with what looked like a river crossing at the bottom. As I walked over it, I spotted a tall narrow house against a dark background of trees farther up a long hill and realized that I'd somehow come around the back way to Connie's property.

The light was coming from the small house next to the open shed. I went around and up onto the porch. The door was standing open, and the front room was empty except for a table draped with dark red velvet against the far wall. On top of the velvet, various items had been arranged in a tiered fashion. About half a dozen candles burned among them.

I stepped cautiously inside. The walls and ceiling were bare boards, and the floor had been painted white, but not very recently. As I got closer to the altar, a whiff of dead fish and paint thinner caught my attention, at about the same time that I realized what the lumpy gray object on the center tier was: the dismembered hand that had appeared behind the bar on Thursday night.

It was lying on a bed of fresh flower petals and surrounded by a collection of cigarettes, money, and candy. There were also some less familiar items—miniature bottles filled with colored water and stones, small bundles of oily-looking cloth tied up with red cotton string, and several pieces of dollhouse furniture, including a table with chairs and a tiny sideboard. Interspersed between these objects were piles of small oval dark green leaves. The flowers and decaying flesh together produced a sharp, raw smell.

Something clamped on to my right biceps, and I started to turn, swinging a fist out by instinct, but was trapped by arms coming around from behind. I brought my heel down as hard as I could on the foot between my own. There was a loud yelp and the arms loosened; I jumped out of reach and whirled to face my attacker. It was Hector.

"Jesus Christ," I said. "You've got to stop with this sneaking-up-behind-me thing."

He'd been knocked off balance against the wall, and now he got his feet back under him, aiming an alarmed look at me. As his eyes moved across my face, I saw something puzzled run across them and quickly disappear into the darkness. He glanced warily at the open door, then back at me. "How'd you get out here? I didn't hear a car."

"Truck broke down on the ridge up there," I said, waving toward the river. "I saw the lights and walked down. I think I knocked a hole in the oil pan."

His eyes widened. "Did it seize up?"

"You don't think I know better than to drive with the engine light on?"

We stood there staring at each other for a minute, then Hector wiped both hands up over his face with a heavy sigh.

I lifted my chin at the altar and asked, "How'd you get hold of that thing? I thought Teresa sent it off to a forensics lab somewhere."

He turned his head away, not saying anything. I waited, but he didn't crack.

I tried a change of subject. "Maines is getting a warrant for your arrest."

"Screw Maines," Hector snarled. "He can arrest me all he wants. I didn't kill her."

I looked pointedly over at the hand, then back at him.

"You think I did it?" he demanded, his eyes flashing up like black firecrackers.

"No, but my objectivity is in question." It sounded a little querulous coming out of my mouth. I started to clarify, but then stopped. Let's see what he did with it.

Hector's ferocious expression evaporated. He clomped across

the floor, out onto the porch, and crackled off through the dry grass.

It took me a while to realize that he wasn't coming back. I stepped out of the dim room onto the porch to think.

Down here, below the road, the only sounds were of a light breeze moving and the occasional growl of cattle in the distance. The clouds had moved off and the moon was frosting everything with cool light. The inside of my head felt like an empty echo chamber.

Twenty minutes passed while I tried to make sense of the altar and the hand. Plainly Teresa hadn't sent it off to the lab as promised, but that didn't explain how Hector had gotten hold of it, or why. Naturally the thought occurred—again—that he'd killed her for it, but the radar still wasn't having it. Which reminded me that I hadn't yet figured out whether or not it could be trusted in my new circumstances.

Realizing that standing out here alone in the middle of nowhere wasn't going to solve that problem, I decided to walk up to the main road to see if I could hitch a ride back into town. As I stepped off the porch, I caught a whiff of fragrant smoke and saw a small orange glow arc through the darkness down near the river. I aimed for the light and found Hector leaning against one of the big cottonwood trees along the bank.

"I've already gotten one person killed," he said, continuing our conversation as if he'd never pretended to leave. "I'd rather you weren't the second."

"Look, I'm not going to let that half-wit sheriff lock you up for something you didn't do," I said. "I'll keep pushing on this thing until I get to the bottom of it, and I could really make a hell of a mess if I don't know what I'm dealing with."

Hector sighed out a cloud of fragrant smoke, dropping his cigarette butt on the ground and crushing it with the square toe of his boot. "Please, just leave it alone."

"No, you don't understand," I said. "I'm not offering you a menu of options. I'm telling you what's going to happen. I can't help it. It's the way I'm wired."

I'll give him credit; once he made up his mind about it, he didn't hesitate. I was mashed up against him, getting the daylights kissed out of me, before I realized what was happening. Things moved fast from there. It was like rushing to put out a fire, our clothes tearing off, breath coming fast, hands and mouths all over each other. We sank to the ground, his hot weight pressing me into the prickly grass. He rolled away briefly, and I heard the crinkle of a condom wrapper; then that delicious first plunge—and it was over.

"Damn it," said, sitting up.

I flashed to the backseat of a '72 Barracuda and the humiliating revelation that my paramour was performing for a shot at Joachim's good graces, not because he liked me. An old, hot anger rushed up as I felt around for my jeans.

"I'm sorry," Hector said, tending to himself. "I'm just—it's been a while."

"Yeah," I said. "Two days is an eon."

He frowned over at me. "What are you talking about?" He was sitting with his elbows on his knees, still breathing hard, a sheen of sweat showing at his collarbone.

I fought the urge to grab him and lick it off. "Come on, Hector. They found your DNA inside Teresa's body."

He peered at me, baffled. "*My* DNA?"

I nodded, and he sat there with a frozen expression for a minute, then got up quickly, muttering, "God damn it." He caught a look at my face while yanking his jeans on. "Maines and Richard are setting me up."

"Wait a minute," I said, trying to grab him. He was whipping around, jamming his arm into the wrong shirtsleeve, getting his socks half on. "Your DNA doesn't prove anything except that you two were having an affair, which isn't exactly a secret—"

"We weren't having an affair," he cut in. "We sort of dated, before she met Richard, but that's been over for twenty years."

"So why does everybody in town think you two were—?"

"Because she wanted them to," he groaned, a scratchy desperation coming into his voice. He stopped dressing, closed his eyes and let his head fall back. "She liked pissing Richard off, and God help me, so did I. So I went along with it. It was just a joke, between old friends. He must have found out about her roof thing—"

"What 'roof thing'?"

"She used to come across from her private office above the café sometimes. It was—she was—I don't know, she just liked doing stuff like that. It was all part of the joke, for her."

"Why didn't you tell Maines that? It explains how she got up there."

Hector wiped a hand up over his forehead again, shaking

his head mutely. I was standing up now, half dressed, a ripple of sorrow lapping at my ribs. It had a little undercurrent of derision in it. "This looks really bad for you."

"You don't think I know that?" he snapped.

We glared at each other; then he reached over and laid his forearms on my shoulders, cupping the back of my head in his hands. He didn't say anything, just pulled me forward until our foreheads touched, and closed his eyes. I felt the heat go out of him.

"Come on," he said. "I'll give you a ride home."

I stepped away, twitching my head toward the cottage. "I'm not going anywhere until you explain that."

Hector pressed his lips together, pushing his chin forward. It was a gesture I was starting to recognize.

I said, "If Maines has gone so far as to fake a forensics report, do you really think he's going to hesitate to do worse? You're going to need people on your side, and I'm not joining up unless I know exactly what I'm getting into."

"Fine," Hector said, bending down to tighten a buckle on one boot. When he stood back up without saying anything else, I realized he didn't mean it the way I'd hoped.

"Listen," I pressed, "I'm not being altruistic here. Maines told the feds that I'm somehow involved in Teresa's death, so they've cut me loose. If I don't get to the bottom of this thing, I could end up in the clink right along with you. Or worse."

He stood there in the moonlight, mulling it over. It wasn't easy to read his expression in the half darkness, but it seemed to me that he didn't like the idea of being responsible for someone else's troubles. I was counting on that.

He sighed again, pushed his hair behind his ears, and started back toward the cottage. I followed.

The candles on the altar had burned down, and he got some fresh ones from under the velvet drape, setting their wicks on fire with his chrome lighter. He murmured something I couldn't hear, then turned and beckoned me forward.

"Come on in and meet my father."

MONDAY, NOVEMBER 5

I stumbled into the room, trying to get my head around what Hector had just said. After a minute, I realized that I was staring at the hand, looking for a family resemblance. The absurdity of it forced a short laugh out of me.

Hector put a finger to his lips and whispered. "You got a dollar? It's not polite to talk until you've given him something."

Mechanically, I opened my wallet and took out a bill, laying it on top of the stack at the edge of the table. The smell of hot wax, decaying flesh, and flowers floated through the room. I couldn't figure out what question to ask first.

Hector saved me the trouble. "It's traditional in my culture to keep your relatives with you even after they're dead."

"Your culture?" I managed.

"I'm Aymara, from Bolivia. We're native to the Altiplano, the high plains of the Andes. Up there, it's so dry that bodies don't decay, so we have this whole tradition around mummified ancestors." Hector smiled. "We even build little houses for them. *Chulpas.*"

I was only half listening. A vague sense of misalignment kept flashing at me from the altar, like one of those puzzles where you have to figure out what's different between two seemingly identical pictures.

"Wait a minute," I said, seeing what it was. "This isn't the same hand we found behind the bar. The thumb's on the wrong side."

"Yeah, it's the other one."

Hector paused until I looked at him again, then said, "It was with Teresa's body when I found her. I took it down to Lavon's and threw it over onto the hotel roof before you came up. I went over there and got it yesterday."

Speech failed me again, and Hector turned toward the altar, pinching out the candles. As he did so, he murmured something unintelligible and held a few of the small green leaves up in a gesture of benediction.

Then he turned back to me. "Let's go outside," he said in a low voice. "I don't like to talk about this in front of him."

We stepped out onto the porch and he locked the door. Then he dropped onto the top step. I sat down next to him and waited.

"They were stolen from my apartment during that break-in last week," he said when we'd both settled. "Thursday night, after I threw that drunk out, Richard called and told me I could have them back if I'd sell Jesse the bar. I didn't have time to answer him before Connie—"

I'd jumped up, unable to suppress a jubilant "Yes!" Hector's expression went alarmed, and I said, "I knew they were colluding on this Milestone Properties deal, but I haven't been able to find anything to prove it."

He gave me a look that was half tenderness, half pity, and reached into his shirt pocket. "You can't tell anybody any of this."

It felt like the beginning of a long story. I sat back down.

Hector fired up a cigarette and took his time putting the lighter away. Then he pointed a frank look at me and said, "The only reason you're hearing this is because I've got something just as big on you. Got it?"

I made the sign of the cross over my heart and zipped my lips, throwing away the key.

Hector said, "You ever heard of a guy named Jorge Escobar?"

I thought for a second, then shook my head.

"He was one of the head guys in the Medellín drug cartel, back in the '70s and '80s. You know about them, right?"

"Who doesn't?"

"OK, well"—he took a deep breath—"Escobar and his guys killed my mother and my two younger sisters—my entire family at the time—for refusing to sell him our coca crop."

My eyebrows headed north. "Your family were cocaine farmers?"

"Coca isn't cocaine," Hector said, a tired patience coming into his voice. "It's a medicinal plant that's been used by indigenous people in the Andes for centuries. Yeah, you can turn it into cocaine with enough processing and chemicals, but in its natural state, it's just a mild stimulant, like nicotine or caffeine. That's how we use it."

He watched my face to make sure I got it, then looked back toward the river. A long time went by without him saying anything. When he went on, his voice had sunk to a low monotone. "I'd gone to town to get some medicine for my mother. Coming up the road to our house, I saw her and the girls being marched out of the house by Escobar and his men. I knew right away what was happening. I dived into the bushes before they could spot me." A quiet pain lifted his monotone a notch. "I can still smell those flowers."

He choked off and stopped. I waited awhile, then snaked my hand across his thigh. He took it, squeezing hard. His voice was looser when he started to talk again.

"After they were gone, I went around to our *chulpa*. In the old days, whole *malquis*—family mummies—were kept in them, but we just had my father's hands. When I came back around the house with them, Escobar was there. He saw me and hollered for his men. I ran like a son of a bitch. I still don't know how in hell I got away."

I'd drawn closer and set my cheek against his shoulder, lulled by the vibration of his body as he spoke. "They must have been lousy shots," I said.

Hector looked at me. "They didn't have guns."

I frowned up into his face.

"Machetes," he said.

Nausea rattled at the back of my throat. "That's what they used to kill your mother and sisters?"

He nodded. I closed my eyes and took a slow, deep breath, willing myself not to visualize the carnage Hector must have witnessed.

"I think I made it to La Paz on pure adrenaline," I heard

him say. "I got on a train heading north and rode it until I ran out of money. Red found me a couple of months later."

I opened my eyes. "Why didn't you just go to the cops, after you got away from Escobar?"

Hector scoffed gently. "Escobar and his men *were* the cops. That's how it was those days. The drug cartels ran everything."

"OK, but the Medellín Cartel was dismantled in the '90s," I remembered aloud. "Those guys are all in jail now."

"Escobar worked some kind of deal," Hector said. "I think he served five years or something, then he went in with the Mexicans. Now he's second in command of the Gulf Cartel."

The bottoms of my feet went cold. Two hundred miles south of where we were sitting, men, women, and children were being slaughtered on the order of hundreds daily by an organization grown so brazen that even the military wasn't safe. Joe and I had sold guns to drug mules coming up from Baja, and I knew that the cartels were a vast international network worse than any Mafia. They never forgot an enemy, never let a transgression go unpunished. If they were looking for him, Hector was indeed in mortal danger.

"Escobar's distribution route runs right up through here," Hector was saying, watching me. "If he tracks me down, I'm a dead man."

I started to protest that finding someone of Hector's description in Central Texas was probably about as easy as picking out an individual pebble at a gravel mine, but then I realized that publicly associating him with a pair of mummified hands significantly improved Escobar's odds. That's why Hector had tried to hide the one he'd found with Teresa's body.

"Ever thought about moving to Canada?" I said.

Hector's hand strayed up toward the pocket where his cigarettes were, but he didn't get another one out. "Yep."

Before WITSEC, I wouldn't have thought twice about
giving him shit for not going, but now I knew better. There's a
reason the U.S. government devotes an entire program to helping people disappear effectively: it's not something that's easy
to pull off by yourself. Most people who get away with it on
their own do so only because nobody is very interested in finding them. Once you escape the immediate threat, the safest
thing to do is stay put and blend into the woodwork as quietly
as possible.

"So how does Richard know about all of this?" I asked after
a minute.

"I wish I knew. Teresa's the only person I ever told, and
she would never have said anything, especially to Richard. She
understood how dangerous the situation was for me."

"Maybe Tova or Connie said something without thinking,
and it got into the local gossip pipeline."

"There's nothing for them to say. They don't know anything
about it."

"That you know of," I corrected with a smile. "Take it from
me, little girls are nature's crack detectives."

Hector shifted on the worn board steps, making them creak.
"No, look. When Red found me in Managua, he just assumed I
was Nicaraguan, and everybody in the family followed him." He
fixed his dark eyes on my face. "There hasn't been a moment of
my life, since that day, that I didn't understand what the stakes
were. I've always kept the *malquis* out of sight and under lock
and key, and nobody—in the family or outside it—has ever said

or done anything to make me think they knew anything about them. If they had, I'd have split and taken them with me."

I digested this for a few minutes, trying to decide if the Amazon could have let something slip unintentionally, but I'd known within thirty seconds of meeting her that she didn't have an unintentional bone in her body. Even if I were wrong, she'd surely have warned Hector that his secret was out, had she been the one to spring it.

"Maybe Richard doesn't know all the details," I said. "I mean, obviously he knew about the *malquis* and where they were before the break-in—you don't open a wall safe with a pocketknife." Hector's eyes lasered over to me, and I went on quickly. "It's possible all he knows for sure is that you don't want people knowing you kept a pair of mummified hands in your apartment."

"No," Hector insisted, shaking his head. "He'd never have taken the risk of leaving that second one with Teresa if he thought there was any chance I'd report it."

"Why not? I assume that if you could make a connection between him and the break-in, you'd have done it by now."

"It would have been enough for me to make the accusation—everybody in town knows how their divorce was going. He had to know, for a fact, that whatever the *malquis* meant was problematic enough that I'd let him get away with murder. He's not the kind of person to take a risk that big on a wild guess."

I wasn't convinced, but Hector's chin was starting to get that stubborn look to it. "So, what *did* you report about the burglary, if anything?"

"I told Teresa everything—confidentially—but that was before Richard's phone threat on Thursday night. I was getting ready to call her when Connie screamed and all hell broke loose."

That explained the hateful look he'd given the Amazon. Maybe it hadn't been so much hateful as terrified. "So you went over to her place after we closed, to fill her in?"

"No, I told you," he said, impatient. "Whoever you heard talking to her that night, it wasn't me. The last time I saw her was when she left the bar with you that night." His face went suddenly haggard, skull-like in the darkness. "I never thought Richard would kill her. I figured I'd catch her up in the morning."

The buzz in my stomach turned sour. I got up, extending a hand, and he looked up at me, those beautiful eyes pits that went all the way down. "Do you think character is hereditary?" he asked.

It was an odd segue, and I wondered if talking about all this was ramping him up to a PTSD episode.

"I wouldn't know. I was raised by wolves," I said, hoping to put an end to the story for now. I wiggled my fingers at him. "Come on, let's get out of here."

Hector was gazing muddily off into the darkness. "When *Mami* got mad, she'd always say that I was just like my father. Self-centered and arrogant. She's right. All I've cared about in this thing is keeping my own ass out of the fire."

I dropped my hand to his shoulder. "Look, you don't need to work at making yourself feel worse. Things are bad enough on their own. Put it away for a couple of hours. Sometimes things clarify themselves if you stop thinking about them for a while."

He didn't say anything. I felt him struggling against something tidal, and then his shoulder solidified under my hand and he got up. "I'll call Nathan in the morning to come tow the truck to his shop," he said. "It'll be OK up there tonight."

11

Back at Teresa's, Hector parked under the oak tree and held the bike steady as I got off. I didn't stop to say good-bye, hoping he'd follow me up the back steps and into my apartment. He did.

"Whoa!" he exclaimed as I went over and turned on the lamp. "Not too big to keep clean, is it?"

My cardboard box full of money was still sitting there. I got myself between it and Hector and took it over to the kitchen cabinet, my heart pounding. I'd been so distracted when I came back upstairs after prowling the basement that I'd just grabbed Richard's keys and run out. I was lucky the box was still there.

Hector passed behind me to look into the bedroom as I shut the cabinet door. The place seemed even smaller with him in it, as if the family Rottweiler had just trotted into the kids' playhouse. The thought made me smile. He saw my grin and came over to slide his arms around me.

The light from the shaded bulb in the bathroom fell on his face, illuminating the sparse black beard coming through his skin. There was something enthralling about looking at him up close, like having a private audience with a famous work of art. Behind his back, my fingers ran through the ends of his hair. It was coarse and supple, like a horse's tail.

"Are you staying over?" I asked, watching him watching me.

His face went surprised. "You want me to?"

"I thought you might like a chance to improve on your previous performance." If he was going to sex me up to try and keep me quiet, I might as well get his A game.

His dark eyes moved down to my mouth, with a smile in them. "Yes, please."

This time the fire was a slow burn, and Hector worked it like a man with something to prove. He was deliberate and thorough, hard and soft in all the right places, and deliciously filthy without being vulgar. I wasn't quite sure how he managed it, until I realized that he'd almost certainly had a lot of practice. He'd probably been beating women off with a stick since puberty.

The moon had gone down when we finally exhausted ourselves. Hector, lying next to me with one leg heavy across my hips, ran a hand over my bruised side.

"Where'd you get this?" he asked.

I squirmed, eyes closed, reluctant to dilute my afterglow. "I fell down some stairs."

"Were you on fire at the time?" he chuckled, holding up my burned finger.

I covered a yawn. "It's kind of a long story. I'll tell you later."

I felt him sit up. "OK if I take a bath?" he asked.

I nodded, and he nudged me. "You coming?"

"In a minute," I murmured, smiling.

I heard the water turn on; then I don't remember another thing until the sun crossing my pillow woke me, some time after noon.

III

I was in bed alone. I lay there savoring my memories from the previous night for a few minutes, then got up.

Hector wasn't in the apartment, and a look out the kitchen window told me his BMW was gone. He must have gotten up early to go take care of the truck. I appreciated the fact that he'd let me sleep, but a note would have been nice.

I put some water on for tea, then went back into the bedroom and dialed Hector's cell. He didn't answer, so I left a short message asking him to call me back. As I hung up, I wondered if the PTSD attack I'd felt coming the night before had gotten hold of him. I liked that better than the depressing thought that he'd gone off somewhere to formulate his "let's be friends" speech, but I knew less about how to handle it.

While the tea was brewing, I sat down at the laptop to do a little research. Not that the Internet is all that useful for that purpose anymore. I remember a time when you could type in something like PTSD and get actual information. Nowadays you're just as likely to land on a site selling time-shares in the Australian outback or a conspiracy theory page advising you that the government has planted a chip in your head. I sifted through these online gems for a couple of hours, spending most of that trying to discern whether or not what I was reading was reliable.

Before I shut the computer off, I went to check my e-mail and saw that there was a message to Margaret Ness from Pete's nom de plume, Uncle Vito. I clicked it open and read:

Here's another picture of Olmos—I got it too late to include in our recent correspondence.

There was an attachment, a digital photo of a squat Hispanic guy in his mid-sixties, in front of an office building on a city street. It looked like it had been taken from a car about half a block away. I didn't recognize him.

Puzzled, I went and got the cardboard box out of the cabinet. A white paper corner peeked up from the scramble of crinkled money, and I wondered why I hadn't seen it the day before. It was a plain letter-sized envelope, sealed. Inside there was a note, handwritten in Pete's spiky scrawl, folded around a single color photo. The note read:

J.—

We discovered after you left that one of our northern suppliers, Nick Olmos, was an undercover federal agent. He went over the wall after it broke and might be looking for trouble. This was taken in San Antonio. Keep your eyes open.

—P.

The photo was of the same guy from Pete's e-mail, only here he was thinner, better groomed, and without the wire-rimmed glasses. He was talking to a familiar-looking woman at some sort of outdoor vegetable stand. I peered closer, and my stomach dropped through the floor. It was Silvia Molina.

She was using better posture, wearing younger clothes, and her hair was pulled back into a high ponytail that made her look closer to fifty than seventy. I checked the camera-stamped date in the lower right corner. It had been taken six days ago.

I stood there staring at the photo until my eyes watered, then laid it on the table and went out into the backyard. I wanted to feel that big sky lifting the top of my head off. I needed something to release the pressure.

My first coherent thought, when the brain made its way back into my skull, was to pack my stuff, go find the truck, and just start driving. I had fifty grand sitting on my kitchen table and a clean slate. I reminded myself about the woodwork and went back inside to try Hector's cell again. He still wasn't answering. I doubted that he was at home, but I didn't want the possibility nagging at me, so I called the bar.

Mike answered. He told me that he hadn't seen Hector since Friday.

"Any idea how I can reach him?" I asked. "He's not answering his cell."

"Sorry," Mike said. "What's up?"

Wishing I knew the answer to that question, I moved on to logistics. "You don't happen to know a mechanic named Nathan, do you?"

Mike recited a number, apparently from memory, which I scribbled down on a paper towel. While I did it, I heard him rummaging around with something clinky on the other end of the line.

"What are you doing at work in the middle of the day?"

"I thought maybe somebody had turned in my phone. I don't see it in the lost and found here, though."

I remembered Tova bringing it to him on Thursday night. He sure did lose things fast.

Something jingled, and Mike muttered, "Well, I'll be damned. Richard's keys."

"The ones he lost on Thursday night? Are you sure?"

"Well, there's a medallion thing with 'R.E.H.' on it, and a Lexus key. Somebody must have turned them in on Friday, because we tore the damned place apart looking for them on Thursday night, after you and Connie left."

Tweaked as I was at the moment about Pete's e-mail, I needed a second to remember why I cared about Richard's keys. The whole issue seemed absurdly meaningless now.

"You still there?" Mike asked.

"Yeah. Sorry. Listen, if you see Hector, ask him to call me, will you?"

He agreed and we hung up. I punched in the number he'd given me, and a man with a deep Texas voice answered. He'd gotten a message from Hector first thing that morning, he said. He told me his shop was a few blocks north of the square, on Main, and that I could pick up the truck any time.

IV

After retrieving my wheels, I got to work freaking out, alternately planning my escape and talking myself out of it again.

Silvia's changed appearance in the photo told me that she was a field operative of some kind, undercover either here or there. Several million possibilities branched out from that one, all of which I spent some time with that afternoon, narrowing down to the two most likely: She'd gotten her information about me from Olmos, and they were now colluding to squeeze me for some cash; or his appearance in the vicinity was a fluke, and they were working together on something completely unrelated to me. Given Silvia's behavior toward me since I'd hit town, I was betting heavily on the former.

At some point in the proceedings, I ran a background check on her through one of the online services and discovered that she was a Cuban national who'd been granted asylum in '94. She appeared to have come straight to Azula and lived here ever since, which smelled funny to me. She was sixty-two and widowed, with no children, so I doubted that she had family here, and it didn't seem like the most likely destination for a Cuban expatriate. Maybe she'd been pressed into service with the feds as part of her asylum deal. The thought gave me a little hope; if true, it had happened long ago enough that I wouldn't be at the top of her food chain. Of course, everything I was reading about her could all be government-sponsored bullshit, just like the stuff anybody looking me up on one of these databases would find.

I almost let six o'clock go by, but I was thinking clearly enough by then to realize that the local underground might be my only resource when this Silvia/Olmos shit hit the fan. Not only that, if I could make nice with the Kings, maybe they'd share whatever was currently floating around on the airwaves about me. That would give me a big leg up. Not to mention the gun.

V

The Inca's place was at the end of a dead-end gravel road, a crooked board-and-batten house that backed onto open pasture. There were three pickups in front, parked at various angles on the dry grass, and I smelled meat cooking when I got out and went up onto the porch.

The door behind the screen was open, giving a view all the way through to the backyard, where a dozen or so people were milling around under a canopy of white Christmas lights. Not expecting anyone to hear me, I rapped on the screen door, and almost jumped out of my skin when a hand reached immediately out of the darkness to open it.

The guy attached was maybe thirty-five, short, and solidly fat, with a red and black bandanna riding low on his forehead, covering his eyebrows. Every visible inch of skin except for his face was adorned with indigo tattoos. He was dressed in an oversize black T-shirt and baggy black jeans, and wore a pair of what looked like welder's glasses—thick black plastic frames with nearly opaque round lenses—despite the dimness of the room.

He gestured politely for me to come in and sit down, asking, "Can I get you something? There's beer, lemonade. . . ." He had a low, melodious voice with a thick accent, and spoke with care, as if testing each word for accuracy before pronouncing it.

"No, thanks," I said.

He nodded, and waited for me to take the worn tweed chair facing the sofa. The room was cozily illuminated by a single floor lamp, and the homey sound of children playing and people laughing and talking filtered in from the backyard.

"Cabrito's almost ready," he told me, dropping onto the sofa after I sat down. "It's been cooking all day."

I waited. It was his party.

"You lied to Alex about having a police record," he said.

I hadn't expected that, and replied almost automatically, "It was in California, under another name."

The Inca smiled, showing a gold grill with a diamond on each canine, and said, "You are Jaana Rizzoli, yes?"

Time stopped moving. High up on a back shelf somewhere, the brain noticed that he'd pronounced the name correctly—*Jane-ah* rather than the flat *Jah-na* that always drove me nuts. The black lenses remained trained on me for what felt like a century; then the Inca shifted one hip forward and brought out the Kahr ACP I'd seen with Alex. I waited for it to point at me, but it went down onto the coffee table, on its side.

A little girl about five years old came trotting into the living room from the back of the house. She went around the coffee table, showing no interest in the gun, and pressed her little body against the Inca's knee, saying something in Spanish. He put an arm around her, leaning his head down to listen, then replied in a low voice and gave her a gentle push. She looked at me curiously as she sidled out.

"My daughter," he murmured, smiling.

There was a long pause; then he went on in his ponderous way. "I consider it my duty to make sure that she grows up in an environment devoid of the nonsensical bullshit groups like the Aryan Brotherhood perpetrate. I take my parental responsibilities very seriously."

The flat lenses glinted toward me again, and I felt a hot surge of hope.

"It's my understanding that the Brotherhood doesn't operate in this area," I said, amazed at how calm my voice sounded.

"You understand correctly," he replied, leaning back against the sofa with his chin lifting. "I don't allow those *coños* in my territory."

"How do you keep them out?" I asked, genuinely curious.

"The chief of police, she was a woman of great insight. She understood that allowing my organization to operate without undue interference had benefits to her position."

I felt a twinge of respect for the Amazon. She was more than just cop. She'd had some sense.

The Inca seemed to be waiting for me to say something, and when I didn't, he asked, "She was helping the government to hide you?"

I couldn't see the harm in him knowing it now that she was dead, so I nodded.

He continued looking at me, his head to one side.

"Did she tell you who I am?" I asked when the silence started to stretch out.

He shook his head. "I assure you that my source is of no danger to you. Please honor me with your trust on that." The "please" didn't make it sound any less like a threat.

I slid to the front of the chair and looked at the Kahr, then at him. He nodded. I picked it up, holding myself tight. A spasm of revulsion clutched at my stomach, then receded. I checked the chamber and magazine and slipped it into my front pocket. It felt like a block of ice pressed against my hip.

"I wonder," I said carefully, "if you've heard any other interesting things that might concern me."

"Do you refer to this captivity of the policechief's husband?" The Inca frowned, puzzled.

I didn't, but he had my attention. "Richard's alive?"

He nodded, sneering, "He hired some white boys for a job and then failed to pay them for their work. They are holding him at their compound on Flat Creek, just across the county line west of here, hoping that someone will pay a ransom for his sorry ass." He paused to run a finger under one eye, chuckling softly.

I was still sitting on the edge of the chair, my elbows on my knees, and I felt a faint tremor run down into my hands. I pressed them together so that it wouldn't show. "Do you know what Richard hired them for?"

"Yes," the Inca said simply. I waited, but he didn't go on.

"Did it have something to do with Milestone Properties?"

"Yes," he said again.

A thrill of satisfaction shot through me, making me less careful. "How about Teresa? Did he have them kill her?"

The Inca made a derisive noise. "Those cowards can't even kill a man who deserves it."

"So who did it?"

"I do not know," he said, looking off to one side with annoyance twisting the part of his face that I could see, "and I am not much pleased by that fact. There has never been a hit in my territory of which I was not made aware beforehand." I shifted in the chair, and he added quickly, in his peculiar, formal cadence, "It was not the Brotherhood—this I know, from my informants—but neither was it another of my known competitors." He sighed. "Things will not go so well with my people now that she is gone."

I considered showing him the photo of Olmos that I'd gotten from Pete, but the radar told me to keep it in my pocket.

"May I request a favor of you?" the Inca asked.

There was no requesting about it. He held all the cards. "Of course."

"This man Maines, is it true that he is to become the next chief of police?"

"I don't know," I said, surprised. "I wasn't aware that he wanted the job."

The Inca retrieved a black lacquer card case from his hip pocket. It was the real thing, not a plastic knockoff. Crime pays. He removed a card, checked the back, and held it out. "If you learn of anything more concerning his future plans, I would appreciate knowing."

I nodded, taking the card. The name MAURICIO TORRES was printed on the front, and it had a phone number handwritten on the back.

VI

I drove out to a sporting goods store that I'd spotted on my trip to Johnson City, bought a box of Tritons, and loaded the Kahr in the parking lot. It didn't feel quite so repellent in my hand now—a tamed basket of adders rather than the stinging wild bite it had given me before. I sat there holding it, letting my hand get used to a gun again while I considered the best approach to use with Silvia.

There was nobody home at the botanica when I got there. I thought about waiting around, but the late night with Hector was beginning to catch up with me, and I was afraid I'd fall asleep if I parked. Until I got more information on this Olmos character, I didn't want anyone getting any kind of drop on me.

I got back in the truck and aimed it toward the corner store on the square, to pick up something with caffeine and sugar in it. As I came around the courthouse, I saw that the lights were on in Hector's apartment.

I pulled up and parked at the curb, let myself into the bar, and vaulted up the stairs. The apartment door was standing open, and the radar stopped me on the landing to listen. There was a quiet step in the hall; then the sheriff's lanky figure came into view with its back to me, moving toward the kitchen table.

"I hope you have a search warrant," I said from the doorway.

He turned slowly, not surprised. "Don't need one. Exigent circumstances. Guerra was stopped in Galveston this morning. Trying to hire a boat to Mexico."

A curious sensation washed through me. It felt a lot like relief. I hadn't even been aware that I was worried. Immediately behind it, though, was disbelief. "To Mexico? Are you sure?"

Maines had been casting his pale eyes around the apartment, and now he turned them on me. He didn't say anything, just waited for me to continue talking.

"What time did they stop him?" I asked, coming in.

The sheriff savored his ten seconds, then said, "Eleven eighteen."

That meant Hector had left my place near dawn, which would have come shortly after I'd fallen asleep.

"Bail hearing in the morning," Maines was saying. "He's cooling his heels across the square until then."

"How long has he been in there?"

"DPS released him to me about eight." As if it were an afterthought, he added, "He probably wouldn't mind a visitor. Judge isn't likely to grant bail, given his flight."

I gave that the look it deserved, and Maines's phantom smile appeared. "No tricks. I already got all the evidence I need."

I didn't beg to differ.

Headlights splashed across the face of the courthouse, and Maines stepped over to the bay window to look out. Then he turned with his index finger to his hat brim, saying politely, "Excuse me."

I watched him go, then took a walk around the apartment. Nothing appeared to have changed since the last time I'd been in it, except that the cat food bowls were empty again. I filled them up, and Luigi materialized at the top of the stairs as if by magic. He complained about the slow service, then started to eat.

I went over and lay down on the bed to think, which I realized, too late, was a mistake. The sheets smelled of Hector, and my body started making decisions. I fought it for a while, then decided it couldn't do any worse than my head, and got up.

VII

The jail was a dirt-colored stone behemoth standing flush with the curb, its front door recessed into an arcade of massive arches. The hall inside had a '60s-era green terrazzo floor, with a small office of the same vintage on the right. In it, a tan-uniformed kid with a Taser on his hip sat with his legs up on the desk, playing online poker.

He finished the hand before he got up. "You wanna see Guerra?"

I looked him over. He was maybe twenty-five, white-blond, clean-cut, skinny. I'd never seen him before. "Maines told you I was coming?"

He went past me into the hall, jingling keys. "Only prisoner in the place."

Another hall ran down the center of the building, parallel to the street. It was divided from the front section by an iron gate that looked original.

The kid unlocked this and held it open for me. "He's right here," he said, gesturing to the first cell on the left. "You need anything, just holler." He shut the gate and locked it.

"You're leaving me alone with a murder suspect?" I said, just to egg him. "What if he tries to kill me?"

The guard shrugged. "Holler loud."

Hector was lying on the bunk with his feet toward the front of the cell, in the same clothes he'd been wearing last night. There was a straight-backed chair standing against the hallway wall, which I pulled over and sat in, side-on to the cell. Hector didn't move, just lay there with his arms folded under his head, looking at the ceiling.

"You OK?" I asked after a couple of minutes had ticked by. I saw a muscle in his neck twitch, but he didn't say anything. His eyes were open, but he wouldn't look at me.

I've experienced the flighty male often enough not to take it personally, but there was obviously more going on here than a guy trying to avoid an unwanted romantic entanglement.

"Listen," I said, "I don't know what you're really hiding from, but it's obviously not some South American drug lord with a summer home in Mexico." I paused, in case he wanted to respond. He didn't. "You know, if you told me the truth, I might be able to get you out of here. I've got access to stuff the cops don't."

Hector's visible eye jumped toward me before he could stop it. He stayed quiet, though.

The hallway was tall, maybe twelve feet, and about eight feet wide. There were six cells on both sides, all standing open. At the far end was another iron gate just like the one behind me, and another plate glass door.

"I should have brought you a cake with a file in it," I mused aloud. "Wouldn't take much more than that to break out of here."

Other than the rise and fall of Hector's broad chest, there was no sign of life from the bunk.

Right about the time I'd decided to leave, the guard jingled around the corner with a serious-looking Mike Hayes in tow. Mike gave me a silent chin-lift greeting as the kid let him in, then stepped over to the bars separating Hector from the rest of the world.

"Hey, man," he said through them.

Hector sat up quickly, and began speaking to Mike in a language I didn't recognize. It sounded like Spanish, but none of the words were familiar, and it seemed to involve more vowels. Mike listened, then, to my surprise, replied in the same language. They went back and forth for a little while, then stopped, staring at each other through the bars and breathing like they'd just run a marathon.

"What's going on?" I said.

Both men turned guarded eyes on me, not saying anything, and suddenly, just like that, I'd had enough.

"You know what? Forget it." I got up, grabbing my wallet off the floor. "Good luck."

Neither of them tried to stop me as I called for the guard, or when he unlocked the gate.

The square was dark and silent, except for the hotel, gushing light onto the sidewalk from the night lobby. The buildings peeked at me like old ladies behind lace curtains, murmuring their censure to one another. I wanted to scream at them.

TUESDAY, NOVEMBER 6

I

I took a long bath when I got home, lying half submerged like a lazy crocodile and sneering silent epithets at the brain when it tried to do anything but keep my skull from caving in.

I'm not sure why I was so pissed off. My situation was completely self-generated. I should have just kept my head down after finding Teresa, and let the chips fall wherever they were headed. Although, even if I had, I probably would have ended up in the same place. I'd just know less. That depressed me even more. All the shit I'd gone through over the last week, for nothing.

The thing that stung the most was how gullible I'd been about Hector. Who the hell knew what his story really was? All I was sure of now was that it wasn't the one he'd told me, which meant that my worries about the radar were probably well founded. Having my libido engaged always makes sussing out a con a little more difficult, but I can usually look back and see where I ignored signals, and I couldn't find any with him.

The warm water finally started to relax me enough to feel

sleepy. I closed my eyes and leaned back, considering the pros and cons of heading for Mexico myself. I could probably make the border before anybody even realized I was gone, and sixty thousand would set me up pretty well there. For a while, anyway. I could find someplace way off the grid and build my own little hacienda. There were some interesting new adobe technologies floating around that would be fun to play with, although that meant spending more on the foundation than—

The brain picked that moment to lob a fact up into my consciousness, where it exploded like a Molotov cocktail: Richard had been keeping Hector's *malquis* in Teresa's basement. That's why he'd been so freaked out when Jesse told him he'd found the door open.

I sat up in the tub, my pulse accelerating. That meant whomever I'd heard going in there around four on Thursday night was after the remaining hand—to leave it with Teresa's body—and it couldn't have been Richard. He was still with Benny Ramírez at four.

I willed myself to stay calm until I'd thought it all the way through.

Richard wouldn't have hired someone else to kill Teresa and leave the second *malqui* with her body—his whole scheme with Hector was dependent on secrecy. If anyone else found out, all his leverage would be gone. The only other person who might be in on it was Jesse Reed, but the only reason Jesse would kill Teresa was if she'd found some evidence connecting him and Richard, and that didn't seem to be the case. Unless Maines was keeping it quiet to protect his cousin.

My fingers were turning to raisins, and the bathwater had gone cold. I opened the tub drain and got into a towel, feeling schizophrenic. Knowing that the Inca and his crew had my back had bought me some breathing room regarding the Silvia Molina–Nick Olmos thing; I should be spending it figuring out how to save *my* ass, not Hector's.

I made an industrial-strength cup of tea and took the laptop into the bedroom, forcing my attention back to the problem on the top of the pile. Fifteen minutes into researching how to cross the border undetected, I was asleep.

My dreams were weird, Freudian snippets of a trip to Mexico with a man who was supposed to be my father. He had Red Bradshaw's face, and machetes where his hands should have been. We raced through surreal streets on an old BMW motorcycle, pursued by a doll with an apple head and steel-colored braids.

I woke up early with that weird sense of heavy time having passed that you get after an epic dream, and milled around for a while, waiting for my head to clear. I still couldn't decide whether to cut my losses and take off for parts unknown, or stay put and see which way the wind blew.

After a couple of cups of fresh tea, I decided on a third option.

II

Pulling up to the stop sign at Silvia's cross street, I saw her getting out of her car with Alex Méndez. I idled there, my stomach knotting. Not because Silvia and Alex knew each other—in this little town, that seemed to be the case with everyone—but because Silvia was striding around the car upright, shoulders back, looking fifty instead of seventy. With him there.

I shifted into first and made the corner. As I pulled up, Silvia shrank back into her *curandera* persona. I parked the truck and got out, not bothering to arrange my face.

Alex gave me his mack daddy once-over and lifted his chin. "What you want?"

"I want to know what the feds are doing in town."

He glanced quickly up the street. Silvia took a fast, light breath, staying in character, and said, "We should go inside."

Alex nodded wordlessly, and the three of us trailed up the narrow sidewalk and into the fragrant botanica. We passed through the small front room into the bigger room off the kitchen, where Alex stopped in the middle of the floor and turned to give me a bright, hard look.

Silvia eased onto the sofa, muttering, "I told him it was a stupid idea."

Alex crossed his tattooed arms over his chest, looking away from us.

Silvia said to me, "We were supposed to scare you into thinking you'd been clocked, WITSEC would shut you down at the other end, and you'd go right to Torres." She gestured at the ceiling. "This was the brilliant plan."

I didn't point out that things had gone almost exactly that way; I just said, "Plan for what?"

"We're information-mining the narcotics distribution route through here from Mexico, trying to get a handle on the situation along the border," Alex said. His O.G. accent had disappeared. The tattoos still looked real. "I fucked up pretty good a couple of months ago—that's why Torres put me back on shit detail, working street deals. I may have to be rotated out, and we needed a replacement that we knew Torres would accept immediately."

He watched me with those flat, bright eyes, leaving the rest unsaid. I was so focused on the intersections with Hector's cartel story that it took a couple of heartbeats for Alex's meaning to sink in. When it did, I almost laughed, it was so absurd. "You think I'm going to work for you?"

"It's that or do your time."

"That's not the deal I made."

"So call a lawyer."

When I felt like I could talk without screaming, I asked him, "You're Torres's source?"

"He'll never know it's you narking him," Silvia said. "They're careful not to hit close enough for him to figure out that the leak is from inside his own organization."

"And what's the plan once the feeding frenzy for his territory starts?" I said. "With Teresa gone, it's going to be open season, and I'm walking around with a target pinned to my ass."

Alex shook his head. "The feds supply more money and soldiers than we know what to do with. We let Torres think it's his reputation bringing everything in, and he makes sure to crow about it wherever he can. The smart guys know it'd be suicide to try and move in here."

My irony receptors were going off. "Let me get this straight. I put a bunch of skinheads away in California so that I could come down here and help you guys keep another crew in business?"

"What, you're growing a conscience now?" Silvia mocked.

Alex held up a hand, glaring at her. "The point," he said to me, "is that your federal protection contract is with us now. So it's play ball or walk."

I got the photo Pete had sent out of my wallet and handed

it to him. Alex peered at it for a few puzzled seconds, then went over to the sofa and showed it to Silvia. He watched her eyes widen, then asked, "*¿Quién es?*"

"*No sé,*" she said, lifting her shoulders. "Just some guy I see at the farmers' market down in San Antonio. He's one of the vendors, I think." She lied well, but then, you'd expect that from somebody in her line of business.

"Try again," Alex snapped, flicking the edge of the photo with one finger. "You're not in drag there." I saw a flicker of something dangerous cross Silvia's face. "*¿Qué pasa, amiga?*" Alex said. His voice was quiet, but he was clearly not in the mood for any foolishness.

She sat back on the sofa, cutting her black eyes at me. "Mama put me on another operation down there a couple of weeks ago."

Alex tsked, turning his head. "Without letting me know? Come on."

"They wanted a closed set," she said to him, lifting her shoulders again.

"Why?"

"How the hell should I know?" she scoffed. "You know they don't tell us field meat jack."

Alex was wavering, but he didn't have everything yet. I gestured at the photo and said to Silvia, "Now explain the fact that this guy was one of the Rizzoli suppliers back in California."

Alex's eyes shot back to Silvia, who was staring at me with her mouth open. She held up both hands, protesting, "No. No way. I got the assignment through the usual secure channels and ran all my checks and balances. Nothing pinged."

Alex rubbed his hands down his face and stood with his

fingers on his chin, then said to me, "How sure are you about this?"

"As sure as I get."

"Damn it," he muttered, turning away from us to take a walk around the room. I gave Silvia a knowing look. She pretended not to notice.

"You got a name?" Alex asked me. His voice was thin and grim.

"Nick Olmos. My information is that he went AWOL when he left California. That should be easy enough to check."

Alex went over and stood in front of Silvia, arms crossed, feet planted. "You'd better fucking hope she's wrong."

"Like I said—everything came through legit," she told him, eyes wide, then looked at me. "Maybe he's part of the big scare plan that they didn't tell us about."

"What was your assignment in San Antonio?" I asked her.

"It hasn't dropped yet, which is standard. We always meet first to establish contact."

"That was taken last Wednesday," I pointed out. "Teresa was killed the following night."

Alex shot Silvia a look that would have fried bacon, and she stood up and put some distance between them. "I didn't say nothing to him about her."

He blew a fast sigh out through his nostrils and crossed his arms again, looking away. "I'm going to have to get with the home office, find out what the hell's going on." He glanced sharply at Silvia again, holding up a pair of crossed fingers. "Until I do, you and me are gonna be like this."

Silvia shifted on the patterned rug, giving me a *thanks for nothing* look, which I might as well have given myself. By trying to play hardball with Alex, I'd effectively placed Silvia off-limits to further interrogation for the time being. One of these days I'm going to learn when to shut up.

III

The brain did a few laps as I drove back to the apartment. Maybe there was some truth in Hector's story. The feds might have figured out who he was, and sent Alex and Silvia—and me—down here to keep an eye on him, in hopes of snagging Escobar. It would explain a lot: the nonregulation arrangement with Teresa, how my identity had gotten out so fast, the push to employ me at Guerra's despite my lack of experience.

What it didn't explain was why Hector had headed straight into the arms of the cartels in the middle of the night. The brain speculated that he might have run without thinking too hard about where he was going, but my gut didn't like it much, and I still didn't know how he'd gone from postcoital bliss to flight mode in less than an hour.

How Olmos fit in was anybody's guess. Getting me yanked was just a phone call—it didn't require a trip to San Antonio. So maybe Silvia was right and he'd been brought on as part of the scare-me-crooked-again campaign. That worked only if Olmos was still in good standing with the feds, though. In which case, it sure seemed like they would have clued Silvia and Alex in.

When I turned in at Teresa's, there was an unfamiliar vehicle—a white Jeep—parked under the oak tree. Mike Hayes was sitting on the porch steps, waiting for me. He looked tired, and didn't get up as I walked over.

"Tough night?" I asked him.

"I need to talk to you," he said.

"So talk."

He seemed nervous. "Can we go inside?"

"No," I said.

He put his elbows up on his knees, squeezing one fist and then the other. His knuckles crackled like popcorn. "Hector thought you were in with them," he said, squinting up at me, "but I talked him out of it, after he told me who you were."

"Call me when there's a 'For Dummies' version," I said, starting up the steps.

Mike jumped up and got in my way. "If you really want to help Hector, tell me what you know about this guy Olmos."

"Olmos?" I frowned, then saw it. "Hector read my e-mail?"

"You searched his apartment," Mike shot back.

I was trying to recall exactly what Pete's message had said. "Why are you interested in Olmos?"

"He's one of the guys who hacked up Hector's family," Mike said.

I snorted. "I don't think so. Olmos is—or was—a federal agent of some kind." Mike shuffled on the step, looking impatient but not surprised, and a thrill chased up my throat. "Are you saying that's who Hector is really hiding from?"

"When he heard you were coming, he thought maybe—"

"I could help him? Find out what the feds know?" I shook my head as the facts rattled into place. "If I ever had an in, it's gone now. Maines told WITSEC I'm mixed up in Teresa's death somehow, and they threw me out."

Mike fell back against the railing. I paused, then asked, "So this Escobar story that Hector told me, that's all bullshit?"

"No. Olmos is Escobar."

I held up a hand while I got the photo out and pointed to Olmos. "This guy? This guy is Jorge Escobar?"

"Yeah," Mike said. "He went in with the feds as part of his deal when they broke up the Medellín Cartel."

"Hector told me he was with the Gulf Cartel."

"Yeah. He's a government mole."

"So why's Hector heading right into Escobar's territory, after seeing this picture? That doesn't make any sense."

"He wasn't heading into his territory."

"Maines said he was trying to hire a boat to take him to Mexico."

Mike chewed his lip, then said, "You can't go direct to Cuba from the U.S. He was gonna go down to the Yucatán and cross over from there. That's safer than trying to go across the border. The Gulf Cartel operates along there but not further down."

That made sense to the radar, as did his choice of Cuba, given who was after him. It did tickle my curiosity a bit that Silvia Molina was Cuban, but I was frankly too relieved that Olmos/Escobar wasn't here to get me killed to care much.

"Marie Hooks says you were out at Richard's looking for him the other day," Mike was saying. "Did you find him?"

I hesitated, puzzled. "You mean Charlie's girlfriend? How would she know that, and what's she got to do with Richard?"

"She's his housekeeper," Mike told me.

The radar found that interesting, but—as usual—it didn't tell me why. I put it on the back burner and said to Mike, "Hector's not seriously going to try and play ball with Richard, is he?"

Mike looked off across the yard with an impatient frown. "Just tell me where he is."

"Listen, giving in to blackmailers is just extending your torture. You show them your soft underbelly, they just take their time tearing you to pieces instead of doing it all at once."

"I know how to shut him up," Mike said. His hands were squeezing open and closed at his sides.

I gestured at them. "All that'll do is make him take a bigger bite later."

"I'm not gonna *hit* him."

"Then I hope you've got something else to keep him quiet," I said.

Mike made a face that told me I'd accidentally hit pay dirt, and I went a little giddy. "Is it something to do with Milestone Properties?" Mike twitched, and I grinned. "Son of a bitch. What is it?"

Mike hesitated, then got out his phone. He messed with it for a second, then held it up. Voices started coming out of it.

"You're gonna *what?*" one of them said. It sounded a lot like Jesse Reed. The background noise made it clear that he was in the bar.

"The holdouts will be begging Milestone to buy, when I'm through with them," Richard's nasal twang answered. "They won't be able to get out of town fast enough."

"Richard," Jesse sighed, "it's a really stupid idea. Those guys are gonna ask questions, and that's four people with information that could fry us. It's too dangerous."

"I'm not going to tell them anything—," Richard began, but Jesse cut him off.

"You think you can just wave a couple of bucks in front of some local mouth-breathers and they'll just do whatever you tell them, without saying anything to anybody else? Please. Just be the political guy and leave the crunchy stuff to me, will you?"

The recording stopped. Mike lowered the phone and put it back in his pocket.

I said, "I don't know the exact location, but Richard's being held at a compound just across the county line west of here, probably by whoever he was talking about there."

Mike had turned and was heading for his Jeep. I caught up and got into the passenger seat as he started the motor. "You'll need money."

IV

I explained the ransom situation as we headed toward the square. Mike stopped at the bank and returned to the Jeep with a zippered bag after about twenty minutes.

"Sorry about the wait," he said, tossing it into my lap.

I looked inside. There were twenty bricks of new Cs—a hundred thousand dollars. "Jesus Christ. Did you rob the place?"

"I'm a cosigner on Tova's account," he said. I gave him a look, and he tilted his head away from me. "It's for Hector. She'll get it."

He aimed the Jeep west, and after a couple of miles we were slingshotting along the winding two-lane strip of asphalt like we were too young to die and too old to care. He seemed to know where he was going.

I sat back, trying to ignore the ride, and said, "What was that language you guys were speaking last night?"

"Some local dialect that Hector used back home," Mike said. "He taught it to me and Teresa while he learned to speak English. Came in handy when we didn't want teachers or any of the other kids to know what we were saying to one another."

"Probably came in handy for dodging the feds as well," I said as a prologue to grilling him about it, but a flash of red and blue had caught my eye. We were cresting a low rise, and a Confederate flag fluttered from a galvanized pole fronting a group of mobile homes in the wash down below.

"Is that it?" I asked Mike, grabbing his arm. He nodded and pulled to a stop on the shoulder.

There was one large trailer facing the loop at the end of a gravel drive, with four smaller ones farther back. A new red pickup was parked alongside this main trailer, and a couple of late-model cars near one of the smaller ones.

"You'll have to go in without me," I said, swallowing the boulder at the back of my throat.

Mike put the Jeep back in gear. "Hon, people around here fly that flag like it's a Six Flags banner. They don't got no more idea of what it means than my dog does. These jokers aren't the guys who are after you."

I tried to reply before survival mode kicked in, but my limbs were already going cold and nerveless. I checked the Kahr in my front pocket, to make sure that the safety was off and a round was in the chamber as we rolled up the driveway.

Mike stopped at the chain-link gate and got out. I stayed

where I was. A man came out onto the wood stoop that had been built up to the main trailer's door.

"What you want?" he called over, not friendly.

He was youngish, maybe thirty, with stringy blond hair hanging out the back of his ball cap. He had on a Western-style plaid shirt and creased, starched Wranglers, with a huge silver rodeo buckle belt. His boots were sharp-toed ostrich hide, dyed red.

"Got a proposition for you," Mike said.

The man came down the wood steps and over to the chain-link fence, squinting. "Now, what'd you say?" he asked, drawing a pack of cigarettes from the snap pocket on his shirt.

"I'd like to buy Hallstedt out," Mike said steadily. He didn't fidget, just said his piece, nice and plain.

The man lit a cigarette, took a deep draw, and blew the smoke over to one side with a contemptuous air. "You gonna have to speak up, man. I don't hear too good."

Mike strode to the Jeep and got one of the bricks from the zipper bag, which was shoved down tight between the front seats. He went back over to the fence, holding the cash at shoulder level. I could see Blondie's eyes glitter from where I was sitting.

"Owes us a lot more than that, brother."

"How much?" Mike asked.

Blondie glanced toward me, then walked over to the gate and started working on the padlock. "Y'all better talk to Gene."

Mike got back in the Jeep and we drove through the gate. Blondie pointed us toward the trailer at the very back, a battered red box with a rickety shed porch across the front. A man was sitting there in a plastic folding chair. He had a summer hat on, straw, with a ventilation band around the crown. Below it, his hound dog face moved in a slow chewing motion. He had a round, low paunch in his lap, and stringy legs propped wide in front of him. A shotgun leaned against the trailer on his left side, between him and the door. He took hold of it leisurely as we drove up, and laid it across his knees. Blondie ambled up behind the Jeep and came around on my side as Mike turned off the motor.

"These folks say they wanna buy our boy."

"That a fact," said Gene, looking us over.

Mike had remained in the driver's seat and was leaning forward slightly, his wrists stacked on top of the wheel. He didn't say anything, just waited.

Gene chewed for a second, then said, "He ain't fit for much."

"That's all right," Mike replied, "we don't need him for much."

Gene stood up and came to the top of the porch steps. His belly looked like a basketball shoved up under his shirt. "Who's your friend?"

"Just along for the ride," Mike said.

Gene nodded with a sneer. "She looks kinda proud of herself."

I can't help the way my face is put together. I let my eyes drop toward the floor of the Jeep, hoping it made me look demure. I doubted it.

"You oughta teach her to look at a man when he's talking," Gene said, his voice growing louder.

Mike waved at him. "She knows. She's just nervous. You know how women are."

"Seems to me she needs a little tap," Gene told him, his jowly face spreading into an ugly grin. "Just a little tap, to remind her."

Mike made an impatient gesture. "We gonna sit out here in the heat all day, talking bullshit?"

"Half a million," Gene said.

Mike snorted. "Get real, man. That sorry sack ain't worth nothing like that."

"You know he let a wetback fuck his wife? Just let him do it, make a pussy bitch out of him, in front of God and everybody."

Mike shook his head in mock opprobrium, and Gene made a satisfied noise in the back of his stringy throat. "Come on up here, brother," he said to Mike.

He was holding the shotgun horizontal across his midsection, one hand supporting the barrel, the other looped loosely under the stock. Mike didn't look at me, but took his hand off the keys in the ignition with a deliberate air, and climbed down out of the Jeep. He walked over to the steps and up.

"You, too, sister girl," Gene said. "Be good for you to see what happens to a man with no self-respect."

Blondie was immediately to my right. Hoping he wouldn't notice the bulge of my jeans pocket under my shirt, I got out and climbed up, staying one step below Gene. He struck me as the kind of man who wouldn't like a woman at eye level, and I didn't want to get much closer to that shotgun. He backed up and turned, going over to the trailer door. He swung it open and gestured us in.

Trailers always smell wrong to me, and this one was worse than most. Rotting garbage and urine with a top note of stale cigarette smoke. The floor had an orange and brown shag carpet, and the walls were covered with fake wood paneling. A folding table stood under one of the aluminum windows along the back wall, and what was left of Richard Hallstedt was propped in one of the plastic chairs next to it.

His nicely pressed khaki pants were now soiled and torn, and he reeked of excrement. Both eyes were swollen shut, his mouth a bloody maw with teeth floating in it. The nose was definitely broken. He was shoeless and nude to the waist, bruises and cuts covering his narrow torso. One large gash near his right armpit appeared to be infected, red and swollen with pus. Gene gazed at him with amused pride, cradling the shotgun. I had to clench my teeth to keep from saying what I thought of him.

Mike's face was impassive as he stood looking around the trailer, seemingly bored by the specter at the table. "Stinks in here," he said. "Y'all should clean the place once in a while."

Richard's head moved at the sound of Mike's voice, and an indecipherable gurgle came from the vicinity of what had once been his mouth. Gene said mildly, "Shut it, boy," and Richard stiffened, going silent.

"All right, let's just cut to the chase," Mike said with a sigh. "I don't have half a million dollars. I've got fifty thousand. I know he don't owe you more than that."

"You do, do you?" Gene was still chewing a nameless something, his jowls swaying gently with the movement. "You can have his carcass for fifty." He pumped the shotgun and raised it in Richard's direction. My gut clenched.

Mike gave the appearance of considering it for an instant, then shook his head. "I need him alive, at least for a little while."

Gene hitched the shotgun in Mike's direction. "Then the price is half a million."

Mike looked at me and shrugged. "Guess we'll be going, then."

Richard cried out at that, and Gene turned toward him again, shouting, "Shut up, I said!"

Before he could come back around, Mike had hurled himself at the shotgun. He hit it in the middle, pushing it against Gene's skinny chest, and both men went over backward, Gene howling, "Floyd!"

Mike rolled to the side, keeping hold of the gun's barrel, twisting it away, and brought the butt down on Gene's face. It made a sound like ice cubes breaking out of the tray.

I felt a quick slap at my hip and noticed that the Kahr was now in my hand. Boots sounded on the porch, and as Mike lurched to his feet, I swung toward the door. Blondie was standing there, his right hand rising. I didn't wait to see what he had in it. I gave him all seven: two in the face, five in the chest.

I didn't hear the shots; I didn't hear anything. I was high up, away, somewhere else, only dimly aware of Mike moving over to the table to drag Richard from the chair. They stumbled out and around Blondie and down the steps toward the Jeep. I floated behind like a disembodied spirit, my eyes sliding across the man lying on the porch without seeing him.

Mike shoved Richard into the backseat and swung behind the wheel. As we ran the gauntlet out, a figure materialized from a shaded corner, a .38 braced in both hands. I heard a round ping across the hood, and the report of several others, all wide. We got through the gate without losing anybody, and Mike stood on the gas.

My right hand was burning; I flexed and shook it and heard something heavy thunk onto the Jeep's floor.

"You think he needs the hospital?" I heard Mike say, very faintly.

My head floated around toward him, and a voice I didn't recognize said, "Who?"

Mike's hand swam toward me; as it landed on my shoulder, I felt myself fall and jerked, bracing for impact.

"You all right?" Mike said, peering hard at me while trying to watch the road at the same time. His voice sounded normal now. I didn't feel floaty anymore.

I twisted my head to look at Richard, curled up on the backseat. He was breathing noisily, eyes closed.

"I don't know," I said.

Mike fumbled in his far side pocket and passed me his phone, reciting a number. "Doc Harman. Tell her to meet us at Richard's house."

V

The front door opened as we pulled up under Richard's porte cochere, and Marie Hooks stepped out onto the stoop.

"Oh my gawd, what happened?" she cried as Mike helped Richard around the Jeep. She pulled the door open wide and said, "To the left."

We passed through a big archway at the end of a foyer that was lined in something that was supposed to look like marble but didn't. Beyond this was a sunken living area about the size of Dodger Stadium, littered with overpriced furniture. Marie led us into a bedroom almost as big, with a king-size bed dressed in frilly shams and a designer duvet.

"What happened?" Marie asked again as Mike eased Richard onto the bed.

"Doc Harman's on the way," Mike told her. "Keep an eye out, will you?"

Marie flicked an unfriendly look in my direction and disappeared. Mike got Richard stretched out on the bed, propping him up with a couple of the effeminate pillows. Richard lay with his head back, breathing raspily through the ruins of his mouth.

I was still feeling slightly supernatural, and stood there mutely as Mike leaned forward and said quietly, "Hey, Richard? Can you hear me?"

Richard made a series of noises that sounded affirmative. Mike got out his phone. As the recording played, Richard began to roll his head from side to side on the pillow.

"You keep quiet about Hector, and nobody else'll hear this," Mike told him.

Richard's head stopped moving, and his eyes flashed through the swollen lids. He performed a painful nod, going still.

Voices exploded in the foyer, and the doctor bustled in. She stopped at the foot of the bed to gape at Richard before setting her bag on the floor and getting out a stethoscope. She examined him, then turned cold eyes on me and Mike and said, "What happened?"

"Some local heroes have been using him as a speed bag for a couple of days," Mike said.

"Why?"

Mike shrugged. The doctor's look shifted to me. "I'll have to report this to the sheriff."

"Whatever you gotta do, Doc," Mike said, his voice amiable. He got out his keys and put a hand on Richard's shoulder. "I'll be back later to look in on you, man."

There was something oddly merry in Richard's pained nod, as if he were accepting a challenge he relished. It put a bad taste in my mouth.

"Listen," I murmured to Mike as we headed out, "maybe this gets Richard off Hector's back, but what about Maines?"

"They're a package deal," he said.

I wanted to ask how sure he was of that, but Marie was waiting in the foyer and had surged toward us as soon as we cleared the bedroom door. "Is he going to be OK?"

"Depends on your definition of 'OK,'" Mike said.

She gave him an annoyed frown and flounced officiously to the front door. Her concern was ostensibly natural, but something about it was making my radar tweak. I stopped on the doorstep and asked her, "Do you live in?"

"The household arrangements are none of your business," she informed me.

"I'm just wondering why there was nobody here when the cops brought Richard home on Thursday night."

Her severe look grew distinctly hostile. "I have a personal life."

"Where were you?"

She pressed her lips together, shoving at us until we'd cleared the threshold, and then slammed the door behind us.

"What was that all about?" Mike said as we got into the Jeep.

"She's got a drinking problem, doesn't she?" I asked him.

"Understatement of the century," he scoffed.

"Did she know Teresa?"

"Yeah, she used to work for them. Teresa let her go after Richard moved out, and Tova hired her on at the hotel, but she was such a mess that Tova gave up on her after a couple of weeks. I think Richard hired her back just because he felt sorry for her."

"Does she run errands for him?"

Mike snickered. "I doubt it. She can barely tie her own shoes."

So why had she been coming down Teresa's driveway in Richard's Lexus on Wednesday night? OK, I wasn't positive it had been Richard's Lexus, and I hadn't paid enough attention to the driver to be sure it was Marie, but I kept thinking about that patch of green minty stuff on the box in the basement that smelled suspiciously like peppermint schnapps, and Connie's remark about her not having a driver's license. If she'd waited for Richard to fall asleep and then come over to Teresa's to retrieve an old basement stash, she'd have seen the *malquis*.

The brain didn't care much for the idea that the Amazon had been killed over something as banal as firing her maid, but the bizarre circumstances of her death felt less bizarre when I looked at them through beer goggles. I knew from personal experience how hugely out of proportion a slight could grow in the alcoholic mind, and the illogical lengths to which the same mind might go for revenge.

"He'll need some time to consider his situation," Mike said as we pulled away from Richard's house. "Tomorrow I'll make sure he knows that part of the deal is him getting Maines off Hector."

"What if Maines won't do it?"

"He'll do it," Mike assured me.

"OK, but what if he won't?" I insisted.

"Then this goes to the D.A.," he said, patting his pocket, "and Richard and Jesse go to jail."

"So does Hector, unless you've got them copping to Teresa's murder on there somewhere," I pointed out. Mike didn't say anything, and I asked, "What do the feds want him for?"

"It's something to do with his family, back home."

"I thought they were all dead."

"He's never gone into specifics about it with me," Mike said, looking away. "Too dangerous."

I gaped at him. "We nearly got ourselves killed and you don't know why?"

"Hector and I have been friends for almost twenty years," Mike said. "He asks for help, I give it to him."

I leaned back in my seat, speechless.

The sun was down and the big sky was filling up with stars when Mike dropped me off at the apartment. We hadn't said much else on the drive back to town from Richard's, and as I got out, he broke the silence. "Look, I know it don't make any sense to you—"

"You're damned right it doesn't," I said, reaching in to pick up the Kahr, which was lying on the passenger-side floor where I'd dropped it. My head spun as I touched the gun's polymer grip. I shoved it into my pocket and straightened up. "If Hector doesn't want to get picked up by the feds, why's he so willing to go to prison for Teresa's murder? It's the same difference."

"Not quite," Mike muttered, putting the Jeep in gear. Before I could say anything else, he popped the gas and shot off down the driveway. I watched him fishtail into the street, wondering how long until the first really bad wreck. Maybe he'd already had it.

VI

It was going on ten by the time I'd settled down enough to hear myself think. Mike's last remark was still pinballing around in my head, and I got to work on figuring why, which didn't take long: if Hector went to jail for killing Teresa, it would be because the *malquis* stayed out of it. He was trying to hide them, not himself, which meant that they must be evidence in the feds' case against whomever he was related to.

Around eleven thirty, my phone rang. I let it go to voice mail, then dialed in and listened to the message. It was Tova. She wanted me to come see her at the hotel in the morning.

As I set the receiver down, I heard footsteps on the porch. They went up the rear stairs and across the ceiling of my bedroom; then a door opened and closed.

I put the Kahr back in my pocket and my feet back in my shoes.

The wide hall on the second floor opened into a lofty foyer at the front of the house, with a grand staircase winding down into it. There were two doors on either side of the hall, and the one closest to the foyer had a tin letter B nailed to it.

Jesse answered my knock with a cigarette hanging from his lips, dressed in a wife-beater and a pair of absurdly tight black jeans. When he saw me, he stepped back, taking the door with him. It opened into the kitchen, which was essentially a sink and a hot plate alongside a small section of laminate countertop.

Through an archway to the left was the main room, looking out over the town and beyond. There was a foldaway futon, not folded away, and a comfortable-looking chair. Everything else seemed to be stored in piles.

"To what do I owe the pleasure?" Jesse said through a cloud of tobacco smoke, gesturing toward the chair. He folded up the futon and sat down, rolling the cigarette between his thumb and forefinger.

"I ran into Richard earlier today," I said, staying in the archway.

Shock leaped onto Jesse's face. "Jesus Christ. That was you?"

He'd heard it from someone other than Richard, or else I'd certainly have been identified. That gave me more navigating room than I'd expected.

While I thought about what to do with it, Jesse got up and went into the kitchen for another cigarette, lighting it from the one he'd just finished. He took a deep draw, throwing the butt in the sink, and crossed back over to the big windows. His bony shoulders rose and fell heavily as he stood there looking out at the featureless darkness. There was a long silence.

Finally, he turned toward me again and said, "I've got everything I own tied up in this Milestone deal. I can't afford to let that crazy bastard fuck it up."

He was looking me steadily in the eye now, and I realized why he did it so infrequently. His gaze had the amoral flatness of a wild animal. There was life in it, but only of the most elemental kind.

"The owners were selling," he said, leaning toward me as if whispering a secret. "Everything was moving ahead nice and smooth. But Richard, he can't just sit back and let me drive—

he's got to get in there and dick around, be a *player.*" Jesse shook
his head, the yellow light from the side table lamp skittering
across his sharp chin and collarbone. A sudden realization cut
through the murk in my head like stomach acid rising after a
bad meal. "You set this whole ransom thing up with those Flat
Creek guys, didn't you?" I said. "To keep Richard under wraps
until the council vote. You knew he wouldn't be able to pay,
because Milestone's got all his money."

Jesse came back over and sat down on the futon, his hands
sliding up his long thighs. He aimed an innocent expression at
me, then showed me his snaky grin, almost reluctantly. "It's
going to be damned hard to prove that."

"I'm not interested in proving it. If you and Richard want to
play Monopoly downtown, I don't care. I just don't want Hector getting sucked into any of it."

Jesse kept his feral gaze on me, his smirk slowly dying. "So
why the smash and grab?"

"Hey, if your guys had actually been interested in a deal,
none of it would have happened."

Jesse sat back, blowing a stream of smoke at the ceiling. After
a minute, he twitched forward again. "*Damn* it!"

I could feel the ions in the room shifting polarity, and held
still, waiting.

Jesse said, "You've got a thing for Hector, huh?"

He didn't want an answer, so I just gave him a smile.

"Tough break," he said. "Looks like conjugal visits from here
on out."

"Oh, maybe not. You and Richard might decide that laying
off him is the lesser of several evils."

Jesse's wandering eyes came up to my face, the tips of his

fangs catching the light. "Hey, I never wanted to lay *on* to begin with. Richard is fucking nuts. Who in their right mind tries to scare a grown man into selling off his bread and butter with a dried-up old cadaver hand? Dude's been watching too many reruns of Vincent Price or something."

The radar wasn't picking up any deception, but Jesse was one of those people who knew how to lie convincingly. There are actually two methods: the first is to lie with the certainty that you'll be caught at it, which relaxes you enough to put it across, and the second is either to tell part of the truth, or believe what you say enough that it feels true when you tell it. Unsure what type I was dealing with, and still not convinced my secret superpowers were in working order, I made the mistake of pressing a little further. "He didn't tell you some kind of story about why he thought Hector would make a deal?"

Jesse's oblique animal eyes shifted at me, suspicious. "What do you mean?"

At least the superpowers were working well enough to let me know I'd just put my foot in it. If I wasn't careful, Jesse would figure out what he obviously didn't know yet—that that dried-up old hand was the kernel of this whole thing. Backing off now wasn't going to work; I'd have to finesse it.

"We found another cadaver hand with Teresa's body," I said, feeling as if I were jumping out into rush-hour traffic. "Richard must have clipped a pair from the hospital."

The look of astonishment that drifted down onto Jesse's face told me that the existence of the second *malqui* was completely new information to him. He searched the empty air in front of him, then beamed those lupine eyes at me again. "How come nobody's heard anything about this other hand?"

"Maines is keeping it under wraps," I hazarded, and when Jesse didn't call bullshit, kept going. "You know, so he can maybe trip somebody up with knowing about it."

His face sharpened. "Is that what Richard was keeping locked up in the basement? These hands?" I nodded, and he sat back with a wondering laugh. "Well, I'll be damned. The son of a bitch actually did it."

"After you gave her the roofies, right?" I said. Jesse frowned at me, and I added, "If you testified against Richard, you could probably take a lot of years off your jail time."

Jesse's frown cleared, and his man-eating grin returned. "Oh, I'm not talking about Richard." He slid his right foot forward, wriggling his fingers down into his front pocket. "I found this on the basement floor, right before Richard drove up."

He held his fist out toward me, and I stepped forward, taking care to stay out of grabbing range. Then he turned his hand over and uncurled his fingers, displaying a small gold object on his long, pale palm.

It was Hector's *chakana*.

WEDNESDAY, NOVEMBER 7

—— ◆ ——

1

A slicing shock shot through me, which got my attention more than the thing in Jesse's hand. Apparently, the radar had really believed that Hector was innocent until that moment. I put on my poker face, but it felt dry and foreign. The eyes that rotated up to look at Jesse felt like oversize marbles riding in their sockets.

"It's Hector's," Jesse said, turning it over idly. "He must have dropped it when he went in there to get that other hand."

My memory had already told me that Hector wasn't wearing the charm when I'd ogled his almost-exposed nakedness on Friday morning.

"I honestly didn't think he had it in him," Jesse was saying, smiling down at the *chakana*.

Disoriented, I took a step back toward the kitchen. Jesse got up, and the Kahr came out. He froze in his tracks, staring at the pistol with that mixture of curiosity and terror common to people who don't spend a lot of time around firearms.

He got his worldly expression back in place with some

effort, laughing softly. "Man, you are something. I got a policy against fucking fat girls, but I might make an exception in your case. I bet you're a party and half in the sack." His smile lingered while his eyes wandered down across my chest, but when they flickered back up to my face, he went solemn.

"Too bad I got a policy against fucking skinny assholes," I said, moving a couple more steps away so that I could take one hand off the gun without worrying about it. "Toss me that thing."

Jesse lobbed the *chakana* toward me in a low arc. I caught it, sidled over to the door, and slipped out; backed along the hall and ran down the stairs to my apartment, shutting and locking the door. My fingers and legs felt boneless, my head like a dried orange on a peppermint stick.

Keeping my ears tuned for the sound of feet on the stairs, I threw my box of money, some clothes, and the laptop into my suitcase, then got into the truck and headed downtown, watching the rearview mirror.

II

I drove directly to the jail, where the blond kid told me that Hector had been transferred up to Johnson City in preparation for his arraignment the next morning. He added that the sheriff wasn't letting anyone talk to him except his lawyer.

I went out and got back into the truck, but I didn't start the motor. I just sat there trying not to disappear. When I felt like I could do it without leaving the planet, I let my mind slide gingerly over the possibility that Hector might actually have killed the Amazon.

The idea was unexpectedly tolerable. I poked at it, trying to replicate the reaction I'd had up in Jesse's apartment. After a few minutes of self-examination, I realized that, holding the gun on him while forcing myself not to drift off onto autopilot, I'd felt a near-irresistible impulse to pull the trigger—to kill him—just because I could. It occurred to me that I might have chosen my life for that very reason. The constant consciousness of danger might be what had kept me functional all these years.

I sat there sucking air and pumping blood until it was clear nothing else was going to happen north of my collarbone, then got the suitcase and walked over to the hotel. Kathleen was behind the desk, and I asked her to fix me up with a single. I could tell that she wanted to ask questions, but my face was stopping her. If it was anything like the inside of my head, I didn't blame her.

I was about halfway through filling out the registration card when I heard a familiar voice.

"We're full," it said. Tova was coming down the wide corridor. She was wearing a white satin robe, her platinum hair down around her shoulders, her face bare of makeup. She shimmered against the dark hall behind her like a ghost.

Snatching the card out from under my pen, she snapped, "I don't want your business. You'll have to find accommodations elsewhere." I stared at her, dumbfounded, as she ripped up the card and tossed the pieces onto the desk. Her blue eyes were colder than usual. "I don't care to have criminals as guests in my establishment."

My heart froze in my chest.

"You don't seriously believe that I would fail to notice a

withdrawal of a hundred thousand dollars from my bank account, do you?" Tova said, propping a hand on one of her vine-
ripened hips.

"I didn't take that money," I managed, relief making my
voice weak.

"Oh, I know you didn't," she said, "but please don't attempt
to convince me that you're Little Bo Peep and Michael was the
Big Bad Wolf."

The fairy-tale reference cut in, reminding me of a girlhood
when I'd been able to trust myself not to kill anyone. Tova
didn't wait for me to answer. She spun away and strode back
down the corridor.

"I don't suppose there's another hotel in town," I said to
Kathleen.

"San Marcos," she replied in an apologetic voice.

Fine, I thought. San Marcos, and to hell with this place.

Out in the fresh night air, the wash of light from the courthouse showed me the dark front of Guerra's, and I remembered
that Hector's apartment was empty and still had a broken door
lock. In my current state of mind, I didn't really feel like driving forty miles to overpay for a funny-smelling room, and maybe
sleeping with Hector's pheromones would help me settle down.

Luigi was lounging on the big plank table when I came into
the apartment. I gave him some kibble and water, took my
travel kit into the bathroom to brush my teeth, then stretched
out on the sofa. The bed would have been more comfortable,
but I didn't want to risk sleeping so soundly that I couldn't get
up in a hurry if I had to.

It was turning cool, and I pulled the red and black blanket
over me. It had a woolly, animal smell that made me feel like I

was bunking down next to a campfire. Luigi sidled up and jumped on top of me, spiraling down into a relaxed curl on top of my pubic bone.

I lay there for a long time listening to the cat purr and watching time pass. The brain still wasn't doing much more than filling out the space between my ears. Strings of meaningless content floated across my consciousness like motes on the breeze. I fell asleep watching them.

III

Some barely heard sound woke me early. I was on my feet with the Kahr out before my eyes were fully open. When complete consciousness hit, I realized that I was aiming the loaded gun at Hector, who was coming toward me from around the kitchen table.

He took it out of my hand without slowing down, burying his face in my neck. His mouth came around to mine before I could say anything. There was something almost desperate in the force with which he held me against him, as if pleading with me not to stop him. So I didn't.

Afterward, we lay back on the pillows, our skins cooling. The sheets felt good. The bed felt good. Everything felt good. I rolled my head to the side and saw that Hector was watching me with half-open eyes.

"Four gold stars for you," I murmured.

He rubbed a hand across my stomach with a sleepy chuckle. "It's not me, *jeva*. It's us."

I was too dopey to argue. I just smiled and let my eyes close.

Some time later, noises from the kitchen woke me. Hector, showered and barefoot in a pair of faded navy sweatpants, came over to the bed with two cups and passed me one. He was so beautiful in the white light streaming through the bay window that it almost hurt my eyes to look at him. Remembering the *chakana* made everything else hurt, but at least my gears were working again.

"What are you doing here?" I asked. "Last I heard, they were going to throw away the key."

"Tova talked her way around the judge," he said. He brought his foot up on the bed and showed me a GPS anklet.

"Wow," I murmured. "How'd I miss that?"

He just smiled at me like a well-fed animal. His face went serious again as he sat down. "Mike says y'all talked."

"We did a hell of a lot more than talk."

Hector nodded, and I took a swallow of tea to brace myself before reaching down to get the *chakana* out of my jeans, which were lying on the floor next to the bed. "Jesse Reed found this in Teresa's basement on Friday morning," I said, holding it toward him.

Hector couldn't decide what to look at, my face or the *chakana*. Finally he stretched out a hand and took it from me.

"Richard was keeping the *malquis* down there," I said. "Hiding them in plain sight."

Hector went over to the sofa and got a cigarette from the box on the table. He sat down, lighting it, and stared into the space in front of him with eyes that seemed to have gone completely black.

"Maybe I did kill her," he said after a long time. His voice was wondering, almost childlike.

He sounded genuinely baffled, and I was back on that razor's edge of not knowing whether I could trust my perceptions. Irritated and unsteady, I said, "Look, that shit might play to a jury, but please, stop trying to sell it to me, will you?"

Hector made a evasive motion with his head, like I was a gnat buzzing around his ears. "This morning, listening to the lawyers, I got this weird feeling in my feet, like I was walking on gravel, and then this—not even a memory, just, like—a *flash* of crossing Teresa's driveway." He looked over at the bed, where I was rolling the rim of my teacup along my chin, watching him. "Then I remembered the argument." His lips flinched, like he was tasting something foul. "I went over there to get the *malqui,* after we closed the bar, and she said she'd give it to me if I'd have sex with her."

I'd been sitting in the bed with my knees drawn up, the sheet tucked under my arms, and I felt a cold thrill run up my bare back. Not that I was surprised. The whole fake affair thing had always struck me as wishful thinking on somebody's part.

"I didn't even think about the repercussions of turning her down, it was so ludicrous," Hector said, sounding weary. "When I got home, she was up here waiting for me—she'd done her over-the-roof thing, and said she wanted to apologize."

"Did she bring the hand with her?"

Hector shook his head. "We had a couple of glasses of wine and talked for a while." He closed his eyes. "Everything after that is gone."

My ears felt like a million tiny insects were nibbling at them. "You mean from the bottle that was on the counter when I came by on Friday?"

"Yeah, why?"

"It was doped," I told him, amazed that he didn't know. Why was Maines telling me shit that he wasn't even giving the lawyers?

Hector's face snapped open like a searchlight had hit it. I watched him run through it, stunned, and then he balked like a horse refusing a jump. "No way. Teresa would never do a thing like that to me."

I couldn't help an exasperated snort. "Hector, she'd just tried to blackmail you into having sex with her."

"Come on," he said, doubt shading his expression. "You can't date-rape a guy."

"Why not?"

His face flushed. "Because I'd have to be conscious to—you know."

His embarrassment made me smile, in spite of what we might be talking about. "You've never had a wet dream?"

He paused at that, then tried, "If that's what she was up to, why'd she drug the whole bottle? She was drinking it, too."

"They put a dye in that stuff now," I said. "If she'd just done your glass, you'd have noticed the color difference. She was a big enough woman to ingest a little bit and still be functional, and she had the advantage of knowing it was there. You'd be out before you realized she wasn't keeping up with you. That's why they found it in her system."

Hector sat back on the sofa and stared at me. I gave us both a little time with it. It's a hell of a thing to have to comprehend. After a long silence, he looked over at the *chakana*, lying on the coffee table next to his cigarettes.

"When's the last time you remember having that on?" I asked him.

"Thursday night, when you looked at it back in the office," he said. "I noticed it missing Friday, after I got home from the gym."

"Jesse claims he found it around five in the morning," I said, half to myself. "I mean, he could be—" Another bomb exploded behind my eyeballs. I held my breath, not believing what I was thinking, then let it out and looked over at Hector. "Are any of your clothes missing?"

"My clothes?" he repeated, looking baffled. "Why?"

"Just look, will you?" I didn't want to put words to my idea until it proved itself worthy of the effort.

Hector heaved himself off the sofa and went into the bathroom. I wrapped myself in the bedsheet and followed him. He pawed through the hamper, paused, then went over to the chest of drawers and dug through it. "The shirt I was wearing that night. I don't see it anywhere."

I dropped down onto the toilet seat, closing my eyes while I thought out loud: "The *chakana* must have gotten tangled up in it when Teresa undressed you." When I opened my eyes, Hector was leaning on the sink, looking a little sick. I went on quickly, "Richard came down here and got your shirt to cover up with before he went over to get the other *malqui,* so that nobody would see the blood on his clothes if he were spotted."

"I thought Richard was in the clear," Hector said.

"Only because he didn't have time to give Teresa the roofies," I said. "Since she gave them to herself, that's off the table now." The brain was racing ahead, trying to keep up with itself. "You were lying with your head toward the window when I came by on Friday morning, so if Teresa was on top of you—" Hector turned his head, closing his eyes. I hurried to finish.

"—she'd have had her back to the door. You were more or less unconscious, and she was—busy. Richard could have grabbed the knife from your kitchen, if he was quiet, without either of you clocking him."

"What would be the point?" Hector said. "If he wanted to hang this thing on me, killing her down here would have sealed the deal way faster than doing it on the roof. I couldn't remember what happened, and she'd be lying there with my DNA all over her and my kitchen knife in her chest. It'd be a slam dunk."

The brain screeched to a halt. "You're right."

"Hell of a time to turn agreeable," Hector grumbled. I looked up at him and he pushed himself off the sink, giving my hair a friendly rumple on the way out.

My scalp was feeling overheated and greasy. I turned on the shower and got in, giving up on trying to see the logic in what Hector and I had just figured out. The brain was cranking busily around on it; I'd know soon enough.

While I lathered, rinsed, and repeated, the sequence of events started to take shape. First: opportunity. Whoever killed Teresa couldn't have planned it ahead of time, because she had no regular schedule for going across the roof to Hector's. They must have seized the moment. That meant they were on the square, or somewhere in the vicinity, a good hour after the bar had closed. That ruled out a lot of people.

Second, who wanted to kill her? Richard and Jesse were the only possibilities I knew of, and as Hector had just pointed out, they wouldn't have done it on the roof. I could guess at motives for the rest of the population until I was blue in the face, so I left off and moved to the nuts and bolts.

The bar would have been locked, meaning the killer had gotten on the roof some other way. Maybe Teresa had left the alley door at the café unlocked, and they followed her. Killer climbs up, goes across and down; sees what Teresa is up to, grabs the knife . . . I closed my eyes, visualizing myself standing there. Why do I go back up to the roof? I've got a perfect opportunity to kill Teresa and make it look like Hector did it.

As I got out of the shower and into a towel, it occurred to me that maybe the killer hadn't wanted it to look like Hector did it. But then why not wait over at the café building and kill her there? Close the roof hatch, and nobody would ever know she'd even been at Hector's. Well, except for the DNA. But that could have been explained away by their "affair." Still, the difference between Hector's roof and inside his apartment felt critical.

I found a comb on top of the medicine cabinet, and as I reached up to get it, caught sight of some new muscle definition in my arm, which made me smile. I flexed it a little, and it hit me: Teresa was big enough that even an average-sized man would have balked at attacking her without some kind of advantage. If the killer was a small man, or a woman, there was no way they would be able to just sink a knife into her without getting a hell of a fight in return. That's why the roof. They'd gone up there to wait because they'd seen the two-by-four on their way in, and realized that they could whack Teresa as she came up out of the attic hatch, then stab her while she was down.

I dressed and went back up front, where Hector was on the sofa, smoking and looking out the window.

"Somebody small," I said, "with a reason to kill her. Who fits that description?"

He made an impatient gesture. "Aren't you forgetting something?"

I started to tell him that I was leaving the *malquis* out of it for the time being, but the brain had caught up. I dropped into the side chair. "Marie Hooks. She saw the *malquis* in Teresa's basement on Wednesday night, so she knew that Richard was hiding them down there. She didn't know why. She just thought that if she left the remaining one with Teresa's body, it would implicate him in her death."

Hector boggled at me, then said, "OK, I'll admit that when Teresa let her go, she was pissed, but Jesus, not pissed enough to kill her. Even if she was, leaving the *malqui* doesn't make sense—she'd have to expect the cops to believe that Richard was, like, carrying it around in his pocket or something, and it just fell out by accident without him noticing. It's absurd."

"Not to an alcoholic," I said. "That's how they think. Come on, you must have listened to plenty of drunks over the bar— you know what I'm talking about." I felt Hector's certainty starting to yield, and leaned forward. "Marie was here that night, late—I saw her. She was lit up and bitching about Teresa ruining her life. Connie couldn't give her a ride, so maybe she hung around the square, saw Teresa coming across the roof to your place, and decided to come up here and give her a talking-to. Instead, she catches her date-raping you. Hell, I might have tried to kill her, too."

"That doesn't track with what you just said about going up to the roof to wait," Hector said.

"She'd probably sobered up a little by then," I mused. "It was at least an hour since the bar had closed. She saw her opportunity to get rid of both of them in one go—kill Teresa and frame Richard for it."

Hector smoked in silence for a while, thinking. Finally he said, "It answers a lot of questions, I'll give you that, but even if you're right, I'm still in the same fix. If the feds hear about the *malquis*—which they will, if anybody but me goes to trial—I'm cooked."

I moved over to the coffee table, where I could watch his face. "Look, tell me the truth," I said. "I was married to the mob for eleven years. I can forgive a lot, and maybe I can help."

"If I could, I would," Hector replied. "It's just not safe."

"Why isn't it safe?"

He made a frustrated gesture with his head, pressing his lips together, and the guard went up in his dark eyes. He kept quiet. I was suddenly furious.

"Last chance," I said, keeping my voice low and even. "You can tell me voluntarily, or let me make a mess."

I watched him calculate his odds and pick the wrong horse. It was too bad, but at least I wouldn't have to be careful anymore.

IV

I stopped downstairs to call Mike on the bar phone. "Have you been back out to Richard's yet?"

"This morning," he said. "I doubt he'll so much as mention Hector's name for the rest of his life."

"Did you by any chance talk to Marie while you were out there?"

"Marie? No. Why?"

"She might be mixed up in Teresa's death."

"Look, don't fuck with this. Everything is settled."

"Did Richard give you somebody to take the fall?"

"No," Mike said, "we don't need that. Richard will pull Maines off the case, Tova's lawyers will take care of Hector, and that'll be the end of it."

"Except he'll go to jail."

"Not for long," Mike said, "and as we've discussed at length, it's the lesser of many evils."

I couldn't agree, but Mike wasn't the person I had to convince.

V

Richard's huge house looked deserted, except for a large bald man standing to one side of the front door. He was wearing an athletic-cut blue sharkskin suit, and flexed impassively as I pulled into the porte cochere and got out.

"Is the boss at home?"

His laconic gaze moved over my face. "Who's calling?"

I told him, and he put out a long arm and rang the bell. Marie opened the door. When she saw me, her thin lips twisted with aversion.

"She's on the list," the bodyguard rumbled at her.

Marie didn't like it, but she stepped back and let me in. I gave her a gander as I passed. She looked sober.

Richard was sitting on one of the sofas in the enormous living room. His face was badly bruised, but the caked blood was gone, and both his eyes, blackened, were open now. As I came in, he picked up a checkbook from the side table. Marie made a derisive noise and headed for a swinging door in the wall behind him, but I stopped her with a question. "Did you ever decide where you were on Thursday night?"

"I don't have to talk to you," she said, stopping behind the sofa.

I looked at Richard. He made a placating gesture over his shoulder, and she huffed but stayed put. "You know where I was. You saw me."

"After that," I said.

"I went home."

"How?"

"I don't remember."

"Do you remember palming his keys?" I said, pointing my eyes at Richard.

His head came around at her faster than I'd have said was possible with his injuries.

Marie's expression turned hateful. Her hands started to shake. "You're crazy!" she said, crossing her arms. "I don't know nothing about no keys."

"You run the household here. You know that Richard's keeping some stuff in Teresa's basement. You found out exactly what when you went over there on Wednesday night to look for a bottle you'd stashed down there."

Richard returned, painfully, to looking at me. It was hard to tell what his eyes were saying.

Marie tugged at the hem of her apron and squared her narrow shoulders. "So what? It's none of my business. He's a doctor."

"So you knew right where to go, when you needed something to implicate him, after you killed Teresa."

She widened her eyes at me, then started to laugh. Richard glared over his shoulder and she shut up, but kept grinning.

"Go do the patio," he said. His words were slurry around some wiring in his mouth, and his voice sounded raspy.

Marie gave him a scornful look and pushed out of the room.

Richard opened the checkbook, clearing his throat. "Before we go any further, I'd like to express my gratitude for the actions that you and Mr. Hayes undertook on my behalf."

Marie appeared beyond the plate glass windows with a bucket and broom. I sat down on the sofa opposite Richard. "You can write me a check if it'll make you feel better, but I won't cash it." He lifted the pen and raised his head. A glimmer of hostility passed across his ruined face. "You can't buy her out of this," I told him.

His swollen, purple-ringed eyes flickered from side to side; then he raised and dropped his shoulders and replaced the checkbook on the side table. He cleared his throat again and said, "Perhaps you'd be so good as to specify why you think I can't."

"Because there isn't enough money on the planet."

Richard regarded me silently with a disparaging smirk. Then he said, "I realize that people like you enjoy fraternizing with your social inferiors in an attempt to appear egalitarian, but you fail to understand that not everyone shares that predilection."

The statement didn't appear to be related to anything I'd just said, so I kept quiet. He seemed disappointed, but went on, "Azula is dying. Ten years ago, it was a pretty little town— quiet, law-abiding, a place people felt safe and enjoyed living

in. Now, it's overrun with immigrants, white trash, hippies—"
He waved toward the ersatz Sherwood Forest outside as if it
were to blame, which—ironically—it partially was. "Some years
ago, I determined to put my considerable resources to work in
an effort to reverse that trend."

"Oh, I see," I said, leaning forward. "You're a reformer."

I didn't try to make the word sound anything but contemptuous, and his face reddened behind the bruises. "Naturally,
you wouldn't understand. You haven't worked hard all your life
to make a decent living for your family, only to see it all stripped
away."

"That's true," I admitted. "I haven't clung to the antiquated
ideal of having two-point-five kids and a plastic house in the
suburbs. Maybe you could explain how that makes me your
'social inferior.'"

Richard saw that he was getting into an unproductive area,
and swerved back to his original point: "What I'm attempting
to convey to you, Ms. Kalas, is that I occupy a respected position in this little town. You may find it difficult to make your
accusations stick to someone associated with a person of my
standing." He smiled, exposing the metal in his mouth. "Especially without any concrete evidence."

I glanced out at the patio, where Marie's alcohol-shriveled
form was laboring. "How long do you think she can hold out?"

Richard didn't answer me. I got up and left.

VI

I spent the drive home compiling a list of possible reasons for
Richard to protect Marie. A love affair seemed out of the ques-

tion, but I've seen stranger couples. Or maybe she knew something, from working for him, that Richard couldn't afford to let get out.

There was a tan county cruiser leaning off the driveway at Teresa's when I drove in and parked. As I got out, the big deputy who'd brought me home the night Hector and I found Teresa's body ambled over to meet me at the foot of the back steps. "Sheriff wants to see you," he said.

I wanted to pursue the Maria Hooks angle, but I know better than to argue with enforcers who can break me in half. I followed him to the car, wondering how much Maines knew about the whole mess.

The sheriff was vertical and conscious when we got to the sty. He pointed his eyes at the side chair and said, "Have a seat."

I pulled it around and parked myself side-on to the desk, facing the office door. Maines had his notebook open in front of him, which he continued to look at for a couple of minutes in silence. Then he breathed deeply, closed it, and creaked back in his chair.

"Did you find that Milestone file out there?"

I kept my expression neutral. "Out where?"

He lowered his chin and looked at me over the tops of his glasses. "I'm givin' you self-defense on Floyd Garnier. Push me, I'll make you prove it."

My stomach jumped, and I couldn't help a mirthless grin. Richard hadn't talked to him. I wondered if Mike knew.

Maines continued to look at me without comment for another minute, then asked, "Did Torres say anything about Milestone at all?"

"Who's Torres?"

The sheriff examined the ceiling, then returned his pale gaze to my face, saying, "You want to make life hard for me? You just go right ahead on and do it. I guaran-damn-tee you won't like the results."

"I don't like the results now. How much worse does it get?"

"That file has got to be somewhere," Maines said, pinning the blotter to the desk with a rigid index finger. "It's none of the places it should be. If you don't have it, and those west-side yahoos don't have it, and Richard doesn't have it, where is it?"

I noticed that he wasn't pausing endlessly between questions and answers anymore. His face, too, had grown more animated, showing actual expression for the first time since I'd met him. It was making the back of my stomach itch.

"Why do you care?" I asked, genuinely curious. "You've got your case against Hector all sewn up. You've done your job. Take a day off."

"Physical objects don't just disappear," Maines said. "Somebody's trying to hide that thing. There's got to be a reason."

"You can have your very own copy, you know," I told him. "All you need is a warrant."

Maines's eyes fluttered away from me. "Judge won't give me one."

I was surprised to hear him admit it, until I remembered his earlier bouts of loose lips. I felt my attention swerve away and congeal around the memory, making my stomach hurt in a completely new way. "Richard can't make that happen for you?"

Maines twitched in the creaky chair like something had bit him. "You think I'd be stuck covering seven hundred square miles of territory with just myself and a couple of deputies if I had that kind of pull?"

Baffled, I said, "So why have you been trying so hard to shove me under the bus all this time?"

"I been making lemonade," he drawled, one of the level corners of his mouth lifting a hairsbreadth.

When I realized what he was saying, I had to get up out of the chair and put enough distance between us that I wouldn't reach across the desk and punch him in the face. Once the urge had faded, I turned back and said, "If you tell me that you're in on this thing with Alex and Silvia, I swear to God I will go postal on your ass."

His fractional smile evaporated. "What thing?"

"Alex is a federal agent of some kind—DEA, if I had to guess—and Silvia's his local. They're working the drug route up through here from Mexico, and are trying to rope me into working with them. Not very nicely, I might add."

I left Olmos/Escobar out of it for now. Maybe if I made Maines mad enough, he'd run the whole bunch off before they could finish whatever they'd started.

The sheriff absorbed what I'd said with his usual impassivity, gazing through me for a few long minutes before sitting up and grabbing his pencil. He made a couple of notes, then said, "The chief know about this?"

I shrugged. He lifted one of his long hands to his forehead and drew it across. After a while he muttered, "Lots of gopher holes to step in there, all right."

He sighed and took off his hat, revealing a thicket of strawberry curls so at odds with his personality that I almost laughed. He leaned forward and watched his hand drop the hat on the blotter, saying, "You know that thing about most homicides being solved within the first forty-eight hours? It's because the obvious person usually turns out to be your killer. If not, you go on to the next obvious candidate. And so on. Until you find your guy. It rarely takes more than a couple of days. Because most murders aren't planned, and the ones that *are* planned—well." He turned over one hand. "How much practice does the average person get?"

He looked almost human without the hat. I couldn't tell if that's what was tweaking my radar or not, so I just asked, "What's your point?"

Maines looked up. Light fell through his glasses into his eyes, showing them sharp and transparent in his colorless face. "I think the complexity of this crime is a kind of evidence. Your garden-variety criminal—somebody like Torres—he doesn't want to fool with logistics like limited-access rooftops and drugging his victims. He just wants to get in, get the job done, and get out."

"Nobody drugged her," I said. "She drugged herself."

Maines's sandy eyebrows appeared above his glasses. "Say again?"

"She's the one who put the roofies in that bottle of wine," I said. The sheriff made a skeptical noise, but I kept talking. "She made up the whole affair with Hector to piss Richard off. Hector went along for the fun of it, but then Teresa decided that she wanted the real thing. Hector turned her down, so she took matters into her own hands."

Maines was still looking doubtful, but he was paying attention without interrupting me now.

"Part of their fake affair thing was that Teresa would sneak over to Hector's across the roof from the café building from time to time—probably making sure that somebody on the square saw her, so that they'd gossip about it later. On Thursday night, she used that route to get into Hector's apartment, cajole him into sharing a bottle of wine she'd doped, and then have her way with him while he was passed out. That's why you found his semen in her body."

Maines's expression went horrified, then his face split open and emitted a long staccato laugh, revealing a set of big, round-edged teeth. He looked like a gawky high school kid who'd just gotten the punch line of a dirty joke. "That's the most ridiculous thing I think I've ever heard."

"What's so ridiculous about it?"

He gazed around the room, his merriment subsiding. "I wouldn't know where to start. If you knew her at all, you'd laugh, too. It's just not something she'd do."

My eyes jumped to his bare left hand, and he leaned forward to put his hat back on. "I know sex can be a powerful motivator. But you might as well tell me she was from another planet. That gal was straight. To the bone."

"I was, too," I said, "until life made me different."

That bought me a disgusted look. "After what it cost you, you can joke about that?"

I was getting tired of matching wits with the poorly armed. "Look, you tell me how that stuff got into her."

"Guerra doped the bottle." He shrugged. "Raped her. Then took her up to the roof and killed her."

"Again—," I began wearily, but Maines cut me off.

"I don't explain things," he said. "My job is to deliver the most plausible suspect to the legal system. That's what I've done. You want to get creative with the whys, talk to the lawyers."

The strawberry-curled kid companionably complaining about his job had disappeared. We were back to Mr. Hard-ass.

"You're such a fucking fraud," I said, getting up to leave. I heard the chair creak and turned back to make sure he wasn't coming after me. "You *wish* you didn't care, but you're just as hooked on getting to the bottom of this thing as I am. Why else are you chasing this Milestone file around?"

The sheriff was sitting forward against the desk, watching me narrowly with his ropy forearms lying on the blotter. He didn't answer my question.

VII

Coming around the courthouse, I saw Tova going into the hotel. I wasn't exactly eager to answer her summons, but it was something to be gotten out of the way, so I steeled myself and followed her. She'd already gone up to her suite when I came into the lobby, so I rode the elevator up and knocked.

She answered the door with a sheaf of papers in one hand and stepped back, beckoning me in. "I put in roughly four hours getting everything together for the closing on the Ranch," she said, sitting down on one of the velour sofas. "Since you neglected to give Connie any earnest money against the possibility of your backing out of the deal, I'm forced to ask that you compensate me for that time."

"Forced, huh?" I went around the sofa facing her, getting out my checkbook. As I did so, my eyes flicked over at the big arched window, which perfectly framed the second floor of the café building. The western sun was blazing against the side street wall, turning the window glass solid gold; at night, with no curtains to interrupt her view into the lighted interior, Tova had a front-row seat to any doings on the second floor.

I brought my eyes back around into the suite, measuring the angles. The main room was about twenty feet long; the bathroom and closet would add another ten. This was probably the only room in the hotel that could see what it did.

"Something wrong?" she asked, noticing that I hadn't sat down.

I finished my circuit around the sofa and joined her. "Just admiring your view."

She jumped up and went to the kitchenette, getting a can of soda out of the small refrigerator. She popped the top with nervous fingers, pouring about half out into a juice glass and adding some ice. I had the feeling she wished it were something stronger.

"Five hundred should cover it," she said, leaning against the edge of the counter. Her voice was cool, but I could smell fear coming off her.

"You saw Teresa going up to the roof on Thursday night, didn't you?"

"I wonder if you wouldn't mind getting the hell out of my apartment," she snapped, going over to the door and yanking it open.

I put my checkbook back in my wallet and got up. As I passed her, I saw a droplet of sweat streak down her left temple.

I stood in the corridor for a few minutes after the door had finished slamming, then walked down and rang for the elevator. I rode to the lobby and went to the front desk, where Kathleen was slouched, tapping on her laptop.

"Were you working on Thursday night?" I asked her.

She gave me an uncertain look. "The night Chief Hallstedt was killed, you mean? Yeah."

"What time do you get off?"

"I don't. I mean, I do an eight-to-eight shift, eight at night to eight in the morning."

"Did you see anybody leave here around three a.m.?"

Her eyebrows shot toward the ceiling. "Like who?"

I shrugged, not wanting to lead the witness, and she said, "Not that I can remember. I bunked down for a nap around two—slept for about an hour—but the elevator will usually wake me up if somebody comes down." She gestured toward the hall next to the desk. "Sometimes people use the fire stairs. It's not the fastest elevator in the world."

I glanced down the hall, remembering the steel exit door out into the alley. The fire-stair door would have the same kind of hardware, a metal push bar that retracts flush bolts at the top and bottom of the door leaf. Noisy.

"You didn't hear anybody going out that way?" I asked Kathleen.

She screwed up her face, thinking, then shook her head. "Honestly, I can't remember. This week has been kind of a nightmare."

Fucking Maines. If he hadn't been so quick to decide that Hector was his killer, he'd have been out questioning people when their memories were fresh.

As I turned to go, the brain burped an idea at me, and I pointed at the old phone booth. "Does that thing work?"

"Sure," she said, sounding relieved at the apparently innocuous question. "Dial nine for an outside line."

I shut the booth's folding door and dialed my own number, keeping the receiver to my ear until a hotel customer came in. When Kathleen got up to meet him at the desk, I stepped quietly out of the phone box and ducked down the corridor.

The door to Tova's office was unlocked.

It was past sundown, and the fading light coming through the French doors wasn't doing much for my eyesight, but I didn't want to turn the lights on, lest a sliver of light give me away. I went over to the desk and flipped quickly through the stack of papers and folders sitting on its corner, without finding anything interesting. Then I tried the filing cabinet. Still nothing.

I started to move away, then turned back and pulled it open again, parting the hanging files to look below them. Sure enough, at the very back of the bottom drawer, the face of a manila folder gleamed up at me. I pushed the hanging files farther apart and saw MILESTONE PROPERTIES handwritten in green ink on the tab.

I couldn't suppress a grin. As I reached in to take it out, though, I hesitated. If I took it with me, I'd never be able to prove that it had been here, but if I left it, Tova might try to get rid of it. Especially after what I'd just said upstairs.

As I crouched there, trying to decide, I heard footsteps coming down the corridor. I grabbed the folder, jumped toward the French doors, and slid out, plastering myself up against the exterior wall. The office door opened, throwing a rectangle of light onto the pale carpet. I heard a faint fumbling at the French doors. A pair of small white hands was closing the flush bolts. I was locked out.

I heard the filing cabinet open, and did a quick, desperate survey of the courtyard. There was an exit-only gate on the alley side, and I was standing on a rubber welcome mat. I lifted one corner and slid the folder underneath, then sidled silently to the gate and out.

VIII

Hector was behind the bar with a book, as usual, when I came in.

"I need to make a quick phone call," I told him, barely slowing down. "OK if I do it from the office?"

He didn't say no, so I kept walking.

"I found that Milestone folder in Tova's office," I told Maines when he answered. "I stuck it under the mat in the courtyard. Public domain. If you get over to the hotel right now, you might find it before she does."

"Where are you?" Maines asked.

I told him I was at the bar. He hung up without saying anything else.

Hector was leaning on the serving top when I went back up front, talking to an older guy whom I recognized as Mel's drinking buddy from Thursday night.

"What are you doing here?" Hector asked as I came through the flip-top.

"Reporting for work," I said, nodding hello to the older man.

Hector stared at me for a few long seconds, then said, "Herb, this is Julia Kalas, my new bartender."

"Kalas?" Herb's opalescent blue eyes brightened. *"Mistä olet kotoisin?"*

"Um," I replied.

"Ah, nobody teaches their kids anymore," he complained. "I knew some Kalases back home in Kainuu. Maybe you're related?"

"I might be," I said, then, knowing I shouldn't: "Any of your Kalases named Timo?"

Herb thought about it, his eyes wrinkling. "Maybe. I'd have to ask my nieces."

Hector said deftly to me, "It's pretty slow. You could take the night off, if you want."

A pair of shadowed figures were crossing the square from the courthouse, moving toward the hotel. One of them wore a cowboy hat and had a high stoop.

"Trying to get out of paying me?" I said to Hector.

He shook his head, giving up, and lifted his chin at Herb's glass. "You want a refill?"

Herb pushed the glass forward with one finger. Hector took it down the bar and dumped it in one of the bus trays, setting up a fresh glass for the new round.

"What part of Finland?" Herb asked.

"I'm not sure," I lied, sorry I'd brought it up now. "He and my mom met in the States, back in the '60s."

He gave me a shrewd look. "She wasn't Finnish." His faded blue eyes were merry, like he was doing a magic trick. "If I hadda guess, I'd say"—he scrutinized me—"Mexican."

I relaxed at the incorrect guess and went back to watching the square. "Not bad. What gave me away?"

"That cultural anthropology degree still comes in handy sometimes," Herb chuckled, hooking his thumbs under his overall straps.

I kept him going, asking pointless questions and giving

inaccurate answers, while I did a fair imitation of being at work and kept my eyes peeled for Maines or his wingman. By eleven thirty, I was about ready to jump out of my skin, and nearly did it when the bar phone rang. The place was almost empty, and Hector had gone back to the office for something, so I grabbed it.

It was Maines. "Meet me at the church in fifteen minutes," he said, and hung up without waiting for me to answer.

I buzzed the office and told Hector I was going out for a break, then hit the sidewalk.

IX

I found Maines sitting in the second pew from the back, gazing meditatively toward the altar.

"You're supposed to take that off in here," I said, glaring at his tan-hatted head.

He turned and laid his arm along the pew back, lifting that mouth-corner of his. The hat stayed where it was. As I sidled into the pew behind, I spotted a manila folder lying on the seat next to him. He picked it up, opened it, and handed it to me. The page I was looking at listed Milestone's investors, and there was only one name.

Tova Bradshaw.

THURSDAY, NOVEMBER 8

1

I stared at the page for a minute, then sat down.

"She was underwriting the whole damned operation," Maines said.

I closed the folder and handed it back to him. "I didn't see anybody leaving the hotel in handcuffs."

The sheriff tossed the folder back onto the pew seat. "I can't make an arrest on this. It's her money. She can spend it any legal way she damned pleases."

"If Jesse and Richard are colluding on this development thing, it's not legal."

"She could easily say she doesn't know anything about that. Assuming I ever find anything to prove it."

I tried again. "Why was she trying to hide that file, if she didn't want people finding out?"

"Tova Bradshaw cares about her reputation more than any human being ever should," he said. "If she were seen to be making money off the backs of her neighbors, she'd never live it down."

"That gives her motive," I insisted.

"Not if anybody with a warrant could get a copy of this," Maines said, gesturing at the file.

"Anybody can't," I reminded him. "She must have called in some of the favors she inherited from her father to make it difficult."

Maines made a face at the folder, not answering.

"Tova's got a direct view into the second floor of the café building from her suite at the hotel," I said, leaning forward to rest my arms on the back of his pew. "That file was in the desk when Richard dragged me out of there on Saturday night, and it was nowhere to be found when I got back to town a couple of hours later. She went up there and got it after we left."

Maines's eyes came up to my face.

"That also means that she saw Richard holding that gun on me," I went on, "and she didn't report it. Now, maybe that's not DNA or fingerprints, but it proves to me that she's no law-abiding citizen."

Maines reached into his shirt pocket and got out his notebook. He flipped back through a couple of pages, looking grim.

"Where did she say she was on Thursday night?" I asked him.

He recited, "In and out at the hotel, then in bed, asleep."

"She told Mike earlier in the evening that she had something to do that night, and that she'd see him the next day."

"It's not against the law to lie to your boyfriend."

I sat back in the pew to think.

"That's only half of what I wanted to talk to you about, anyway," Maines added before I could get started again. He paused and looked toward the altar to make sure that we were alone.

"Alex Méndez isn't DEA," he said when he came back around. "He's CIA. They're using the drug thing as cover for tracking some Bolivian from an old international case they been trying to close since the '60s."

I swallowed the thrill that jumped up into my throat. "What case?"

The sheriff gave an irritated shrug. "That's all my guy would tell me. You know how the feds are."

Well, that was that. Talk about making a mess. I hadn't known the half of it.

"Do you think they're involved in Teresa's death?" I asked Maines.

He laid his arm along the back of the pew. "I doubt it. They usually clean up after themselves pretty damned thoroughly. No body. No clues. No nothing."

I let the brain play with this for a second, then shoved it onto the back shelf and asked Maines, "Did you have forensics check Teresa's office? That would at least tell you whether Tova's ever been up there or not."

"No cause to check it, at the time."

I leaned forward again and gestured at the folder still lying on the pew in front of me. "You've got cause now."

"Judge wouldn't give me a warrant to get *that*," he said, waving at it. "He sure ain't gonna give me one for what you're talking about."

Frustration pushed me up out of my seat and down the aisle. After I'd done a couple of laps back and forth, I found myself thinking about Hector's shirt and the mid-crime trip to Teresa's for the second hand.

"How about between Tova's suite and the bar?" I said. "Did you check for a blood trail?"

"It was raining," Maines pointed out.

"Not inside the hotel."

Maines went dour again, but before he could protest, I said, "You could check the public areas—the lobby and the corridors—without a warrant. If you find something, surely that opens a door the judge can't shut."

Maines's crystalline eyes focused on me thoughtfully. "You ever thought about going into law enforcement?"

I frowned at him. "Don't be insulting."

The big wood door at the back of the church creaked open and a stout elderly woman came in, dipping her hand in the bowl of holy water and crossing herself. Maines stood and touched the brim of his hat as she passed us.

"Listen," I said, stopping him outside before he got into his car, "if Tova confesses, does she have to tell you all the details?"

He paused with one foot inside the car. "Why?"

"Just curious."

I could tell he didn't believe me, but he played ball. "I'd certainly expect it. The law will go easier on her."

He waited for my answer, his eyes blank in the dark behind his spectacles.

"You'd better make tracks," I said.

II

The courthouse clock showed two fifteen when I got back to the square. It hadn't felt that long. The lights were off in the bar, and the front door was locked. I let myself in and went upstairs. Hector wasn't there.

It was just as well. I didn't think I had the mental energy left to cope with telling him about Tova. I scribbled a note apologizing for my extended dinner break and saying I'd call him in the morning.

III

The phone rang around ten. I was still in bed, but I answered it.

"Got some things to discuss with you," Silvia said.

"Your friend Olmos, I hope."

She made a spluttering, shushing noise. "*Cállate*, you idiot!"

"Hey, you're the one who wanted to talk."

"Just get over here. Damn." The line went dead.

This was going to be interesting. If Silvia and Alex knew that Hector was their Bolivian, they wouldn't be bothering me. I doubted that I could hold the dam alone for long, though. With Teresa's case coming to a head, his true origins were eventually going to get out.

I had a leisurely breakfast and bath before I obeyed the summons, not wanting anybody to get into the habit of ordering me around before noon. When I pulled up at the botanica, Silvia was sitting out on the porch in her rusty chair, as before. The big yellow dog greeted me with the same tongue-flapping enthusiasm.

"The sheriff searched the hotel this morning," Silvia said as I stopped at the bottom of the porch steps.

"Yeah?" I said, peering through the screen into the house. "Where's your keeper?"

"He's been reassigned."

I stepped up onto the porch and parked myself in the other chair. The dog clacked over and dropped onto the board floor in front of the screen door with a satisfied snuffle.

"What happened?" I said.

"First things first," Silvia replied. "What's Maines after?"

"You'll have to ask him."

"Come on," she growled.

I gave her as little as possible. "Tova Bradshaw."

She formed a silent whistle and looked out across the street, toward a vinyl-clad double-wide bleaching slowly in the heat.

"That'd be just about perfect," she murmured. "He'll never work in the county again, if he locks her up. Is it gonna stick?"

I shrugged.

She had something folded into the lap of her dress, some herb or other, which she was tearing away from its dry stems. Her hands continued this work as she asked, "Anything you can do to make sure it does?"

"Oh, probably," I said.

She looked over at me.

"Is it the feds or the Kings that don't want him to get the police chief's job?" I asked her.

"Same thing," she said. "What's good for them is good for us, and vice versa." She didn't say anything else, so I prompted, "What about Olmos?"

She came forward in the chair, resting her elbows on the arms and peering hard at me with those little black eyes. "I've known Nick for almost twenty years, since before he joined the service. He hooked me up down here. It's part of his job to make recommendations to the feds for people he thinks will be useful in certain situations."

The back of my neck twitched. "You're saying he 'recommended' me for this?"

"The Brotherhood connection was just too good to pass up," she said. "Mama needed somebody fast to replace Alex, and they figured Torres would eat you up with a spoon."

Something about that made the radar jumpy. I gave it a minute, but it was back a ways and I couldn't get to it, so I stuck to the subject at hand. "Did they tell Teresa to get me the job at the bar?"

Silvia gave me a sharp look. "You had to work somewhere."

I paused to consider whether getting confirmation on Olmos's identity was worth pushing her. I decided it wasn't.

"All right," I said. "So what'd you get me over here for?"

"That hand y'all found behind the bar," she said, keeping her eyes on the herbs in her lap. "What'd it look like?"

Making myself sound puzzled, I said, "Why?"

Silvia's shrug was fairly convincing. "Might be somebody trying to move onto Torres's turf. Was it a man's hand?"

"Search me. Teresa was going to send it off to the lab, but who knows if she got around to it before she was killed?"

Silvia got up, shoveling the mound of plant matter in her lap into a ceramic bowl on the small table next to her. She dusted off the front of her dress and said, "Find out."

I smiled, managing to make it look perplexed rather than triumphant. "Surely you guys can do that without my help."

She gave me an annoyed look. "Just do it, all right?"

"You and Olmos are working off the books, aren't you?" I

said. "Otherwise, you'd be able to find all this out through of-
ficial channels. How'd you get Alex out of the way?"

"Listen," Silvia barked, "I can put you in the graveyard just
like that. So do what I tell you."

That's the kind of thing that makes me stubborn on
principle—but in this case, pretending to obey would get me
closer to what I wanted.

"You're the boss," I said, getting up.

IV

I found Hector half horizontal in front of his TV, in a pair of
cut-offs and an elderly T-shirt. The GPS unit was still cinched
around his ankle. I went over and sat down in the side chair.
Hector clicked off the TV.

"So where'd you get off to last night?"

"Maines wanted to talk to me," I said, feeling suddenly nervous.

Hector's face went quizzical. "Kind of late, wasn't it?"

"Tova is Milestone's sole investor," I said, ripping the Band-
Aid off as fast as I could. "She was funding Richard and Jesse's
whole scam."

Hector went still, looking at me with motionless eyes for almost a full minute. Then he asked quietly, "What are you saying?"

"Teresa found out about it somehow," I said. "She got a copy
of the incorporation documents from the county clerk's office a
couple of days before she was killed."

Hector's eyes started going vague. I didn't want him fading
out on me, so I reached over and took one of his hands. He
yanked away from me, jumping off the sofa, and went to the

window. His breathing rasped noisily against the glass, then he turned to me with an agonized face and said, "Money? That's what she died for?"

No.

I almost turned to see who had spoken before I realized that I was only hearing the word in my head. Perplexed, I waited, and the voice came again:

She saw them.

I closed my eyes, shutting everything but the brain out. Saw who? Saw what?

She saw them both.

I opened my eyes. Hector was leaning on the windowsill, watching me.

"Marie Hooks took Richard's car over to Teresa's on Wednesday night, to retrieve some booze she'd stashed in the basement when she used to work for them," I said, following the brain as it groped along, then reminded me of Tova's urgent visitor at the hotel during my visit to buy the truck. "Marie saw the *malquis,* and it freaked her out. She went to Tova the next day, for legal advice about what she should do."

Hector crossed his arms, his eyes folding down and away from me. It didn't matter. At this point, I was just telling the story out loud to hear how it sounded.

"When Tova stopped into the bar that night, she went over to talk to Richard and Jesse, and Richard must have said something that made her realize Marie might not just be babbling. She palmed his keys so that she could go over to Teresa's and have a look in the basement for herself."

Hector had grown more attentive now, and he came back over to the sofa, reaching for his cigarettes. I kept talking.

"Before she was able to get over there, we found the hand behind the bar. So she came back here to ask you about it, and walked in on Teresa assaulting you."

Hector's lighter flame froze. He reached up and took the cigarette out of his mouth, snapping the lighter closed.

"It was a perfect storm," I said, watching it take shape in my head. "She thought that leaving the hand with Teresa's body would incriminate Richard and put you in the clear. She had no idea the hands had anything to do with you."

Hector came around the coffee table and sat down on the sofa with a grunt. "I might buy Marie Hooks overlooking the logic we talked about before, but not Tova," he said. "She's, like, the female reincarnation of Machiavelli."

"She didn't care whether the cops believed Richard had done it or not," I said. "All she wanted to do was make sure they knew it wasn't *you*. She had no idea that leaving that hand with Teresa's body would have the exact opposite effect."

Hector sat looking at his unlit cigarette, pushing his chin out. I gave him a minute, then said, "So. Why does the CIA want you?"

He flinched forward on the sofa, his eyes going black.

"Escobar is working with them, and they're looking for you," I said. "You in particular. And they've been doing it for years. Why?"

Hector had gone so motionless that I paused to make sure he was breathing before going back to work on him. "Is it because you can identify him as one of the guys who killed your family?"

My question dropped into an opaque silence that stretched

into minutes. Finally, Hector leaned forward, put his cigarette back in the flat yellow box, and got up.

V

I followed him down through the bar and out onto the square, where he made for the hotel. When we got to Tova's suite, she and Maines were standing in the hall outside with another man, short and round in a dark brown suit. Suit extended a hand toward Hector as we approached, and Hector shook it, saying warily, "What's going on?"

The skinny forensics kid came to the door of the suite with an impossibly small pair of ladies' athletic shoes. He held the soles toward Maines and said, "These are positive for blood."

Maines did his chin-drop nod and murmured, "Bag 'em up."

"I want those processed in San Antonio," Suit said. He was maybe thirty, with a peaches-and-cream complexion below a head of earnest dark curls.

"OK with me," Maines said. "They're usually faster than Houston anyway."

Tova hadn't reacted to our appearance or the kid's comment. She stood observing with her arms crossed, a little distance apart, one white finger tapping a rhythm against her elbow.

"The whole thing's ludicrous," Suit said. He turned his bright brown eyes on Maines. "Naturally, we'll cooperate with the investigation, but it's clear that someone screwed up pretty royally somewhere."

Hector was watching Tova, who now smiled her closed-lipped smile and told him quietly, "I knew what they were up to."

"Tova," Suit warned, but she ignored him.

"I had complete right of refusal for all buyers," she went on, looking at Hector. "I wasn't going to let them sell us out. If I hadn't invested, someone less scrupulous would have."

Hector's eyes wandered uncertainly through the suite door at the kid, who was logging the bagged shoes on a clipboard.

"The killer could have tracked blood into the street," Suit said as if addressing a jury. "Anyone might have stepped in it."

I heard a woman's voice call to the kid from the inside of the suite, and he got up and disappeared from view.

Suit kept on at Maines, "You can't make an arrest on this—it's completely circumstantial."

Maines's eyes moved behind his glasses. Nothing else did.

"Got positive for blood here as well, Sheriff," the kid said, coming back into the doorway with a dark blue man's button-up shirt. "It's been washed, but there's still reactive proteins."

I recognized it as part of what Hector had been wearing on Thursday night. He put one hand on the papered corridor wall, steadying himself, and looked over at Tova.

Her face had frozen. She stood staring at the shirt for a long minute, then said in a firm, cool voice, "I have no idea how that got there."

"You put it on after you killed the chief," Maines drawled. "To cover up the bloodstains on your own clothes. In case somebody saw you coming back over here."

Suit went wild. "You can't prove any of this! It's all conjecture!"

Maines continued gazing at Tova. "If you'll come voluntarily, I won't cuff you."

She fixed her chilled blue eyes on his pale face, then dropped
her arms called into the suite, "May I have my purse, please?"

The kid handed it out, and Hector said quickly, "I'm coming with you."

Maines did his one-stroke nod, and Tova strode off down
the hall with the three men trailing behind her.

VI

On my way back to the truck, I reflected that Hector's mission
was probably to somehow keep Tova quiet about the *malquis*. If
the CIA was really after him, I understood why, but the whole
thing felt oddly off balance. Hector seemed to care about those
relics more than he cared about his own life. Why not just bury
the damned things out in a field somewhere far away? Why
keep them so close if they were so dangerous? Was it just a
cultural thing I'd never understand, or something else?

It was working my attention so hard I nearly ran over Neffa,
coming down the sidewalk from the direction of the bar.

"What's going on?" she said. "I just seen Tova Bradshaw
heading to the courthouse with the sheriff and her lawyer. Was
that Hector with them?"

I nodded and noticed that she was holding a book, which
she fidgeted nervously with.

"He ain't in trouble, is he?" she asked, her squint tighter
than ever.

"No," I said. Not any more than he had been before, anyway.

She saw me looking at the book in her hand and made an awkward teenage gesture with it. "I been meaning to give this back to him."

"I can take it, if you like," I said. "I'm going back up to the apartment to pick up my stuff."

She seemed puzzled by this, but handed the book over. I noticed the title as I took it: *Metaphor and Ritual in Pre-Columbian Culture.*

"We were doing the conquistadors in history class," she explained. "I was talking about it to Hector one day, and he give me that. It's pretty interesting."

"Yeah?" I said, slowing down. The radar, exhausted as it was, had started to ping.

"You know how people talk about the Indians down there cutting people's hearts out on the pyramids and stuff?" Neffa said. "Fella that wrote that says the church made it all up. The Spaniards didn't want people back home getting mad about them killing everybody. They had to make 'em think they deserved it."

My heart slammed against my chest like a bird flying into a plate glass window. The understanding of what I was really doing here had finally gotten through. Maines hadn't been the only one making lemonade. Olmos/Escobar had "recommended" me because he knew who I was; he knew that I would flush Hector out into the open because he'd watched me pick every psychological scab that formed within arm's reach back in California.

A sharp rap on the café window made me jump, and Lavon put his head around the door. "Girl, you got customers in here. Don't be standing out in the street like you ain't at work."

Neffa rolled her eyes and went back inside with a small smile in my direction. I continued down toward the bar, gingerly pointing the brain back at what I'd just realized. A smaller realization slowed my pulse down a little: if they already knew that Hector was their Bolivian, why the hell had they bothered with me? The question banged around between my ears as I climbed the stairs to Hector's apartment, book in hand.

The red and black blanket had been hastily tossed over the rumpled sheets, and as I approached the bed I felt a sudden urge to lie down and take a very long nap. The world had gone cold and distant, but my head was hot with images of mummies and machetes and sticky rivulets of blood. Luigi came in and jumped up on the sofa. I started to hear my heartbeat inside my ears. The cat and I stared at each other for a long minute; then he opened his fanged little mouth and said, *"Khitis jan wal sarnaqixa, jan walirü tukuwayi."*

I jumped away. The dark corners of the high ceiling undulated. The furniture was poisonous. I noticed that I was shaking.

An eon or a second later, someone who looked like Hector appeared at the kitchen table. A gun hovered into my peripheral vision. The Hector-looking being froze, hands up and open out in front of him. I was aware that something was very wrong, but the brain wasn't doing much to help me figure out what. It was just telling me to get the hell out of there.

I backed out onto the landing and fled down the stairs. The dark cavern of the bar felt safer, but fear that something awful was following pushed me through it and out onto the front sidewalk. There my limbs turned to liquid lead, and I paused to lean against the storefront. A car appeared at the far end of Main. I tossed myself back into the doorway of the bar, crouching and flattening myself into the smallest target possible. The shots were deafening. I clapped my sweaty hands against my ears and waited for the pain to come.

Somewhere very far away, I heard someone saying my name. I kept my eyes closed, my hand pressed against my side where I'd been hit. I didn't want to see Joe again, lying there on the pavement with his brains sluiced across it. I let myself be led away to the ambulance, eyes squeezed shut.

FRIDAY, NOVEMBER 9

———————◆———————

I

I was lying in a bed that smelled familiar. The room was dark and there were people talking in it somewhere.

". . . you should know that, Pops." It was Connie.

Hector answered her in a strained voice. "The doc gave her a couple of these."

I heard a pill bottle rattle, and then Connie's voice again. "Yeah, probably a good idea, until she can get a psych evaluation."

Holding my eyelids open felt like a chore. I let them close. I heard a glass being put down and Connie asking, "What set her off?"

"I don't know," Hector said. "She was standing by the bed when I got home, and just flipped out when she saw me."

There was some more rustling and clinking, and then I heard them again, farther away.

"Well, Liz would have sent her to the ER if she thought it was necessary," I heard Connie say. "Just keep things quiet, minimize stress, let her talk if she wants to, but don't push her if she doesn't. You know the drill."

My body felt heavy and inert. I opened my eyes again, just a sliver, to see how the darkness looked. It wasn't hiding anything scary now. I let go of everything, and sleep took me away.

11

I woke up—or came to—much later. I knew this because the sun wasn't blasting through the east windows, though it was still bright enough to make me roll over and grab for a pillow to put over my face. I got a handful of hair instead. The head attached to it moved, and I opened my eyes. Hector was lying on top of the covers, still wearing yesterday's clothes. There was a book facedown on his belly, and he was watching me through his reading glasses.

I felt down along my side: no new holes. I turned over and looked at the ceiling. It didn't have anything to tell me.

Hector took off his glasses and rolled up onto his elbow. "I think you cured me."

I blinked at him. "What?"

"I was so busy worrying about you that I didn't zone out, like I usually do when shit gets intense," he said.

An urge to cry choked up into my throat. I swung my legs down to the floor, pushing myself off the mattress. Hector's dry, warm hand came gently over and around my elbow.

"Take it easy getting up," he cautioned. "You might be a little woozy."

"Woozy," I repeated, wanting to laugh. All the things I'd seen and heard for the last week—how much of it was real?

A patter of soft, quick steps sounded on the stairs, and

Mike came in, tapping on the door as he did so. "I just saw Connie," he said, looking at me. "You all right?"

"I'm fine," I said, glancing at Hector. He didn't look convinced.

"Anything new?" Hector asked Mike in a low voice.

Mike shook his head and tossed himself onto the sofa. "You know lawyers. He'll figure something out."

I got up, saying, "I'd better get home."

Hector and Mike both looked at me like I'd just told them I was going to jump out of a plane without a parachute.

"I'm fine," I said again, starting to believe it now. "I just need some time to myself."

I found my stuff on the nightstand, stuck it into my bag, and came around the bed.

Hector walked me to the door. "I'll come by in a little while," he said in a low voice.

"I'd rather you didn't."

"No, you don't understand. I'm not offering you a menu of options. I'm telling you what's going to happen. I can't help it. It's the way I'm wired."

His expression almost made me laugh. "Is that word for word?"

He didn't say anything, just pulled me over and kissed me like he meant it.

III

The apartment felt weird and vacant, like I was a visiting ghost. I started a bath running, trying to ignore the brain, which was still making up stories that bore little resemblance to reality.

I could tell the difference now, but the sheer volume of the fictional stuff impressed me. Bits and pieces of the various story lines I'd made up to explain Teresa's death had started branching off and forming increasingly fantastic colonies along the periphery of my consciousness. The inside of my head sounded like a fucking aviary.

Half an hour in the tub didn't help, and as I dried off, I remembered the mild-aired sunset I'd watched on top of Enchanted Rock. Maybe Hector's strategy of getting away from it all would work for me, too. I got dressed and left a note clipped to the screen door.

IV

The shadows were getting long when I turned onto the gravel park road. I pulled well off to the side, locked the truck, and ducked under the gate.

It took about half an hour to hike up to the main trail and another fifteen to climb to the bald top of the main rock. I picked a nice flat spot facing west and sat down on the bumpy granite. The air had gone coolish, and I wrapped the flannel shirt I'd thrown on over my tee around me, waiting for my shoulders to relax. To my relief, the cacophony whirling through my head slowly began to settle, until only one fragment remained:

You saw them both.

I listened to it repeat over and over, waiting for it to die the natural death of its fellows. When it hadn't done so after half an hour, I gave it a poke, hoping to shut it up.

And then I saw them. Keys. Two sets of them.

My neck jerked tight, my pulse jumping back into over-drive. I closed my eyes and ran through the pictures in my head again: Connie dropping her keys into her bag, then taking them out of her pocket in the alley. She'd been in my field of vision the whole time in between, and I hadn't seen her transfer them.

Something rustled off to my left, near the trailhead, and I startled, my heart nearly beating out of my chest. It was just past sunset, getting dark, and the stars were starting to come out. I kept my eyes glued to the spot, and when nothing moved after fifteen minutes, I got up. I was plainly still hallucinating, and too on edge to be out here alone.

I was about halfway to the trailhead, almost dead center in the middle of the rock, when another movement flickered, on my right this time. I whirled, my breath catching, but something human-sized was on me before I could get all the way around to look at it. It hit my right shoulder hard and I dropped to the granite with it on top of me, feeling my ribs crunch as I landed and rolled. The fall knocked some wind out of me, but I came up into a ready crouch a few feet away, my feet planted firmly. The human-sized thing had disappeared.

I held still, squinting into the half darkness, wishing I'd talked Hector into giving me back the Kahr before I'd left his place. There was still enough light to make out shapes, but nothing was visible on the smooth arch of the rock in any direction.

Something crawled down my left arm, and I reached up to brush it off. My hand came away wet. Feeling under my shirt, I found a deep gash close to the shoulder joint, just below my collarbone. The blood was coming in a rapid, pulsing gush, soaking through the fabric and running down my arm. I'd been stabbed.

It instantly dawned on me that I was dead. Any wound close to the heart is dangerous, and the location of this one was such that a tourniquet would be pointless. At the rate it was flowing, I estimated I'd bleed out in about ten minutes. I could slow it down with pressure, but that would work only until I lost consciousness. I was at least half an hour away from the truck.

I took off my flannel and wadded it against the wound, holding it there with my right hand. Ten yards to my northwest was a long ridge of granite about four feet high. I made for this as fast as I could, feeling the blood pump more quickly from my shoulder as I moved. I pressed harder on the sodden mass my shirt had become, but I knew it was a lost cause. My core muscles were already feeling shaky.

"It was too late for me," I heard Connie say in her lilting voice, from the darkness off to my right and behind me. "If he'd come just a year earlier, none of this would have happened."

I pushed myself up and peered over the top of the ridge, into the darkness where I'd heard her. The rock sloped off more steeply there, into a shallow valley populated with the pale shapes of loose boulders. After a few minutes I saw her, coming up the slope. She used her knuckles to steady herself as she climbed, holding the blade in her right fist, point down. She was breathing hard when she came vertical and stopped, about ten feet away. I dropped into a sitting position, with my back against the ridge, one leg stretched in front of me.

"It's called the Westermarck effect," she said, her voice cool and quiet. "Children who live together during the first six years of life are highly unlikely to develop sexual attractions to one another. Tova dodged the bullet. I wasn't so lucky."

She'd come closer now, and I saw that her eyes had gone wild. The contrast to her intellectual tone was unnerving, even in my rapidly fading state of awareness.

"If you could have seen it," she said, her voice dropping to a low snarl. "That pig of a woman, using him like some kind of sex toy." She paused, her fingers undulating around the knife handle. "You'd have done the same thing."

I knew I shouldn't waste the energy, but I croaked, "Maybe, but I wouldn't have tried to frame somebody else for it."

She grew suddenly animated, crouching down within a foot of my outstretched right leg. "No, but see, that was the beauty. That hand—it made me pay attention to Marie's babbling about seeing body parts in Teresa's basement. I never would have, otherwise." She leaned toward me with a chuckle, her eyes bright pinholes in the darkness. "Then I get to the car and *I've got Richard's keys.* I'd somehow picked them up by accident— if you believe in accidents."

A faint regret bloomed in the weakness at the base of my neck. She'd hidden it so well. She'd make a damned fine criminal.

"I went over there and looked," she said, her voice dropping to a singsong monotone. "There weren't two, like Marie said. Only one. It was in this little blue suitcase thing, like the case my clarinet came in, in high school. I knew it had to be related to the one we'd found behind the bar, so I took it, to give Teresa. Then I went back to the bar to put Richard's keys in the lost and found. The lights were on upstairs, so I went up to show Hector what I'd found."

Connie stopped and shuddered. "That disgusting woman." She seemed on the brink of some violent movement, crouching there. When she spoke again, her voice was as flavorless as the wind. "I grabbed the knife from Hector's kitchen, but then I couldn't breathe, so I went up to the roof to get some air. When I heard Teresa coming up, I thought maybe hitting her with that piece of wood would be enough. So I did. But it wasn't."

She turned her pinpoint pupils on me. "Have you ever stabbed anybody?"

I didn't respond. She wasn't really talking to me, anyway. "It's interesting," she said, sounding rational again. "There's something viscerally satisfying about it. That hot flood of blood. It warms up your hate."

"What'd I do to earn that?"

Connie's head came forward in the darkness, like a striking snake. "Don't pretend you don't know. I could smell you on him." I flinched and she pulled back. "I'm not proud of it, but it's not my fault. I can't help how I feel."

My senses were all going loose, but as Connie stood up, they congealed on her proximity to my right foot. As if moved by some outside force, it lifted and hooked around the back of her knee, and I yanked with all the strength I had left. She went down with a grunt, the knife skittering—incredibly— right at me. I rolled away from the stone ridge and got it before she could recover.

She came up to standing again, shaking her head. "You'll be dead in a few minutes. All I have to do is wait."

Unconsciousness was coming at me fast. The faint clatter of distant traffic, which I hadn't been aware of hearing until then,

cut suddenly off. Soon I wouldn't be able to hear or see anything.

A weak, raw fury broke over me. In a photo-flash of clarity,
I saw what would be left when life got done burning away everything I thought was true about myself. I was too far gone to
feel or think anything about it. It just hung there like a ghost.

I gave up fighting with it and closed my eyes, letting myself
go limp as if I'd passed out. A few seconds ticked by; then I felt
Connie come close and lean in, reaching for the knife. I turned
the blade up, fast as light, and drove it into her midsection.

She stumbled back, gaping down at herself. A broad shape
appeared over the crest of the rock behind her. Then I was
gone.

V

I don't know how long it was until I found myself awake again.
And alive. There was a painfully bright light in my eyes, and I
tried to raise my hand to block it, but couldn't remember how.
I began to hear hospital sounds.

"She's coming around," somebody said, a woman. "Can you
hear me, hon? Squeeze my hand if you can hear me."

Thin, cool fingers fluttered against mine, and I squeezed
them as commanded. The voice went humorous, throwing back
away from me. "Dawn, you owe me fifty bucks."

I kept my eyes closed against the blinding light, and her
voice came again. "Just lie still, sugar. You're going to be OK."

She said some other things, but they faded off into mean-
inglessness. My body felt weighted and sore, except for my
shoulder, which was a numb, blank hole in space. The antiseptic

smell and quiet sounds of people moving around lulled me. I fell back into the black hole.

An instant later, my eyes opened again. This time there was no bright light, and I was in a private hospital room. My shoulder was still numb, so the young doctor poking at it didn't bother me much.

"Looks good," he said, folding the dressing back over it. He picked up a clipboard from the bed and made a few notes, then offered me his hand. "I'm Dr. Han. I performed the surgery on your shoulder."

He had a very precise British accent, an odd counterpoint to his Asian features. I shook his hand with my good one.

"You should get full range of motion back, but while you're healing, I'll want you to limit what you do with that arm. The wound was deep, and it will take a while for the inner repairs to heal sufficiently." He looked at the chart. "What sort of work do you do?"

I had to think. "I'm pretty sure I'm unemployed."

His clear eyes flickered with a combination of humor and confusion. "Well, don't take up sculling or anything for a month or so, right? I'll fix you up with a sling before you leave, so that you don't forget."

I nodded, then asked, "How did I get here?"

He referred to the chart again. "It says you came in on STAR Flight—that's the airborne emergency service—via a 911 call."

"But I was dead," I said.

"Then this must be the afterlife," he replied with a grin. "I'll be by in the morning to check you again. If you're still doing well, we'll send you home then."

I nodded again, and the doctor left. A nurse came in to give me an antibiotic pill the size of a kalamata olive and show me how to work the bed call. I turned off the overhead light and went to sleep.

VI

When I woke up later, there was a familiar shape slouched in the chair next to the window, its feet up on the edge of the bed. The only light was a fluorescent spill from the bathroom.

"Dr. Livingston, I presume," I said. My voice sounded dry and scratchy.

Hector got up to pour me some water from the pitcher on the bedside table. "How are you feeling?"

"I've been better," I admitted.

He handed me the cup and stood next to the bed, watching me drink. "You're lucky I saw the truck."

My eyes met his over the rim of the cup, and I felt a tremor start deep in my solar plexus. I put the cup down on the side table with a shaky hand.

"I left you a note," I told him.

He shrugged, shaking his head. "I decided you meant it, when you told me not to come by. I was just out for a drive."

I lay back, forcing myself to breathe slowly. Learning that my survival was the result of sheer coincidence terrified me more deeply than anything ever had.

Hector motioned me to scoot over so he could sit on the edge of the bed, and laid a warm paw on my belly. "Connie's in ICU," he said, his eyes going sad. "She'll be OK. Physically."

The seconds before I'd passed out seemed very far away now, but I doubted anything would ever completely obliterate them.

I knew that I'd dig them up and look at them later, when the brain stopped trying to keep me from doing it.

There was a small shuffling noise to my left. I was half turned on my right side, to keep the pressure off my shoulder, so I couldn't see what had made the noise until a tan-hatted figure came around into my field of view.

"She's not making a lot of sense right now," Maines said, his spectacles glinting in the dim light. He brought out his small notebook. "Tell me what happened up there."

I gave him the sheer factual data, leaving out the things Connie and I had said to each other. He listened without comment, making a note every now and then. When I'd finished, he said, "I still don't get why she came after you."

Hector started to say something, but Maines gave him a sharp look, and he held up both hands, pressing his lips together.

"Jealousy," I said. "Hector and I weren't exactly circumspect about our—activities, and she was in love with him." Maines's face remained blank. When the penny didn't drop, I spelled it out: "Romantically. Not like a sister."

He snorted. "That don't make sense. How'd all the other girlfriends escape?"

"I didn't have any," Hector put in. "Not locally." Maines and I both gave him a look, and he explained, "I knew that it bugged her, so I always kept my love life out of sight as much as possible."

Maines made a tsking noise. "It never occurred to you it was weird your sister was jealous of your girlfriends?" Hector started to answer, but the sheriff closed his eyes and held up a hand. "Never mind. I just heard myself. Common as dirt."

Hector got off the bed and took a walk over to the window. "I never thought she was dangerous."

"Something pushed her over the edge," Maines said.

"Yeah," I said. "She came back to the bar late on Thursday night and walked in on Teresa assaulting Hector."

Maines peered at his notebook. "What brought her back at that hour?"

I said, "Marie Hooks hit her up for a ride as we were leaving. Maria was pretty drunk, ranting about Teresa ruining her life—I guess because she'd fired her after she and Richard broke up. Connie took some time to talk to her before heading to her car, where she discovered she had two sets of keys."

"Two sets of keys?"

"Yeah, she'd picked up Richard's earlier in the evening, by mistake. She came back to put them in the lost and found. Mike found them in there the next day."

Maines made another note, then asked, "Why'd she go upstairs after she dropped off the keys?"

I couldn't tell Maines about the hands, so I just said, "Who knows?"

Hector made an impatient movement, and the sheriff glared at him. "Go stand over there," he growled, pointing his chin toward the side chair, out of my line of sight. Hector huffed and moved out of view.

Now I realized what Maines was up to. With Connie in ICU and unavailable for questioning, he'd had to rely on Hector's account of events, and he didn't trust it. That's why he'd been waiting in the room with Hector for me to wake up. He wanted to make sure we didn't have a chance to compare notes.

Performing a wince, I laid my head back and closed my eyes to buy some rehearsal time. Telling what I knew without identifying Hector as the CIA's Bolivian was going to be tricky, and I honestly didn't know if I was up to it.

"OK," Maines prompted. "Connie walks in on them. Sees what's going on and loses it. Grabs a knife from the kitchen. Why didn't she just kill the chief right there?"

I opened my eyes and gave him Connie's story, minus the *malquis,* but Maines continued to look skeptical. He took his time updating his notes, then closed his notebook and cast an wry look over my shoulder, in Hector's direction. "If she can't make it convincing without your father's hands, I sure can't."

My head whipped around before I could stop it, and I had to grit my teeth to keep from screaming while the throbbing in my shoulder subsided. I heard Hector get out of the chair and come over to the bed. I opened my eyes. He looked like he'd aged ten years.

"What do you know about my father?" he asked Maines. His breath was short and thick.

"I know that the CIA helped get him killed. As an American, I've never been particularly proud of that."

The two men stared at each other across the bed for a while; then Maines stepped out of my line of sight and returned with a small blue case. He clicked the latch and passed it to Hector.

"Found that among Teresa's things," he said as Hector opened it and looked inside. "She wasn't the kind of person to put off sending things to the lab. Unless she had a reason. So I hung fire and did a little research. There's only one old open case that involves a pair of mummified hands."

"You realize what they'll do to me if they find me?" Hector said. "I can identify three CIA agents who killed a woman and two little girls in the most horrific way possible. Not to mention the other shit that bunch did, back home. I'd never see daylight again."

"You guys want to tell me what the hell you're talking about?" I interrupted.

Hector opened his mouth to answer, but Maines cut him off. "It's safer for her if she doesn't know. At least until you've cleared U.S. airspace." He got a look at Hector's expression and said, "A man's remains belong with his family. Not in some museum, helping those clowns in the White House justify their foreign policy agendas. I don't care what he did."

Hector was staring at the sheriff with his dark eyes wide. "I can't get them out," he said. "Security is too tight now."

"You leave the travel arrangements to me," Maines drawled. "I've got friends in high places. We've gotta go now, though. Once Connie comes around and starts talking, all bets are off."

Hector hesitated, then reached over and grabbed the notepad lying on the bedside table. "I brought your laptop with your stuff," he said to me, writing something down. I craned my head toward the edge of the bed and saw my bag lying on the floor next to the chair. "Look this up after we're gone. It'll explain—well, not everything, but most of it."

He leaned over and put his hands on the pillow on either side of my head, gazed at me for a few seconds with those beautiful eyes, then gave me a kiss. It didn't feel like a permanent good-bye, but I wasn't ready to ask questions like if or when he was coming back.

Maines extended a hand at me as Hector went around the end of the bed. "When this all hits the fan, I'm gonna be out of a job. I'm thinking about hanging out my P.I. shingle. Work with me for a few years, you'd qualify to take the exam yourself."

All I could do was stare as he nodded briskly, then turned and left without looking back. Hector gave me a complicated grin and followed.

When the amazement wore off, I rolled cautiously toward the side table and slid the notepad over. Hector had written down an Internet URL and a password.

Navigating slowly because of all the wires and tubes hanging off me, I sat up and slid my bag over with one foot. It took a minute to boot up and navigate the hospital's Wi-Fi interface; then I typed in the address and found myself on a secure page from the Library of Congress. I entered the password and was forwarded to something that appeared to be a digest of information collected from recently declassified government documents, detailing the failed revolution imported to Bolivia in 1967 by Fidel Castro and Che Guevara.

Puzzled, I scrolled down and hit a photo of the three CIA agents who'd been part of the group that had executed Guevara. The man I knew as Nick Olmos was standing on the far right, holding a rifle.

Below the photo, I found this:

```
Although the Bolivian peasants had treated
Guevara's presence in their mountains quite
casually, the United States government
feared that if the whereabouts of his body
```

were known, La Higuera would become a pilgrimage site for his followers, keeping his legacy alive and perhaps leading to a backlash revolution. Therefore, the Bolivian president, acting on a recommendation from Washington, ordered that Guevara be buried in an unmarked grave.

Though all those involved in Guevara's execution were sworn to secrecy, it was revealed in 1995 that Guevara's body had been buried with six others under an airstrip in Vallegrande, about thirty miles from La Higuera. Guevara's remains were ultimately repatriated to Cuba in 2001, but the location of the famous revolutionary's hands, which were removed from the body shortly after death for identification purposes, is still the subject of intense speculation.

ACKNOWLEDGMENTS

John Vehko, Patty Chappell, Janet Reid, Ed Ward, Jesse Sublett, Jessica Alvarez, Toni Kirkpatrick, Theresa Weir, J. E. Seymour, Jack Getze, Julia Stavenhagen, Tim Hallinan, and the rest of you. You know who you are.